The Sandman Cometh

The Sandman Cometh

Stuart G. Yates

Also by Stuart G. Yates

- Unflinching

- In The Blood

- To Die in Glory

- Varangian

- Varangian 2 (King of the Norse)

- Burnt Offerings

- Whipped Up

- Splintered Ice

- Lament for Darley Dene

- Roadkill

- Tears in the Fabric of Time

- Sallowed Blood

For Honey, and our future, which will be nothing like this one!

One

I dreamt of Sandmen last night.

In the darkness, I heard them as they came ever closer, the steady pounding of their feet upon the gravel, in perfect unison, an army, each step a death knell for those who dared to venture out after the last peel of the curfew bell.

My garden was nothing more than a dark smudge, the paraffin lamp from the kitchen too weak to make an impression upon the deep, oppressive shadows. Gripped by cold, I stood motionless, trying to still my breathing, listening out for his approach, knowing I was late, knowing there could be only one outcome.

And I heard him, his great legs eating up the distance between us. The garden door swung open and in he came, eyes huge under the peak of his cap, maniacal grin set upon his silver-grey face, and those arms swinging ever closer.

He threw back his head and screeched, that awful, mechanical voice filling me with dread and I knew death had come to embrace me in its cold, steely grip.

I woke, sitting up, heart banging against my chest and picked out shapes in the gloom of my room, wondering if my dream was real. Holding my breath, I dared not turn away lest the Sandman loomed over me and ended everything I ever knew.

Such dreams often came to me and as I lay with my head pressed into my pillow, their fearful marching dominated every sense, every thought. The steady, relentless beat, drumming hard in my ears. Every night they came and every time I dreamed, I dreamed of them.

The Sandmen

I live on my own. They allow us to do that now. It hasn't always been so, but when they decided to take away our parents we had no choice but to fend for ourselves. Silly things, like buying food, doing the laundry, study. Sleeping. It was up to us how we did things. To a point.

On that fateful day, I was sitting in my room daydreaming as always when the videophone buzzed. It always sounded urgent and I have never been able to stop my heart from missing a beat whenever it shrills into life. This is because of what happened, all that time ago. I remember when the telephone rang the night Dad went missing. Uncle Ernie, sounding so distraught, in such a terrible state, his voice screaming down the line. I could hear him even from where I was sitting.

So, telephones and videophones, they always make me anxious.

It was Yolanda and she sounded deadly dull.

"Hello. I'm just calling to remind you that it's practice tonight."

Her face came up on the screen. She *looked* deadly dull. I told her so, despite the hugeness of her eyes and the stunning loveliness of her features.

"Oh, thanks!" She tried to smile, but it ended up as more of a sneer. "I've just finished the science homework, that's why. It was *so* hard, so I'm really tired. Have you done yours?"

"Of course," I lied, but only I knew that. If any of the Sandmen got a whiff of my non-compliance they would whisk me off to some correctional facility; just like Damien Bridges. Fourteen, top of the virtual class, spent an evening at Wembley Stadium playing in the World Cup final and got himself injured. He should have been completing his metaphysics course work. They took him off to Cambridge and we haven't seen him since. That was almost six months ago. No one talks about Damien anymore, but we all think about him.

"Are you listening to me?"

Yolanda's voice cut through my thoughts like a laser and I gave a little jump, rubbing my eyes. "Sorry, I'm a bit tired as well."

"Tired? You're never tired – have you taken your quota today?"

"Yes." This wasn't a lie, and I felt good about that. Well topped up with my daily barbiturates, as I always am, my body was singing with energy. I've never really thought about skipping a dose. What would be the point? Who wants to sleep for more than four hours anyway?

She smiled. "Good. I'm going off to the Albert Hall tonight."

"Nice. What is it this time? Henry Cooper and Cassius Clay?"

"Who?"

"Never mind. A joke."

"You're weird, Simeon."

"No, I'm just a massive receptacle of facts and figures." She didn't respond, not a single flicker across her beautiful features. So I tried again, "Henry Cooper was a British heavyweight boxer and he—"

"I'm going to see Beethoven's Choral Symphony, conducted by Karajan."

"Ah, yes. I should have guessed." As usual, nothing came back. Sarcasm was always lost on Yolanda.

"Don't you want to come?"

I paused for a moment, contemplating a virtual evening of classical music with the gorgeous, but very dull Yolanda. She had great legs, but a voice as boring as anaglypta wallpaper. "Not tonight," I said quickly, before she could think of an alternative. "I'll see you at practice though."

That brought a smile to her face. Practice was one of the few *real* activities left to us now. Her face moved closer, filling almost the entire screen. "I can't wait," she cooed, her voice becoming low.

I felt a little thrill course through me. She was so nice, I couldn't argue about that, I really couldn't. Loyal, honest, sensible. Gorgeous. Nevertheless, there was something…I don't know. Made for one another, you could say. She so cute, so slim. Me… Well, I was me. But conversations were always very dull, all work and no play. Even so, I liked being close to her whenever I could. At weekends, we usually managed a few moments and she cared for me, helped me with school stuff, held me when the memories got too much and I would cry…But conversations were so limited and always, *always* she had to bring it all back down to reality – as if I didn't know enough about that already. Anyway, I just smiled back, pursed my lips with a perfunctory kiss and was about to click the 'end call' button when she held up her palm. "Wait, Simeon. Did you hear the announcements earlier, about the outrages?"

"Outrages?"

"Oh no, Simeon, why don't you *ever* take notice of what's going on? It's important."

"Well, as long as I've got you to tell me what's what, I don't need to—"

"They blew up one of the sub-terminals last night."

I shook my head, not fully understanding her words. For months – or was it years, I could never be sure – terrorists or agitators, or call them whatever you like, had carried out attacks in regular intervals. I rarely took notice. "So, why is that so important?"

"Because they killed some Sweepers this time. Security is tightening up, everywhere you go. So, just be careful when you come to practice, okay?"

"Yes, okay Yollie. Thanks."

"I love you, Simeon."

Her words hung in the air, tiny, glowing wisps of candy-floss clouds, drifting over me, settling inside, wrapping me up all warm.

She loved me. "Me too, Yollie."

She switched off the connection.

For a long time I sat gazing at the screen, the worry eating away at me – I should have done my science homework,

This was really where it all began, you see – speaking to Yolanda. If she hadn't called me, to remind me about practice, I probably wouldn't have gone. And if I hadn't gone, I would have been in terrible trouble. A Sandman would have called, and everyone knows what that means. However, perhaps even that would have been preferable to what I was about to go through.

So, I made my weary way through the empty streets towards the public arena positioned at the top of the city. My journey was no different to any other time – I moved through silent avenues, passing faceless, characterless and ugly tenement blocks, standing like so many forgotten tombstones. Recently washed down by the automated cleaning machines, everything bathed with an antiseptic smell, masking the filth. The sheen on the tarmac reflected the darkened sky, gloomy like my mood. I had a lot on my mind – namely the science homework. It wasn't that I couldn't do it; it was simply that I couldn't be bothered – it was *so* boring. I kept thinking to myself that perhaps if I asked Kevin Phelps, or that other know-it-all, Roger Kennedy, they might offer me some answers. Especially if I paid them. I had some of that American-style gum that I'd found on a corpse down by the river. They'd do anything for that.

Whilst so engrossed in my thinking, I paused to look around and realised, to my horror, I'd taken a wrong turning. Cursing my own stupidity, I turned to retrace my steps but then stopped. This was a part of town I hadn't been in before. I felt the first stirrings of panic growing in my stomach. I whirled around, trying to find some distinguishing feature, anything which might point me back to the main road. But in the encroaching darkness, all of the side streets looked the same and I soon realized that I was lost. It might take me over an hour to find my way back to the route which led me to the arena. Maybe more. When I thought I heard a Sandman patrol marching close by, I quickly dipped into a doorway. Looking back, this decision was probably my most stupid. I had no reason to hide – I hadn't done anything wrong, had nothing to be guilty about, and it was hours before curfew. The patrol might stop, scan my chip, check my identification, then send me on my way with a D-merit to download into school the following day. Nevertheless, the fear of meeting them in that ghastly place was too much, so I pressed myself further into the doorway. Almost at once, the door gave way, rotten timbers groaning. Worried that it was going to burst inwards, making me look more of a guilty fool than I already was, I tried the handle and quickly stepped inside, pressing the rickety door shut behind me.

I held my breath, the darkness inside complete. I stood there for a few moments, waiting for my eyes to adjust to the gloom, listening. Outside, I heard the Sandman patrol stomping past, the sound of their pounding boots growing louder with each passing second. This was the point of no return, of course. If those Sandmen had seen or heard me going through the door, what was I supposed to say to explain away my bizarre actions? A D-merit would be like a welcome gift compared to an evening being grilled by those evil slime-balls.

When I couldn't hear the steady thump anymore, I screwed up my eyes. Someone told me, or perhaps I'd read it on the net, that if you close your eyes for ten seconds, when you open them again you can pick out the details of the darkest of rooms. I did just that. And guess what, it worked.

At least, I thought it had, because the light I saw had nothing to do with my squeezing my eyes shut. It had everything to do with the fact that there were three or four men standing in front of me and the closest held a torch, directing the beam straight into my face. I gasped and turned my head away, hand coming up defensively. Suddenly, other hands, not mine, grabbed me roughly by the shoulders and pulled me deeper inside the blackened room.

They didn't let me go until I was in another room, situated at the far end of the building. Slamming me down into a chair, one of them must have flicked the mains switch because the room suddenly filled with a sickly yellow glow. I looked towards it, screwing up my face again. A naked bulb hung from the ceiling, covered with a thick film of dust and dead flies. That made everything feel all the more terrifying somehow and I snapped my head this way and that, not knowing what to expect next.

Somebody spoke from out of the gloom. "Who the hell are you?"

I looked towards where I thought the voice was coming from. A big man, bigger than the others by a long way, loomed over me, his face wet with sweat.

Along the side of his mouth ran deep lines, created by either laughter or pain – I couldn't guess which – cut into his flesh, seeming to lend his expression a menacing air. No matter how hard I tried, I couldn't drag my eyes way from his. Hypnotic, that's what they were.

"I'll ask you again. Who are you?"

"Simeon," I replied quickly, hoping this was enough. It obviously wasn't because one of the others stepped forward and hit me hard across the face with the back of his hand. The blow snapped my head back with such force that I almost fell over, my head ringing like a bell smacked by a massive hammer. Before I toppled over completely, the big man grabbed me by the arm and tugged me upright again.

He stared at me and for a long time. I didn't have the strength to speak, let alone move, my terror total.

But nothing could take away the pain. It spread across my face until a red, pulsing heat haze of agony cocooned me. Whimpering and blubbering, I held my cheek where the blow had struck and, wincing, managed to cry out, "What the hell was that for?" I wanted to sound hard, but my attempt proved unconvincing. I can hold my own against someone my own age with no trouble, but these were grown men, and there were four of them. With this lot, pretending being tough wasn't going to cut it.

"For being a smart-ass," said the big guy. "Who sent you here?"

I blinked, not understanding the question. How could I, it was blatantly stupid. "No one," I said needlessly, because no one had. I look beyond his shoulder to the others, lurking there in the half-light. Who were these guys, and why were they hiding in a dark building, away from the prying eyes of the Sandmen? I wanted to ask them, but thought better of it when I saw them exchanging dangerous looks. The atmosphere crackled with tension.

"Get rid of him, Stoker," said the man who had hit me, "or I will." He fumbled inside his jacket. I watched with widening eyes as he produced a black revolver and expertly fitted a stubby, evil looking silencer on the end of the barrel.

"Wait," I shouted, both my hands coming up in a defensive gesture, "for God's sake – wait!" My explanation tumbled out of me, "My name's Simeon, Simeon Allis. I live over on Beckford Estate. I was making my way to practice at the public arena when I took a wrong turning and got lost. That's the truth of it, I promise."

The hitter with the gun paused for a moment, weighing up my story. He glanced over at the others, who shrugged. "It don't ring true. Simeon *Alice?*" I knew he thought it was the girl's name. I didn't feel like putting him straight. "What sort of a name is that?"

"Poofter's name," spat one of the others and they all laughed.

"Shut up," snapped the big man, the one called Stoker. He hadn't laughed. His eyes remained fixed on me, giving nothing away. Did he believe me, or not? "Where's your ID?"

I fished around in my pants and brought it out. Stoker snatched it off me and took it over to the far side of the room. I followed him with my eyes and he switched on a spotlight, holding the ID under the glare of the light. I was surprised to see the mass of equipment neatly stacked up there, including an official government ID scanner. That surprised me more than anything, for those things were priceless – as well as being ultra-secret. I knew this, having tried to find out as much as I could about them by hacking into the Internal Security mainframe and failing miserably. So, how had he got hold of one, unless... No, I shook my head, dismissing the idea instantly – these weren't Government men, they couldn't be. As these thoughts swirled through my fuddled brain, Stoker fed my card into the machine, waited a few moments and read off the information. He came back, chewing his lip, deep in thought.

"It's like he says."

The hitter with the gun sighed in disappointment. He looked at me, his features hard. "So, you got lost? And just by chance, by sheer chance, you came knocking on our door?"

"There were Sandmen," I blurted out quickly. "I'd taken a wrong turning; if they'd have caught me they'd have given me a D-merit. I've already got too many of those, and another might mean I'd have to go and see the Principal."

"What, in person?"

I nodded meekly, knowing this was an outrageous thing to say. No one had real teachers anymore. Everything was virtual; we all stayed at home in our rooms, linked through our imbedded chips with the virtual classroom, our lessons downloaded directly into the cerebral cortex. We hardly ever interacted on a physical level now. Exceptions being, of course, practice and the occasional authority figure. This explained why the hitter appeared so shocked to learn the Principals were real. Nothing more than glorified programmers to be absolutely accurate, probably with no educational background at all. But what did that matter. His task was to keep things running smoothly, not to impart knowledge. That was for the government to do. If there was a system failure, he was the man who fixed it. If a student strayed, or received too many D-merits, the Principal spoke to him. Laid it all out on the table – the consequences of not achieving. Deportation and re-programming in Cambridge.

Moving into the far corner, the men spoke rapidly to one another. For a moment I had a wild fantasy of making a run for it, ripping open the door and catching up with those Sandmen, telling them everything I'd found out...which wasn't much, but I felt sure that they'd be interested. I craned my neck and peered towards the door, nothing more than a black smudge in the darkness, and let out a long breath. Impossible, I decided, not a hope. The bullet would smack into the back of my head before I'd got within two metres and that would be that. So I sat and waited, gingerly touching my rapidly swelling cheek every couple of seconds. How would I explain that to Piperson, the Bandmaster? If I ever got out of this mess, of course. If I ever saw Piperson, or anyone ever again. Especially Yolanda. God, I missed her right now.

"All right," said Stoker coming towards me again. I noticed that, behind him, the hitter no longer held the gun. That was something at least, a tiny sliver of hope. "We want you to do something for us."

I frowned, puzzled. "I...what do you mean?"

The hitter pushed past Stoker, jutting his chin towards me, snarling. "We mean, you little shrimp, that if you don't do as we ask, we'll drop you in it with the Sandmen..."

"Right up to your pretty little neck." Another said, the one who'd called me a 'poofter'. Of all four of them, he was the one I detested the most. An aura of latent wickedness radiated from him, unsettling me, causing me to avoid his penetrating stare.

"It's simple," said Stoker. "We want you to deliver a package to The Protector."

Two

Yolanda smiled sickly sweet as I came through the main entrance. I held up my hand to stop her running towards me, but I didn't need to, she was already slowing down, deep furrows appearing on her brow. For a moment, I wondered what was bothering her, then I remembered – my cheek. I brushed the bruise with the tips of my fingers and simply raised my eyebrows. I hoped that was explanation enough.

It seemed to be, at least for now. She didn't ask, just creased her forehead a touch and, taking me by the elbow, gently steered me towards the group of assembled players. She pressed her head against my arm. We hadn't seen each other in the flesh for a week and I knew that she'd missed me. I often thought that for Yolanda, I seemed to be the personification of everything good and pure in this world. She hardly uttered a bad word to me and if ever I snarled or grunted, she simply smiled, letting me know she forgave me. Sometimes, her attentions proved too much – almost as if she were smothering me. Like a mother's love, perhaps. If anyone was to know a mother's love, of course. Mothers were not necessary now, and hadn't been for some time. But maybe Yolanda was as good and, especially after what I'd been through, I could do with someone to love me.

I wanted to tell her everything, but of course I couldn't. They'd told me, those men, in no uncertain terms, that if I opened my mouth to a single soul, they'd shop me to the Sandmen. Stoker had run a defrag through my chip and had found just enough room to place in there a tiny programme he'd created. He'd punched up the information on his screen and there I was. Everything. I marvelled at his expertise, but the idea that he now owned me filled me with dread. I was his, every bit of me. At any given time, he'd know where I was, who I was talking to, what I was eating, even what I was wearing... I was all sewn up.

"Allis, my divine boy, nice of you to join us."

I looked up and nodded briefly towards Piperson as he strode across the parade ground towards me. As he got closer, I could smell the cheese and onion on his breath, a reassuring connection with the real world, of my old life. Yesterday's life. That afternoon's life.

"Sorry, Captain Piperson, sir," I clicked my heels and brought my right hand up to my temple in a stiff salute. "I was somewhat delayed."

"No matter, Allis. You're here now, so we can begin." He span around and I looked over to the rest of the band and struck a pose which I hoped would force them to turn away from me. The last thing I wanted now was lots of questions. They stood rigid, like concrete pillars, white uniforms gleaming even in the drab, dismal light, all waiting. Without another second's pause, I took the cornet from Yolanda's outstretched hand and fell in beside the others.

Piperson's voice cracked, "By the left... qui-ick... MARCH!"

Bramble Fawlkes beat out the bass drum and the practice began.

Just over two gruelling hours later Yolanda and I strolled through the remains of City Centre Park, pausing by one of the stagnant ponds, imagining ducks still swam there, waiting for us to throw them bread. She stood so close I could breathe in her perfume. I slipped my arm around her slim waist and she cooed softly, put her head against me and I held onto her, wanting that simple, glorious moment to last forever. She was supremely gorgeous, the most divine girl I'd ever known. When I first laid eyes on her, I thought my legs would buckle and bend beneath me. Lithe, long-limbed, cheek bones carved out of ebony and eyes that you just wanted to dive into and lose yourself forever. She was everything anyone could wish for, so why did I never feel satisfied with her? Everything was so in-your-face with her, that's the truth. She had no imagination, no soul I suppose. For her, the world was a simple place. This is what it is, get on with it. I always looked under the surface, forever asking questions, never satisfied with the answers. She thought that was dangerous and, in all honesty, it was. Sandmen don't like questions and Yolanda likes them even less. She was programmed, like everyone else, to accept our world, revel in its perfections ... or imperfections, as I so often said, much to her annoyance.

"I need to talk to you about something," I said, not really sure how to make her understand without actually telling her anything.

She looked at me with those great big eyes of hers. "You can talk to me about anything." She reached out a single finger and gently touched my swollen cheek. "What's the problem?"

"No, no, it's nothing to do with this," I laughed, flicking the bruise as if it didn't matter. But it did. The pulsing ache was a constant reminder of how hard that guy had hit me. But I didn't want to offer her any explanation, for the simple reason that I couldn't think of one, other than the truth. So I plunged on. "No, I've got myself in a bit of a mess, Yolanda. I'm way behind in my schoolwork. I need to take some time out to try and get it finished."

"Oh."

And that was it. I couldn't believe it. No accusations or blame, no tears, just a shrug of her slim shoulders and we were walking again, following the path to the main gate. Her silence was disturbing.

"Are you all right?"

She shrugged again. She was good at that. "Fine."

I knew she wasn't. I knew she thought this was my way of telling her that I didn't want to see her anymore. This was way off the mark. Dull she may be, but when she pressed that body against me, I couldn't give a fig about anything else. Shallow? Damn right – I'm Simeon Allis, one of the last cynics left in this open-gash of a world. I saw everything as it is, and that made me something of a pariah. If the truth had to be told, she was the only friend I had and I didn't want to lose her. So, as we got to the gate, I pulled her round to me, lifted up her chin and smiled at her. "Look, this is no big deal, Yolanda. I honestly just need some time to get myself straight."

"Are you sure?"

So, I was right. She believed I was telling her this was the end. I put my arms around her and held her close. "Of course I'm sure. You mustn't worry, honestly." I'd used that word twice. Strange how easily lying came to me. I held her for a long time, feeling the warmth spread across my stomach, enjoying the sensation her body gave me. Slowly, bit by bit, I brought myself back to the present, took her hand, and we moved out of the park and drifted down to the riverside and her apartment block. It was almost dark now and curfew would be sounding. I had about ten minutes. "Don't forget your visit to the Albert Hall. What was it, Beethoven? Should be good."

But she wasn't interested in any of that now. I'd hurt her and I couldn't tell her why.

She studied her nails, not wanting to look at me. "You'll be in touch?"

I smoothed her hair. "I really care for you, you know."

"Do you?"

I nodded and leaned forward to kiss her very gently on her lips. She didn't respond, but she didn't back away either.

"I'll contact you in a couple of days." I smiled. As I kissed her a second time, her mouth opened, those velvet lips rolling over mine, our tongues playing around inside. Electricity coursed through my body. "God, Yolanda," I moaned, my hand creeping towards her breast.

"No, not here, Simeon."

"Well where the hell else?"

She held my face in her hands. "Soon," she said, turned and glided away.

I watched her moving down the path, my eyes centred on her magnificent butt and I let out a long groan again. We could have a life, Yolanda and me. It wouldn't be intellectually stimulating, but my God it would be amazing physically.

She reached her residential block and disappeared inside without looking back. I knew she didn't truly believe me. Perhaps it was for the best, because tomorrow I had to forget about school and go to the Protector's residence, and that was something I didn't want Yolanda to know anything about, *ever*.

I only just made the curfew. I had to dash all the way, taking the route along the river, which wasn't such a good idea, but it would save me a couple of vital minutes. I had to leap over several bodies and when one of them moved and reached out with a bony, stick-thin hand to grab me, I knew I was in trouble if I stopped. And I wanted to stop – my lungs were screaming and the stitch in my side hurt like sin. I bit down through the pain, kept on moving, breathing hard, forcing myself not to slow down, and certainly not stop. I couldn't stop, I couldn't slow. So I pushed on until at last I left the stinking, filthy river behind and veered off up the slope towards my part of town. I could see my block, lights on near the top, and I almost cheered. Not far now.

The lights made me think. Idiot that I was, I realised I'd made a serious miscalculation over the time. Everyone who lived in my block – and there weren't many that did – were already safely inside. This wasn't good and I calculated I was at least two minutes late. If they caught you outside after curfew, you were dead. No arguments. A Sandman would come, relentlessly tracking you down until he found you, take you in his great scissor hands and tear off your head. Whimpering with the fear rushing through me, I put my head down and sprinted forward. As I made the twisted, broken drive way that once would have looked so attractive and inviting, I saw him out the corner of my eye. Unmistakeable. Huge. Terrifying.

A Sandman.

I didn't wait to check. I hit the main entrance door to the block with my shoulder and blasted inside.

Running up the stairs in a mad dash, I could already hear the steady beat of the Sandman as he came down the street, his huge legs eating up the distance between us, faster than I could ever hope to run. I fumbled for my key card and managed to slap it against the readout panel just as I sensed him coming through the main entrance. With my heart thumping I pushed open the door to my apartment and turned to see him, only feet behind me, his great legs coming over the top step first. God, he could move fast! He was almost upon me and soon those great arms of his would be clamping themselves around my waist, lifting me up…

He gasped as I slammed the door shut behind me, leaning against it with all my strength, eyes squeezed shut, gulping down the air. He was right outside, a thin sheet of aluminium the only thing separating me from certain annihilation. I could hear him, sense his menace, his power. But I was inside now and I was safe. Sandmen did not follow you into your abode, unless on express orders to do so.

I slid down the door and slumped in a heap on the floor, running my hand over my dripping face. My God, how close had I been? Five seconds more and that would have been it. I let out a long, shuddering sigh and heard the Sandman moving away. I grinned in total, utter relief.

Gathering my senses slightly, I climbed to my feet, putting the flat of my hand against the wall for a moment, steadying my breathing before padding down the hallway to the kitchen. I punched out my dietary requirement for the evening. I was late and the voice from the cooker told me so. I ordered it to make me gruel and, some five seconds later, I took it with me into the lounge, slumped down into my entertainment couch and whispered the machine to come on.

The gruel tasted foul, as it always does. I couldn't finish it and my house computer didn't like that. I told it to shut up, that I wasn't feeling too good. That was stupid, because of course it logged my comments and already they were being sent over to Central Control. They would want to check my daily quota, make sure the dosage was correct. I groaned and sat back. As I watched the incessant newsreels and adverts for the armed forces, I must have dozed off, my mind filled with unwanted images, of how it was before I lived on my own, the golden days when my family were with me and everything was normal and good and real. And, how I first came into contact with the Sandmen.

Three

The street in which we lived in those days was wide and sweeping. Terraced housing, but each possessed with that little blush of individuality which made them so attractive. All had front gardens, with little paths leading from the tiny gate that separated our private worlds from the traffic beyond. Not that there was much traffic, as I could remember. The fuel crisis had become a permanent fixture by then and the distant war in the Middle East meant people were conserving everything, especially petrol.

I was about six, I think, on that fateful day, sitting on our garden wall, my Nan beside me talking to Mrs. Roberts from next door. I can't remember what they were talking about, but that wouldn't have mattered anyway – my Nan could talk about nothing for hours on end. She was a lovely woman, so kind, so caring. Tall and big-boned. Spectacles. 'Have you got your glasses case?' my mum always asked her as Nan readied herself for work. 'Handkerchief, purse and keys?' It was a ritual. This particular day, she wasn't at work, so I guess it must have been a Thursday because the shops weren't open on Thursdays. They'd gone back to the 'old days' as Nan called them. Another indication of just how bad things were becoming.

Well, they talked, Nan and Mrs. Roberts and I watched the street. There were two dogs across the road and they alerted us to the danger. They froze, ears standing upright like they were on stalks, eyes shooting down to the left, then they were off, tails between their legs, racing away like greyhounds from the starting gates. I felt Nan tense, then she gestured for me to get off the wall, her hand flapping around like a flag in a gale. She didn't speak, but I knew she was worried. I got down, brushed my backside and she put her arm across my chest, pressing me back against the wall, hard. Both she and Mrs. Roberts stood ramrod straight, like soldiers at attention, eyes set straight, not a muscle moving, as rigid as marble pillars.

The Sweepers came. There were two of them, big men, dressed in long, beige coloured raincoats, collars up, massive coal scuttle helmets on their heads, the neck guards trailing down their backs like lobster tails. Some called them lobster-tails, a throwback to the English Civil War someone at school told me years later. But I didn't know that then. All I knew was that Nan was frightened, more frightened than I thought a human being could be, and that frightened me too.

The lead Sweeper drew close, smiling, seemingly relaxed, but his eyes were everywhere, the reason they bore the name 'Sweepers'. They patrolled the communities, seeking out 'undesirables' – the unregistered, those who were not yet chipped, many of them foreigners. So many people fled from the devastating wars in the east and swarmed into our country, creating a society at breaking point, and despair and fear walked hand-in-hand along every street. Most were innocent refugees, but some were hardened terrorists, drug-traffickers, gangsters. This was what Nan told me. I won't repeat what Dad called them, but I think his sentiments echoed the majority.

Inside the Sweepers' huge helmets ran a mass of technology, feeding a constant stream of information into the cortex of their brains. Scanned, filtered and diagnosed, this enabled them to identify, within a few seconds, the exact whereabouts of any person not authentically chipped. Don't ask me how they did it, but it was fast and it was brutal.

The bigger of the two was ruffling my hair, whilst the other looked along the houses.

"Nice boy, mother," said the big Sweeper in a sickly sweet voice, "you must be very proud."

"He's not mine, sir," said Nan. I glanced at her, frowning. Nan calling him sir? "He's Mabel's."

The Sweeper nodded, knowing that this was the case because of the scan he had made. I noticed the little electric impulses scuttling across the visor that he had lifted up so we could see his eyes. When they went into action, the visor came down, connecting them into the central mainframe. But they could scan with the visor up or down. Their eyes did that. Hot-wired into the helmet. More machine than human being. "Yes, of course he is. Tell me more about him, mother."

"Born and raised here in the street, sir," she answered. I noticed she wasn't looking at him, her eyes locked straight ahead, mouth set in a wide grin. But not a pleasant or friendly grin, more like one engraved into her features. I saw the sweat glistening on her brow and realised she was terrified.

"A good boy?"

"Very good, sir. Doing well in school. "

"Yes. Had problems with the downloads, I understand."

"Yes. I think it was when…" she suddenly stopped, her eyes darting to his and quickly back again. Did I hear Mrs. Roberts take a sharp intake of breath?

The Sweeper's shoulders shifted under his voluminous raincoat. "Heard rumours have we, mother?"

"Nothing that is of any importance, sir."

"No? Why don't you share them with me then?"

For a dreadful, achingly long time we all stood there in silence, so quiet I could hear the processors whirring in his head. With painful slowness, he reached out his right hand and placed it on her shoulder and spoke in the most menacingly soft and sweet voice I had ever heard. "Just the highlights will suffice, mother."

I sensed her body giving way, all the resistance leaving her, his huge paw pressing down with immense strength. A tiny moan escaped from her mouth. "A glitch, sir. Nothing more."

"A glitch. Explain it to me, mother."

The use of that word, 'mother', chilled me to the bone. I snapped my head around. "Please sir, it was a software problem. The connection went down and for a moment…"

He turned his eyes to me, eyes which burned with something not of this world, dissecting and examining every nerve and fibre of my body. Seized with crushing terror, I felt my bowels loosen. "Did your chip malfunction, sweet child?"

I managed to speak, my voice little more than a croak, "Only for a second or two, sir."

"Best run a diagnostic," he said and his eyes closed.

A sudden bolt of searing white light pulsed through my brain, but before I could react, it happened.

One minute we were stood there, hardly daring to breathe, my eyes filling up with tears, my thoughts jumbled up but still managing to wonder why this horrible man talked to my lovely grandma in such a way his words turned her into a quivering wreck, and then…

Two or maybe three men, I can't remember the exact number, came bursting out of a doorway from across the street. Instantly, the second Sweeper was moving, visor down, his raincoat blooming wide open, the massive gyro-controlled laser suspended from his shoulder taking a bead on the running 'undesirables'. The lead man reared up and screamed as the first burst hit him, a single beam of intense light slicing his torso in two. I watched in horror as his legs kept running forward for a few steps before buckling and collapsing to the ground. The top half of his body, a singed slab of charred meat, flesh crackling, spitting fat, lay quivering on the pavement. I could see his face, the eyes wide, terrified, open-mouthed, smoke curling out from between the lips. The whole body in spasm.

I screamed. There was nothing I could have done to prevent it. For a moment I thought I was going to be sick. Nan pulled me down to the ground, her body shielding me. But I could still see.

The other two men cart-wheeled over the pavement as the lasers hit the ground next to them, bringing up their own weapons, barking out their responses. These were older weapons, of course. Ancient. Nine-millimetre automatics, no doubt loaded with dum-dum bullets. Several hit Mrs. Roberts across the chest, throwing her back, making her dance like a marionette as the bullets punched into her body, little explosions of red blood peppering her body – one, two, three, the bullets hit home, like the beat of drum to accompany her dance. She made no sound, just a shocked expression crossing her face before she slumped to the ground.

I screamed again. Nan threw her hand over my mouth, pressed me close. But I had to know, I had to see.

The big Sweeper, the one who had spoken to us, moved fast, cutting across the street, whilst his colleague out-flanked the two men. It was over quickly and viciously, one of the men losing his head in a blink, the other both of his arms. They wanted him alive, that much was obvious. And they had him. His wounds, instantly cauterised, were not going to be the cause of his death. The torture he would endure would do that. But not before he told them everything they needed to know – who controlled them, where their hideout was. How many more of their 'cell' plagued the streets?

Three hover cars and a seemingly endless stream of air-bikes came whispering down the street, blocking off all the entrances, Sweepers disgorging from the vehicles like a swarm of locusts, dozens of them, spreading out in all directions.

But they all froze when the Sandman came.

I'd never seen one before that day. And from the moment I saw it, my waking hours were to be filled with dread, and my sleep dominated by nightmares.

Four

Almost before the Sun rose above the horizon, I made my way down to the square to pick up the first hover bus that would take me to the city outskirts. I touched the bulge in my pocket, reassuring myself that the little package the man called Stoker gave me was still there; the one I had to deliver to the Protector, in person. But as the bus arrived and I stepped on board, things began to unravel. I scanned my identity card, but nothing happened. This wasn't unusual, so I didn't panic. Quite often the technology would fail, a fact which was becoming increasingly common lately. With so many resources directed towards the war in the Middle East, money was tight... non-existent actually. Students, such as myself, received an allowance, paid directly into our virtual accounts on a weekly basis. The Government initially tried monthly payments, but most of us spent every cent in the first week – the lure of playing football with George Best, or staring in *Enter the Dragon* alongside Bruce Lee too good to be ignored. With all our food, drink and drugs freely assigned, we had nothing else on which to spend our allowances. So, in their divine wisdom, the powers that be decided we were simply too stupid and irresponsible to manage our finances, hence the weekly payments. Yolanda, always so careful with her money, engaged a personal, virtual finance advisor to manage every single cent she parted with. It was awesome. Me, I would just scroll through the choices, and hit on whatever I wanted, regardless of the cost. Yolanda would save her credits, waiting until something really extraordinary came online. Like that concert, for instance. The concert I'd ruined for her.

Yolanda. Her face came into my mind, a face like no other, those high cheekbones, full lips, the skin burnished with health. Her body a dream. I made a pact with myself, right there, gazing at the scanning device, that when this was over and I was once more safely back home, I'd take her to bed and we'd make love endlessly. The thought sent a thrill through my loins. I was on fire.

A heavy hand came down on my shoulder, wrenching me from my reverie. I swung around to face a massive Sweeper, fibre optics running across his visor. "Problem?"

I froze, feeling my stomach turn inside out. He was already scanning my chip, probably from the moment the fault on the bus was reported. I tried to laugh, but all that came out was a kind of raspy cough, "No, it's just not accepting my ID."

"Oh?" He reached over and took my card, holding it up to his helmet, scanning it. "It's perfectly fine. Perhaps there's a fault with the scanner?"

He carried out a quick diagnostic and sighed. I still wasn't looking at him but I could sense his impatience. "It's crashed. You'll have to get the next bus." The other passengers began to shuffle around nervously. He held up his hand to them and they all instantly settled down.

I closed my eyes. Damn it! I wanted to get to the Protector's as soon as possible. The journey out of town was a long, sometimes dangerous one. I didn't want to be coming back late.

The Sweeper, noticing my disappointment, gave me a long look. "You have an appointment?"

"Yes, sir. Out of town appointment, sir."

He read through my chip. Stiffening, he turned me around to face him. "Boy," he said, his voice serious, "you have an appointment with the Protector?"

I'd never experienced surprise in a Sweeper's voice. Usually so calculated, planned, deliberate, this one appeared genuinely shocked.

It was the adjustments Stoker made to my chip, something designed to enable me to gain access to the Protector's residence, something the Sweeper had just read.

I nodded limply. "Yes, sir."

"And you're going by bus?" He shook his great head and within seconds a hover bike hissed alongside. The passengers onboard all gasped in awe. "This will take you there."

I gaped. A hover bike? I'd never been onboard a hover bike before. I was both shocked and a little excited. "Thank you, sir," I mumbled. He was still peering down at me. I tried to remain calm. He must have sensed my nervousness, surely.

"Don't fret so," he said in a kindly voice. "Meeting the Protector can be a nerve-wracking experience. But it must be important, so go with all our thoughts and all our grace."

I bowed deeply. "Thank you, sir." I stepped down from the bus and slipped into the seat of the hover bike. I breathed a sigh and readied myself for the thrust. I'd seen the images on the holistic screens, but this was real. My God, I was actually sitting in a hover bike.

"Simeon!"

My head snapped round, my eyes nearly popping out of their sockets and I felt the fear grip me like a vice. The Sweeper loomed over me. Had he realised, had he discovered the truth? Was it all just a terrible ploy on his part to get me off the bus and into the open so he could cut me down with his laser?

His hand came forward. "You forgot this."

It was my ID. I tried not to exhale too loudly, smiled instead, and took the card gratefully.

"Safe journey."

I bowed my head again, fastened the safety belt and tried to relax. The Perspex cover appeared from out of thin air, encasing me in its protective shell and then, without warning, the bike shot off, hitting its top speed within a few, unbelievably exhilarating seconds. The G-force threw me back against the seat and I held on, trying to keep my eyes open but finding it virtually impossible to do so. I managed to turn my head to the side and watch the world rush by in a blur. Blasts of cold air buffeted the bike as it climbed, forcing me to close my eyes and when I did chance another glance, we had already left the grime of the city far behind us, passing over barren, scorched countryside. I was on my way, into the unknown, heading towards the Protector's residence. I was terrified.

It was an imposing building. Even with the tall security walls surrounding it, the upper storeys were clearly visible. Set upon a hill, it commanded views across the entire valley. That valley was once a rich and pleasant place, where workers would toil in the sunshine, harvesting the wheat. Now, it was brown, lifeless and brutalised. The years had not been kind to the earth and now, with it no longer tended, scrub, weeds and harsh gorse took control, conquering it.

I stepped down from the hover bike and walked slowly up to the main entrance. Already the cameras were whining away, searching me, my biographical details scrutinised from somewhere deep within the complex. I waved my ID across the scanner and the doors silently slid open.

The guard surveyed me with blank, soulless eyes. I wasn't sure if he was human, encased as he was in dull, black reactive armour, the lines between reality and virtual blurred, the technology so advanced. He came forward, the great, ugly blaster in his hands dominating his whole person. I gulped but didn't move.

"You are expected." His voice mechanical, without emotion.

The statement took me a little by surprise. Stoker's programming skills were a thing of wonder. I nodded, patting my pocket where the packet still lay untouched.

"I have…"

The guard held up his hand, telling me there was no need for explanations – he already knew. Turning, he motioned me to follow. As I fell in behind him, moving along the intensely white path cutting through the verdant plastic grass on either side, he suddenly stopped his head moving, body tensing, alert. I followed his gaze but, as far as I could tell, there was nothing. Not convinced, he gave me an intense look, scanning me, just to make sure. Satisfied, he moved on and I followed, more warily now. Nothing could shake the feeling I was entering into a situation over which I had little, or no control, and no choice other than to do what was demanded of me – whatever that turned out to be.

Five

The only sound which echoed along the corridor was that of my footsteps, the guard leaving me at the entrance. Above and to the side were arrayed whole banks of monitors, all of them filled with the same image – me, walking nervously along the gleaming white, clinically clean pathway to God alone knew where.

Reaching the end, the corridor split into two directions, a red beam pointing its way along the correct path. I took my time, keeping my breathing controlled and easy, aware that sensors would pick up any change in my heartbeat patterns, and soon I came to a blank, gunmetal door. I waited until it slowly opened to reveal the Protector's private apartment.

It was huge, a vast space with vaulted ceiling and oak panelled walls, its grandeur befitting the Protector's position in the Government's hierarchy. He was the leader, chosen by the Supreme Council, elected for life. And life, for a Protector, was long. Unthinkably long.

No one knew his name, not many had ever seen his face, but everyone knew his voice.

It greeted us every morning, calling us out of bed. "Good morning, boys and girls! Rise up for a new day of learning and opportunity."

Older ones did not receive such greetings. Aged still existed, like the ones on the bus, but these were people with no children, or grandchildren. Often, we saw them visiting old buildings known as shops, a concept we found difficult to grasp, but one which they found comforting no doubt – clinging on to bits of a world that no longer existed. Memories. Their time was rapidly drawing to a close.

Perhaps mine was too…

Something lingered in that huge place, something which wasn't right. I took in the sumptuous furnishings of the rich and powerful around me. Priceless artefacts and antique furnishings filled the many alcoves which separated the large room into smaller areas, each slightly differently decorated. I wandered into what appeared to be study, with real books lining the walls. I'd never seen a book. Not one you could hold, flick through the pages. Feeling brave, I took one down, surprised at how heavy it felt, and read the spine 'David Copperfield' by someone called Dickens. Shaking my head, I put it back and drifted into another space and found myself standing before a large painting. Mesmerised, I couldn't help but wonder how any one person could amass enough money to buy such treasures. Tilting my head, somewhere in the dark recesses of my mind I recalled seeing this painting before somewhere, but its title and name of the artist escaped me. And yet the startling image of a skull like face of a man on a bridge, a vibrant, swirling sky, dark, sinister figures in the background triggered something…

"The Scream."

I jumped as his voice came to me from seemingly nowhere. Deep and strangely comforting, it held no threat or anger, more a calmness, a reassurance that everything was going to be all right. He moved somewhere over on my left. I could sense his warmth, pulsating from his body, like an aura. I lowered my head, averting my eyes, not wishing to gaze upon the glory that was the Protector.

"Simeon," he said smoothly. "Look at me, Simeon."

I gasped when I raised my eyes. He glowed. There was no other word to describe him. He was lit up. Like a candle. Not around him, but from within, as if illuminated by an intense white source, rays of light radiating from the centre of his body. He was sitting inside some form of hovercraft, which purred softly, and he wore robes of the softest, subtlest grey. A smile spread across his benevolent, youthful face.

"It was painted in the dark and distant past, before we had the security of the Sandmen to guard us and keep us. I keep it to remind myself of just how dreadful those times were. Can you feel its menace, Simeon?"

"Yes, my lord." I had no idea how to address him, but 'sir' simply did not seem adequate enough for such a wondrous being.

"Come closer, Simeon. Let me scan your chip."

I did as I was bid and allowed him to read through all of my files, the most private, the most significant, and those less likely to show me in a good light. Everything was there: my innermost feelings, desires, fears. Every secret I had ever had revealed, examined and analysed. I couldn't physically feel anything, yet it seemed to me that I was being laid bare, all of my pretensions being swept away to leave me as open and defenceless as if I were a little baby. When he finished I held my breath and waited for his judgement.

"Well, Simeon," he said at long last, "I see that you are somewhat behind in your school work."

"I am, my lord. Yes."

"And you have plans to enter the Academy when you are older. That is excellent news. But you can only accomplish your ambition if you maintain your grades. School, Simeon, is the single most important thing we have. You can recite our creed?"

"Yes, of course my lord."

"There is no 'of course' about it, Simeon. Many students have stumbled in their studies because they had not set the creed to memory."

I closed my eyes, took a breath and recited what years of schooling had stamped into my subconscious. " 'I believe in the unity of our state, in the benevolence of our Lord and in the sanctity of the Sandman's roll to protect and to serve us all, keeping us safe from our enemies and allowing us to sleep well in our beds.'"

"Impressive. But do you believe it?"

Taken aback, I did not fully understanding the implication of his question. "My lord?"

"You very nearly missed curfew last night, did you not?"

Was there nothing they did not know? With little point in trying to justify anything, I nodded, feeling a little ashamed. "I had taken Yolanda home, my lord."

"Yes, an excellent student." The little hover car circled me before it banked away and transported the Protector to the far end of the room where a raised platform appeared from out of a large hole in the floor. A massive desk dominated the centre of the platform, covered with a vast array of technology: monitors, computers, servers. The Protector took the hovercraft up to the desk and settled himself down behind it. He swept his hand across a digitised array and the hover car simply fell away and folded itself up into a small, compact box of purest silver. Picking it up, he breathed on it and polished its side on his sleeve before putting it into a drawer. Then he sat back and beamed at me.

"Simeon, you have something for me, I understand?"

I promptly delved inside my trousers and pulled out the little package Stoker had given me. Immediately, a great clang rang around the room and from out of the wall emerged a bodyguard. Perhaps it was the same one at the gate, I couldn't tell. He looked the same. Before I could really register anything about him, he took the package from me and held it up, obviously checking its integrity. Reassured, he took it over to the Protector, and placed it gently on the desk before him.

"Simeon," the Protector said, running his fingers lightly over the surface of the package, "where did you get this?"

This was the question I was dreading. If I told him, then I'd have to betray Stoker, and that would mean the Sandmen would interview me, scan my brain, find out everything, including the treasonous crime of tampering with my chip. I'd be dead. Stoker had been fairly emphatic about that. If I didn't reveal the package's source, then how could I explain where I got it, and why I had travelled beyond city limits to come here? It was a nightmare and, simply put, I couldn't see any way out, except telling the truth.

"You were in Alpha quadrant last night, Simeon," continued the Protector without waiting for my answer, "your chip cannot lie. Alpha quadrant is a highly secure area, so you must have powerful friends."

The bodyguard put the heel of his hand in my back and pushed me forward. I almost stumbled and fell.

"You were looking for your parents, Simeon."

I couldn't speak for a moment. What had Stoker implanted in my damned chip?

"And you believed they were being held in the Alpha quadrant. Why was that, Simeon? Did you feel that by going there you would see them again?"

"I – I'm not sure, my lord." The chip revealed everything anybody ever did. The one thing it could reveal, however, was emotions. Hence his line of questioning. If I had gone to the Alpha Quadrant, there had to be a reason. The truth, however, seemed somewhat lame and a little hard to believe. An accident? A turn of fate? "Honestly, I'm not sure."

"No, of course you're not." He folded his hands over his stomach. The light around him pulsated, turning from a bright orange to a much duller, but equally warming yellow-ochre. Perhaps it altered with his mood. He smiled. "How do you know Senior Administrator Taylor Andrews?"

This was becoming more wild and weird by the second. Stoker had put stuff into my head about which I had no knowledge. What was I to do, confess everything, or simply go along for the ride? Another push in the back from the bodyguard. "Yolanda" I blurted. Why had I said that? None of it made sense. Stoker had stitched me up tight.

Smiling even more broadly, the Protector waved to the bodyguard to retreat. Turning, I watched him disappearing into the wall, as if he were part of its very fabric, and the Protector and I were alone again, just the two of us.

"Your honesty is refreshing," said the Protector, gently running a forefinger backwards and forwards across the package. "I believe if you do well at school, Simeon, you shall achieve your ambitions." He looked up, his eyes boring into me. "Perhaps, even beyond."

Not sure what he meant by that, I gave a little smile and looked down to my hands, which I was unconsciously wringing. I stopped abruptly, and snapped my head up to find his gaze boring into me.

"You know what this is?" He held up the little package.

I shook my head. "I have no idea, my lord. I'm sorry."

"It is no matter, Simeon. The important thing is, that *I* know, and that you have delivered it safely to me." He slid a key card into one of his computer ports and placed the little package inside a desk drawer. It slid shut without a sound. Moving his hand over a sensor pad on his desk, the great metallic door through which I'd entered opened behind me with a hiss. "And now, you can go. Goodbye, Simeon, until tomorrow."

"To...morrow?"

He nodded serenely. That was enough. I felt the closeness of the bodyguard materialising at my shoulder and I followed him out of the complex without another word.

The hover bike sat there, waiting. As I clambered onto the seat, I took a glance back to the big house, the solid, impervious walls as blank as the expressions of everyone I had met that morning. Even the Protector's smile held no warmth, no meaning.

On my way back to the city, I tried to gather my thoughts, but there were too many questions racing around inside my head, every single one of them making my brain ache. So, I sat back and let the hover bike whisk me effortlessly to my apartment. I couldn't even be bothered to watch the passing countryside.

Six

My call signal was vibrating throughout my apartment as I came through the door and I quickly opened the messaging panel and Yolanda's face loomed up. She looked concerned, but that was her normal face so I wasn't suspecting anything. She forced a smile.

"I know you said not to contact you, but I was worried."

I settled myself down and smiled back. At least mine was genuine. I was actually pleased to see her, felt a little tingle in my neck, all yummy inside too. I had to swallow that down, mustn't let Yolanda guess that I might have feelings for her. "I'm glad. I need to talk to you."

"Oh." That downcast look again.

"Why do you always suspect the worst?" I was feeling tetchy. The meeting with the Protector had ruffled me and I didn't know what to expect next – a Sandman coming through my door, perhaps?

"Sorry," she said quietly.

I ran a hand through my hair. "Yollie," I always called her that when I was being affectionate. Hearing it now, it made her look hopeful. "Look, I haven't been exactly…honest."

She gazed at me with those big saucer eyes of hers. Her bottom lip began to tremble.

"I…look, can I come round? I hate talking on this thing."

"Okay," she said, without any expression, in either her face or her voice. "Ten minutes."

The screen went blank and I turned away. I didn't even have time for a shower, and this was my water window. One hour of hot water every other day. And now I was going to miss it. Typical.

Now I'd delivered the package, I no longer felt bound by the promise I made to Stoker. The fact that it was a bad promise, made under duress, didn't really enter into it. As I stepped up to Yolanda's door, I felt an enormous sense of relief, and when she stood there, I threw my arms around her, holding her close. Her body tensed, and she resisted for a moment, clearly shocked at my action. Gradually, her body relaxed and she gave a little laugh. I put my fingers under he chin and tipped up her face. I kissed her. "Don't worry so much," I said.

She led me into her apartment, sat me down and gave me juice, which must have cost most of her weekly credit. I savoured every mouthful whilst she tidied up her assignments on the computer. She still did it the old-fashioned way, using written words. I always marvelled at that.

"So," she said, sitting down opposite me. She was wearing a single piece short length dress in white, belted around her slim waist with a brown leather cord. The dress contrasted with the copper tones of her skin and she looked beautiful. "Tell me."

She'd obviously prepared herself for my speech. Whatever she was expecting to hear, she had steeled herself, hardening her resolve not to show emotion. I could it, by the set look on her face.

"I wasn't doing my school work," I said, not having rehearsed anything, knowing honesty was the safest, and best course. "Before I got to practice, I'd got lost. I was daydreaming, as I do, and I must have taken a wrong turning. Anyway, there were Sandmen about and I dived into the nearest building. It wasn't empty."

She frowned deeply, "You mean it was someone's house?"

"No, it was all derelict. Everything was black, the buildings nothing but shells."

Her hand came to her mouth. "No, Simeon – you mean the Alpha Quadrant?"

I nodded, saw her wince. "The whole area was a bombsite. But there *were* people in there – men. Hiding."

"Dissenters? Agitators?" Her eyes grew wide with a mixture of disbelief and horror.

"I suppose. I didn't really get a chance to talk to them much. They grabbed me, threw me in a chair and threatened me. They told me that if I didn't help them they would tell the Sandmen I had deliberately found my way there. I'd be arrested, Yollie. Worse. I'd be vaporised."

"What, for getting lost?" She shook her head, biting down on her lip, pained expression on her face. "Simeon – is this *true*?"

I felt the anger suddenly well up inside, "Of course it's true! Do you think I'd make this all up?"

"I don't know…I suppose you would if you were with someone else."

So, there it was – she suspected I was two-timing her. I put my head in my hands. "For God's sake, Yollie."

"Don't use that word, Simeon." She instinctively looked around, fearful that a Sandman or a Sweeper lurked in some darkened corner. "They can hear, you know. Blasphemy is a crime."

I glanced over to her computer array and nodded. "All right. Sorry. Look, Yollie, there is no one else, all right? You're the only girl for me."

By the look on her face I could tell she didn't believe me. I stood up and went over to her window and looked down into the deserted street. Despite it being hours until curfew, no one moved around outside. "Yollie. This is what happened. I'm not lying, I promise. The men told me that if I didn't help them they would hand me over to the authorities. The Sandmen. You know what that means. It's that simple." I looked at her. "They wanted me to deliver a package. To the Protector."

Her eyes grew even larger. "The…But how? What…?"

I knew I couldn't tell her about Stoker and his tampering with my chip. That would be too much, even for Yolanda to take on board. It was the one piece of the whole story I decided to skip.

"I went there today, with the package. To the Protector's residence."

She was thinking now, thinking about the absurdity of what I'd just uttered. I wasn't anyone special; an A-grader, true – when I bothered to finish an assignment – but nothing more than that. I wasn't in any sense, privileged. Thinking about it, I too doubted the truth of my words.

"Simeon – you expect me to believe that you, Simeon Allis, went to the house of the single most important man on the planet, and was granted entry?" I nodded and she titled her heads, not convinced. "And what did you do when you got there? What did *he* do, give you cucumber sandwiches?"

Quite funny for Yolanda! I didn't smile, however, simply shook my head. "He spoke to me."

Her hands came down on her knees with a slap and she stood up, bristling. "Just get out, Simeon. Why don't you just tell me what her name is, and we can forget all this nonsense."

"You drive me mad, Yollie! I've already told you – ah what's the point…You just stay here, believing what you like and I'll go back home and pretend this conversation never happened."

"Yes, you do that. It'll make things a lot easier for you, won't it?"

That was the last straw. I came towards her at a lunge, grabbing her by the shoulders, squeezing her, pressing my lips to her mouth. She tried to wriggle free, but it was useless, I was far too strong for her. I pulled back, gasping and the tears were tumbling down her cheeks. "Yollie…"

"Just say what you have to Simeon…*please!*"

I was trembling. This hadn't gone well. All I wanted to do was unburden myself, let her know the truth. Instead, I'd almost convinced her I was lying. I looked down to the ground, trying to steady myself. I was still holding her by the shoulders and I knew that this was the time. The moment I'd dreaded, the moment I'd promised myself would never come.

Slowly I looked into her sandstorm eyes. I took a breath.

I said it.

"I love you."

We made love. At first urgent, wild, then loving, gentle, responding to the rhythms of our bodies, the love we both felt. Afterwards, we walked down to the river and sat on an old bench there. It groaned under our weight, but we didn't care. There was no pretence anymore. I told her everything. In a weird sort of way I felt that the weight had been lifted and I honestly felt lighter. More content. It was the strangest feeling. She nuzzled into me, putting her head on my shoulder, and we watched the scum on the water play around the various bits of cardboard and wood that floated by.

"I've been an idiot," she said softly.

"Yes," I said it half-jokingly, but I meant it. She didn't stir, accepting the truth of what I'd said. "Yes, you have. But so have I. For not trusting you. I wanted to tell you, but…"

"It's okay," she squeezed my hand, "I understand everything now."

"I don't want to say this – but I was scared, Yollie. Scared what those men would do to me."

"Well," she must have seen the consequences of what I'd been through in the worry lines of my face. In the quiet I could hear a distant clock chiming the hour. It was thirty minutes to curfew. "I think...I think you should tell the Protector. Tomorrow."

"Really? What, everything?"

"Everything that you've told me. Yes."

In that single sentence, I suspected she knew that I hadn't revealed everything. I'd omitted the part about the chip. I still wasn't one hundred percent convinced such an admission wouldn't pitch her into hysterics. Fortunately, she didn't pursue it but it made me feel uneasy I hadn't been totally honest. Yolanda was just about the most perceptive person I knew, but even she hadn't guessed what Stoker had done to me. "I'm not sure I can tell him *everything*, Yollie. I'll have to think about it."

"Okay. But you have to ask yourself why he ordered you to visit him again, tomorrow. The Protector may already suspect you were set up."

I nodded. I'd thought of the possibility myself. He seemed to know virtually everything else. But, then again, Stoker's piece of programming seemed incredibly good. Whatever he'd done to my chip, it had fooled the Protector. That was some piece of wizardry.

"Maybe we should put in an application to move," I said, thinking out loud. "I hate this city. As I travelled out to the Protector's home, I saw other places where we could live. Make a new life."

"Oh, Simeon," her voice was dream-like. She must have been thinking the same thoughts as me. "I would like nothing better, but ... You're not being very realistic."

"I know. But maybe one day, yeah?"

"Yes. One day."

We sat like that for a long time, then I took her home. We kissed again, the smoothness of her lips causing me to almost faint. Okay, so our conversations would never set the world ablaze, but she set my heart ablaze and perhaps that was more than enough. I'd been fighting against these feelings for too long and now, with everything out in the open, I felt strangely at peace with myself.

We stumbled into her room, not making it to the bed. We ripped away our clothes and writhed on the floor and I yelled out when I plunged into her. Her body, so smooth, so moist. Lost in the throes of desire, it was over too soon and we lay, in a dishevelled mess, both of us gazing at the ceiling, breathing hard.

Some ten minutes or so later, I gave her a little wave and she closed the door. Adjusting my clothing, I went back downstairs, and didn't even notice the many steps, feeling giddy with the thought of her. The lift being totally inoperable, as usual, by the time I got to the bottom, I calculated I had about fifteen minutes in order to get home before curfew. Time enough.

Imagine my terror when, as I stepped out into the evening air, a hand grabbed me and slammed me against the wall of the apartment block. A face loomed up close to me, so close I could see the bristles on his chin, smell the stink of alcohol on his breath. It was the Hitter!

"You're pushing your luck, Simeon," he snarled.

I tried to pull free, but his grip was too tight. He pressed his forehead against mine. I squeezed my eyes shut. I wished I could have done the same with my nostrils. He stank of sweat and something like rotten fruit. My stomach baulked.

"You were told not to talk to anyone – *no one!*"

"But I did what you said," I spluttered. "I delivered the package."

"Yeah, we know. We know everything." He jabbed a dirty finger into my forehead. "Stoker has you wired, don't forget. Nothing you do escapes us." He cackled. "*Nothing.*"

I gaped at him. It was obvious what he meant.

"She's quite a girl isn't she – sex on fucking legs!"

"You bastard, if you—"

"Don't try the hard man act with me, you little shit." His hand squeezed around my throat and, gagging, I tried to wriggle free. "I'll give you another slap if you want me to."

Moaning, I felt the tears welling up. "Please…don't."

"We don't want you telling any more stories, you understand?"

"Yolanda won't say anything."

"She better not." He stood back. "Pretty girl."

My eyes snapped open. "Don't you lay a finger on her," I warned, trying to sound as tough as I could.

He grinned. "Ah…touching. Have a soft spot for her, eh?" Without warning, he hit me, very hard, right in the stomach. The air left me in a rush. I crumpled forward, gasping for breath, retching loudly, dropping to my knees, all the strength draining out of me in an instant. The Hitter pulled my head up by the chin. "Get this, Simeon. You open your mouth once more, and I'll do more than lay a finger on her. You understand?"

I managed to nod and then he was gone, as suddenly as he had appeared, leaving me battling for breath, feeling sick, stupid and ashamed. For the first time since Mum disappeared, I cried.

When I felt able, I got to my feet, clutching my stomach. It was tender to the touch. I had to bite back the pain, not having the luxury of time to wallow in my own suffering. I broke out in a jog and as I weaved along the pavements, slowly the strength came back to my legs and broke into a run, pounding down the street like something possessed, I knew I was going to miss curfew. There was nothing I could do, not this time. But I knew I had to try. So, with head down, arms pumping, legs working like a racehorse, I sprinted towards my apartment block. Already I knew I was too late. As I rounded the corner, there he was.

The Sandman.

With my heart thumping, I tried to phone Yolanda. I didn't succeed. My voice was trembling so much that the damned computer couldn't recognise me. I tried to punch in my password, but my fingers felt as big as sausages so I gave it up as a bad joke and sat there, head in my hands, trying to find some sense of order.

It had scanned me. I had stood there, as all the manuals had told us, rigid, not even blinking. And then it had let me go. Trying to think rationally it was due to either of two reasons. Perhaps, the Protector had logged some order into my chip to allow me greater freedom, or Stoker had done something to negate the Sandman directives. Whichever it was, I was grateful. I could have been vaporised on the spot.

For the second night in a row I didn't eat anything. My stomach hurt and when I lifted up my shirt I saw the purple bruise spread across the skin. I couldn't even swallow down my pills. I knew that this was going to be a big mistake. The lapse would be registered. Unless Stoker had fixed that as well.

I went to bed with my head in a whirl. Too many thoughts and images careering round inside, making sleep impossible. Before I knew it, the day was dawning and I felt that I'd gone ten rounds in the virtual boxing ring with George Foreman. It was all I could do to sit down on my couch and stare into nothingness.

Seven

If I think about it hard enough I can remember the last time we were all together. When I do, it all comes tumbling out and there's not much I can do to prevent it.

It was a Wednesday, the memory is that clear. I'd come in from school, because three years ago we still went to a building where real teachers took us into the computer suites, made sure we plugged ourselves in, before they disappeared to over-see what we did from another room, brim full of monitors. From there they registered our every tic and shrug, and logged every single action we made on the computer. If we ever had a problem, a real human being would come and help us. It seems like an age ago now, so much has happened since, but that's how it was.

Until that Wednesday.

I remember when I came home that day, Nan had already made the tea. We sat around the table and Mum and Dad started bickering, as they always did. The talk was always about the war and how it was all so dreadful and so unnecessary. I remember Nan making her excuses. She'd been through it all before, of course. She told me stories of how it was when China had invaded Taiwan all those years ago. Everyone, apparently, believed it was so far away it didn't matter. No need for us, or any of our neighbours, to become involved. She told me about the Prime Minister – we had such a thing then – appearing on the television screens, calming us all by saying that the 'emergency' meant there might be some disruption to trade, but very little else. No threat of casualties, absolutely no possibility of our troops becoming embroiled in what was, we all believed, an argument that would very quickly resolve itself. Almost immediately, however, the Americans started hurling nuclear bombs around and everyone thought it was the end. But it wasn't.

It was only the beginning.

I didn't understand most of what went on. To be honest, I still don't. All I can remember are images of my parents arguing, talking about moving out of the city, my Nan trying to keep order. Lots of families were going through the same thing. Panic. Some of my friends were telling me that there was a bunker underneath the school, that we'd all have to go in there when the sirens sounded. None of the teachers said anything, so no one really took the rumours seriously. Then, bit by bit, things began to change. Gradually, every facet of life became more controlled, more ordered. I was only small, but I can recall when our first lessons were given by computers, how we all had to go and have special chips inserted under our skin. 'All for the common good', the announcements said. We all wondered why the old people weren't fitted with them.

We soon discovered why.

The first time we logged into the new computers, it was like nothing I'd experienced before or since. Greeting us at the gate, a huge, lumbering guard directed us into the assembly hall – except it was no longer the place we recognised. At the far end, where once stood a stage, a huge screen dominated the wall. We sat in rows, and virtual keyboard emerged in the air-space before us. After logging on, everything went haywire. The computers read our chips, and we found we could go and do anything we wanted at anytime, anywhere. It was all simply stunning, at first. After that honeymoon period of playing at the Master in Augusta, or climbing Mount Everest – which I did lots – it became like everything else: normal. Soon, we didn't even have to attend school. Our rooms were now our classrooms. Everything was controlled and we found we didn't have to go outside, not for anything.

But no amount of technology could protect us from falling bombs. How could any computer tell us how to take cover from enemy missiles? None of us had a clue what to do or how to react if such a thing happened, and I don't think the human teachers did either. We all waited anxiously for more news, but it never came. The tension in my household was so electric as soon as you stepped through the door, your hair stood up on end. Televisions and the new hologram screens were all blank. No one was being told anything. Fear was everywhere. You could almost taste it.

The first time I saw Sweepers was not long after that. Nan had been talking to the neighbours and they had said that a huge bomb had hit the capital. A nuclear strike. The government fell into disarray. Control passed to regional authorities. Nobody knew any of this for certain, it was all just rumour, so when the Sweepers came down the street, everyone stared dumbfounded, wondering what on earth they were.

I saw my first man die not long after that.

We soon learned that we had to be very respectful towards the Sweepers. They purposely created an aura of fear around them. When they looked at you, you had to look down. If they spoke, you had to call them 'sir'. Mr Naylor was a big man. I think he used to be a boxer. Everyone was afraid of him. When the Sweepers swung into our street one morning, the tannoys instructed everyone to stand outside, and we all did as we were bid. Except for Mr Naylor. I saw him hit one of the Sweepers. Well, he tried to. But the Sweeper simply moved out of the way, faster than anything I'd ever seen, and then he shot Mr Naylor with a huge, highly advanced laser which sliced through him as if he were a piece of cheese. One minute the poor man was standing there, the next he was lying in neatly cauterised pieces on the ground, quivering like slices of jelly. Nobody ever argued with the Sweepers again after that.

Months went by and we all learned to live with the new ways. Slowly, piece by piece, the technology came back on line. We no longer went to school. We now had virtual classrooms, all of us hooked up to computers, receiving our lessons in our homes through the chips. Lessons were all software generated. No more contact with human beings, certainly not at school. In fact, for the first few months, they forbad *all* contact with others. We had to stay indoors, not speak to our friends, or even our neighbours. Food deliveries were made in the middle of the night, great hover vans whispering through the streets, placing large boxes of provisions outside each door. Gradually, little bits of normality began to reappear, but with very real differences.

The authorities enforced a curfew, from eight o'clock in the summer, five o'clock in the winter. At first lots of people got caught out, either forgetting the time or purposely ignoring it. The announcements on huge telescreens at the end of each street told everyone that new measures would be introduced to prevent people breaking curfew.

Those measures were the Sandmen.

I remember when we were all told to report to the city Centre Park. In those days it was still a real park, with open fields, ponds, boating lakes. That day, thousands assembled there. It was like a carnival and everyone was very happy and the air was full of expectation. A little buzz rippled through the crowd and a man stepped up onto a large platform. I didn't know it then, but he was the Protector. I saw him, so stately and grand, his arms spread wide, dressed in a simple light-grey suit. He looked like someone's benevolent father, someone you could trust, like. Why then was he flanked by armed guards? The happy atmosphere slowly slipped away, replaced by nervousness and anxiety. He spoke to us, and as he spoke his words brought a terrible chill to our hearts.

"My friends – my people. I must tell you some things which some of you will not like, and may not understand. We have failed, my friends. All of us. The war in the east has not gone well, and we are all in jeopardy." A mournful groan emitted from the crowd, frightened faces turning to one another. I held onto my father's arm. "*Friends,*" continued the Protector, holding up his arms, quietening us down, "please, listen to me. The United States is no longer the power it once was. Countless millions have died. The great cities of New York, Chicago, Los Angeles – and many others – are nothing but rubble now, devastated by nuclear strikes. Across the Far East, the same story is repeated. Shanghai, Beijing, Tokyo, Seoul – obliterated every one. Countless millions are dead, the entire area plunged into the Middle Ages." There were cries from the crowd. I saw some people collapsing, grown men bursting into tears. The Protector waited, his hands waving gently like the wings of a bird, and when silence settled, his voice continued, so soothing, "Europe has emerged virtually unscathed and now it, together with the Russian Federation, is determined to rebuild a new world. A world of security and peace."

There was a trickle of applause and then music erupted from the far end of the field. People craned their necks to get a view. Suddenly, like a wave, the crowd parted and I saw them for the first time. The Sandmen. Ahead of them a band played. Men, tall and angular, dressed all in white, pounding away on drums, others blasting bugle, marching with great precision. They wore black, long-peaked riding helmets and shiny black boots. And behind, towering over them, two metres and more high, came the Sandmen, their great legs striding forward, their heads revolving, huge domed eyes scanning everyone from under the peaks of their own helmets. Their arms were as a spider's, long and black, on the end of which bristled great crooked claws, used, as we all too soon learnt, for seizing and slicing. They were hideous, created to instil terror and on that first viewing this is precisely what they did. Everyone gazing in astonishment, many cowering away, some screaming. I pressed myself against my dad and he held me. But as he did, I could feel him trembling. For the first time in my life, I wasn't sure if he could protect me.

"Good people!" roared the Protector above the din. "You must understand some simple truths." The muttering and mumbling of the throng grew louder and the Protector struggled to make himself heard, despite the microphones. Then, as if by some unspoken command, other figures infiltrated the crowd. These were Sweepers, emerging from behind the Protector, pushing and prodding people out of the way, cursing at them, demanding they remained silent. No one argued. How could anyone? These were Sweepers. Everyone knew what Sweepers could do. Nobody knew what Sandmen could do. Not yet.

"Now that I have your attention," continued the Protector, "you need to be aware of some changes." He paused, looking across the sea of faces turned towards him. "I have been aware for some time that the curfew has not been properly observed. To keep our streets secure and to ensure our children are safely in their beds, the Sandmen will patrol our communities as soon as the curfew is sounded. Anyone who disobeys will be instantly dealt with."

It was then that we witnessed the unbelievably horrific power of the Sandmen. One of them moved, its great legs stretching forward, its arms reaching out to seize one poor man, as if by random. Lifting him high into the air. He screamed, wriggling uselessly in those great, gleaming claws, but only briefly. For then the Sandman simply pulled him apart as if he were nothing more than a piece of soft toffee, strings of intestines trailing between his upper and lower body, the blood gushing out in a roar, splattering those beneath. His remains dropped to the ground in a bloody mess. A brilliant white beam struck out from beneath the peak of the Sandman's helmet, vaporising what remained of the man into nothing, leaving only a blackened, smouldering outline where the human being used to be.

It all happened so quickly, most people were too stunned to react until the terrifying scene came to its sickening conclusion. A moan rippled through the crowd, growing in intensity until the people broke and ran in all directions, screaming in terror, desperate to flee.

"There shall be no resistance!" roared the Protector and the Sandmen spread out amongst the scattering crowd, swiping at people with their razor sharp claws, slicing through unprotected flesh like hot knives. The light beams dissolved people instantly as, all around, the stampeding mass swerved and dodged, panic dictating what people did. Any sense of community or togetherness disappeared as individuals battled to save themselves, wild, high-pitched squeals of terror breaking out from everyone's throats. Even children seemed forgotten amidst the rush, many knocked over and trampled, crushed to death by people too lost in their own desperate urge for self-preservation to worry about anyone else.

I was more fortunate. Being closer to the far edge, at the very back of the crowd, my parents made good their escape without much hindrance, running like athletes with me between them, each holding one of my hands. It was if I were flying. We never looked back and all I remember was my dad shouting, "Keep moving, we've got to keep moving!"

Soon, we left the park and those nightmarish scenes far behind us, and made it back inside our house. Myself and my mum fell onto the hallway floor, gasping for breath, whilst Dad rammed the bolt across the door, and turned to look at us, his face smeared in a sheen of sweat. He didn't speak, just gulped air. Mum held me as she cried.

After a few moments, we all went into the kitchen and gulped down water, regaining some of our composure. Nan appeared from her room and Mum told her what had happened. Thank God Nana had not been there – they ordered anyone over fifty to stay at home. Nan was almost seventy-five and in the frantic rush to escape the Sandman, she would have been easy-pickings for them. I held onto her, hugging her tightly as she summed up all of our thoughts in a voice grave with horror. "What has happened to us? How could we let it come to this?"

That was that Wednesday night. The one I remember so clearly. We all sat still, our eyes unblinking, staring out into nothingness. None of us had any answers to why it had all happened because none of us could understand *what* had happened. And still none of us can.

Eight

The second journey to the Protector's residence was a repeat of the previous day and as I left the city, passing through the great gates without hindrance, I had time to think a little about my past, my family. The memories were painful ones but they were a constant reminder of how life used to be.

We'd be monitored, each and every one of us, after the universal dictate was unveiled – parents and grandparents were to be re-settled, children under eight were to be transported to special educational units, those over eight would be re-educated in their homes through the wonders of virtual technology. Within a few months, the authorities transformed the every day existence of millions. They came and took my own family, or what was left of it, whilst I slept. That night I had gone to bed, worried about my parents, but still clinging to a vestige of hope. When I woke, there was nothing left to show my parents had ever lived. No photographs, clothes, nothing. I stood and stretched, opened my window and peered down the street. Music played, and the giant holographic screens, flanked by silent Sweepers, declared a new dawn. I never even questioned it.

Of course, it was about a year or so later that I discovered why I never questioned it. The young people of society had all fitted with a series of microchips, inserted deep inside our brains, that essentially reprogrammed our ability to think subjectively. Some of these had been implanted years before, without our knowledge. Now, new, updated models brought us online totally. Unfortunately, or fortunately if you took that view, some of the chips were found to be malfunctioning. They didn't completely repress memory, only dull it. Individuals were called into ministry buildings for the process to be repeated. My name seemed to have been overlooked somehow, so I still waited to receive that particular pleasure of having my brain hot-wired in Central Control.

A downdraft buffeted me into the present. I was there – the Protector's house. The hover bike whispered to a stop and I got out. The day was dull, the sky overcast, threatening rain. Noticing the cold, I pulled up my collar and approached the huge, impressive looking entrance. I waved my ID card and the doors opened with no delay, a repeat of yesterday. The guard was the same, only this time he remained silent, standing like a pillar, a huge laser-blaster held tight against his barrel chest. Obviously, I was expected.

Inside, I paused to study the paintings in more detail. 'The Scream' held most of my attention, but others also had a particular magnetism. One, a vast canvas, was of ancient ships fighting, another a curious painting of an enormous vessel pulled by smaller ones, the colours vibrant, the sky a grand sweep of greys and subtle browns. Next to it, a much smaller painting, was of a woman standing by a window in the act of pouring milk into a jug. I wondered why someone would paint something like that, an insignificant moment, captured for all time. I screwed up my eyes and moved closer, peering at the detail, so superbly executed, more like a photograph really. A permanent record of a lost time, long gone, preserved for all to see, study and learn. Not insignificant at all, but I wondered who might portray our world as it was now. Did painters and artists still work, hidden from view, secretly recording the day-to-day life through which we all sleepwalked?

Sighing deeply, I looked around. Of course, none of these fabulous works of art were for us; this was the Protector's private collection and not meant for public display. I wondered if he ever sat and looked at them, if, in a no-doubt busy schedule, he ever found the time.

Time.

Where was the Protector?

Feeling a little uneasy, I moved slowly along the room, wondering if I should call out, make my presence known. The massive room seemed as still as the grave, not even the low hum from the banks of monitors to break the quiet.

The monitors.

I looked up and saw that they were indeed all blank. Completely dead. My unease grew. Was this a new twist, another attempt to frighten me into doing something I wasn't prepared for? Or had I been found out, Stoker's programme having been hacked? I whirled around and ran over to the door and desperately tugged at the handle, the sweat breaking out across my forehead. It wouldn't budge.

Trapped, locked inside, all I could do was wait, wait for the Sandmen to come, interrogate me and smooth my brain.

Trying to calm myself, my eyes swept the room. Apart from the monitors, everything appeared normal, at least on the surface. It was as neat and as tidy as it had been the last time I was there. Towards the rear of the room, I spotted another door. Cautiously, I walked towards it, hopeful it might be a way out. As I neared it, my eyes turned to the raised platform and a tiny flash of memory cut through my growing fear. On my previous visit, it had appeared from out of the floor below, and the Protector sat behind the desk, like an otherworldly Head Teacher viewing a naughty schoolboy. Now, the dais stood from out of the depths, already in its position. The desk, together with the computers and other hardware, waited in silence but of the Protector, there was no sign. Thinking he must be in the room beyond the door, I made straight for it without another thought.

On my way, stepping closer to the dais, I caught a shape from out the corner of my eye. Screwing up my eyes, I tried to make out what it was. It appeared to be a bundle of material, like a rolled up carpet or blanket, stuffed behind the desk, partially hidden by the chair. Cautiously, I stepped up onto the platform and crouched down, pulling the chair back to get a clearer view.

I froze.

This was no blanket, carpet, bundle or anything else. It was the Protector, crammed under the desk, and he was dead.

Nine

I'm not sure how long I sat there, rooted to the spot, staring at him, but it felt like a lifetime. Clearly dead, his body was lodged head first under the desk. Grateful that his face was turned away from me, the sight of thick, gooey blood spreading out like a halo around his caved in head brought the bile into my throat, and I span away, retching.

Someone had taken a heavy club and smashed through his skull. Puce coloured brain matter dribbled to the floor and I sat, whimpering, hand clamped against my mouth, battling to stop myself from throwing up, wondering what I could do.

Here I was, alone with the dead Protector, the most powerful man in the world, in a locked room with no way out. Petrified by the sheer terror of it all, I knew this was the end. No amount of explaining was going to save me. I was dead.

Then it hit me, the realisation wiping away the last dregs of nausea from my heaving gut.

Stoker and his cronies – they'd set me up.

With my mind working overtime, a sudden thought, an idea, a tiny hope struck me. Holding my breath, I closed my eyes, and quickly rifled through the Protector's pockets. Finding what I was looking for, I scanned his key card and the desk drawers opened. Groping inside, my hands closed around the only piece of evidence I had that might keep me from being vaporised.

With my tongue thick in my mouth, I crossed to the annexe door at a run. It came as no surprise to find it locked, so now my dilemma was a simple one – how to get out. A quick glance around the room's perimeter told me that there was no sign of any sensor so, gritting my teeth, I took a few steps back, and charged.

My shoulder hit the door with a sickening dull thud. I winced, almost yelping, more in surprise rather than pain. It hadn't budged, not a millimetre. Sucking in my breath, I prepared to charge again. I had no choice. Again, I charged, this time using my other shoulder. The result was as before – nothing. It held firm. Despair engulfed me and I put my back against the door and slowly slid down to the ground. With my face in my hands, I sat and wondered what to do next.

The answer came to me like a Very light going off in my head.

Climbing to my feet, I ran back to the desk and, careful not step on the Protector's corpse, fumbled underneath, my fingertips searching out the switch which might hold the key to my escape. This was my only option – hanging around, waiting to explain my presence to the authorities wouldn't wash. I'd be dead within about ten seconds.

My fingers brushed across the smallest of buttons. I whispered a prayer of thanks to whatever gods were watching over me, closed my eyes and pressed it.

With a jolt, the platform slowly began to lower itself into the void below. I watched the room as it receded away from me, and the last image was of that damned painting. *The Scream,* staring back at me mockingly, seeming to echo exactly how I felt.

The mechanism came to a juddering halt and then, above me, the gap closed over slowly, plunging me into darkness. Not daring to breathe, I remained still, trying to adjust my eyesight to the gloom. Gradually, softly glowing red lights all along the walls came into focus. Perhaps they were a form of emergency lighting, and they gave me a slight feeling of reassurance. At least I would be able to find a way out.

With no idea in which direction to go, I stepped down from the platform and groped towards the wall, using the soft lights to guide me. Keeping my hands flat on the surface, when I reached the wall I followed it, hoping I would come to a door.

There was nothing.

I stood, forcing myself not to panic, trying not to think there was no exit, that this was nothing more than a basement, with no means of escape. Perhaps the only way in or out was through the hole in the ceiling down which I'd just come?

I convinced myself this could not be the case – what if the platform malfunctioned, or the systems went down? There had to be a service entrance, surely. The platform was lowered using some sort of gearing mechanism – if it broke down, access would be required to fix it. Someone would have to be able to come down here and sort out the problem. All I need to do was persevere until I came across...

Whilst I was thinking all of this through, I heard the unmistakeable shuffle of feet. Human feet. I froze, breathing quietly through my mouth, trying to focus on the direction from which the sound had come. Carefully, I lowered myself into a crouch, emulating the many first-person simulation games I'd played, which instructed me to make myself as small as possible in order to minimise the chances of my being shot at. A crouch did this, but still allowed me the opportunity for a quick dash out of harm's way. Well, okay, that was a game, but virtual games are almost the same as real life. When I got shot once, in the shoulder, I couldn't move for a week afterwards.

But this was no game and the fear gripping me was real. In a game you always know, unless you're very unlucky or haven't taken the correct medication, you're not going to die. Right now, I was in the middle of a very serious reality, and in the real world permanent injuries are all too common and, as I'd just recently discovered, so is death.

"Stay very still."

The voice was so close I could feel the breath on my skin. A man's voice; it sounded tense. Stifling a yelp of terror, I complied, hauling myself upright.

He moved nearer. Not a Sandman, Sweeper or guard. Any of those, I'd already be dead.

I could hear his breathing, smell the thick tang of sweat from his body. His shape came into view and I slowly turned my head to face him.

Rocking back on my heels, I groped for the wall to prevent myself from collapsing as I took in the features of his face.

The face from my nightmares. The face of the man from that terrible room, of the man who gripped me by the throat outside Yolanda's apartment and shook me like a rag doll.

The Hitter.

Ten

Preparing myself for another blow, I screwed up my eyes and waited.

No punch arrived.

I snapped my eyes open and stared into his ghoul-like face, the lips drawn back over his teeth. Snarling, his hand closed around my throat, and he drove me back against the wall, hard. I grunted as I hit the solid surface, trying to take in a breath. I failed, his hand like a vice, crushing my larynx. I panicked, started beating away at his grip, squirming around, trying to pull free.

"Stop wriggling," he hissed menacingly. I could see his burning eyes, a fraction away from mine. If he wanted to kill me, he would have done so by now. So, slowly, I conformed and remained still. His grip relaxed a little. "We're going to get away from here and I want you to follow me without a word."

He released me and I slumped to the floor, clutching my throat, massaging it, gagging for air. I coughed and knew instantly it was the wrong thing to have done. His body jerked into action, his fist striking me a ringing blow across the side of my head, slamming me over. I lay there, on my knees, spluttering, hot blood dripping from the corner of my eye.

"I said *without a word.* Now, shut up!"

Gripping my collar, he hauled me up to my feet. The blood splattered onto his hand and he wiped it across my shirt.

He snarled, "You're a bloody idiot"

I stood there, swallowing down the whimpers welling up from deep inside, desperate not to let him see how much pain I was in.

Grunting, he held me by the hand and, dragging me like a reluctant toddler, we moved deeper into the gloom. With my head still spinning, I didn't notice the crumpled figure lying in the corner until my boot brushed against it. I gagged, staring at it in disbelief. Through the eerie half-light I managed to pick out the details. I could see the long, spindly legs, the tweed jacket, the black horse-riding helmet.

It was a Sandman. I was stunned.

It was dead. If a robot could be classed *as dead*. Confused, I turned my gaping face towards The Hitter. "How…?"

His hand moved into his jacket and I instinctively threw up my hands, expecting another blow. Instead, he produced a small, black device, about the size of an old fashioned computer-mouse. "This," he spat. I frowned and he let out a deep, impatient sigh. "Multi-directional immobiliser. It disrupts any technology within a radius of five metres."

It took me a second to register the implications of what he'd just said. "Permanently?"

"So Stoker says. The man's a genius. It's taken him months to create this," he waved the immobiliser. "But now that we have it, and it's proven to work…If we can disable a Sandman like this," he kicked the inert figure viciously, "then we could be in business."

"They'll work it out. Readjust their software."

He tilted his head, his eyes burning with rage. "Then we'll just have to hope that they don't for the next hour or so. Otherwise, we are going to be in a spot of bother."

Unconvinced, I looked again at the body. If one Sandman went down, the entire section, linked together through the technology which controlled them, would respond. This probably meant that they already surrounded the Protector's residence, just waiting for us to emerge.

"Stop worrying about it, and follow me." He put his shoulder against a door I hadn't even noticed, and it sprang open, daylight flooding into the room. Squinting, I followed him outside.

There were no Sandmen here. I breathed a sigh of relief. The Hitter was already moving along the little path, a sort of alleyway, with very high sides. It must have been a service entrance, the one I'd already guessed existed. No longer holding his hand, I followed him, some steps behind until the gently winding path ended at a solid, old-fashioned wooden door at the far end. The Hitter stopped, turned and gave me a meaningful look. "On the other side, you're on your own. Keep low, moving in a zigzag, and make for the far end. There'll be bodyguards and I'll do my best to knock them out."

"They're robots too?" He nodded. I sucked in a breath, knowing there was something far worse than robots to worry about. "Sweepers? What if there are Sweepers?"

"Then we're dead." He held up the black immobiliser, "This won't work against them." As if to underline the fact, from under his coat he pulled out a hefty looking handgun. "For them, I'll use this. Colt forty-five automatic, army issue, circa nineteen-hundred and eleven. Invaluable against modern technology. It'll do for them Sweepers, don't you worry."

Despising him as I did, I nevertheless had to admire his courage. He was fully prepared to blast his way to freedom and I marvelled at that. Perhaps he realized he had no real choice. If they captured either of us, they would extract every piece of information we had before they vaporised us. They'd discover everything – most importantly, who and where Stoker was. If Stoker could build a device such as the immobiliser, a device that could knock out a Sandman, then he was a very real threat to the powers-that-be. They'd trawl through his brain for every ounce of his technological know-how before sending him to oblivion.

But I didn't know then that they had no intention of capturing the Hitter. I only wish I had.

Giving me a wink, he handed me the immobiliser before pressing down on the door handle and pushing it open.

Immediately, all hell broke loose.

With the Hitter's orders to keep myself low burnished into my brain, almost on all fours, I broke into a swerving run, keeping my eyes fixed directly ahead. I soon spotted the main entrance. My heart leaped as I realized it was open. I didn't stop to think why.

As I moved, I gradually became aware of the noise all around – cries, shouts, the blast of lasers and the dull crack of the Hitter's automatic pistol. I dared not stop, all my attention on moving, twisting and weaving this way and that, but as I drew closer to the door, something caught my attention over to my right. Craning my neck, I saw it and my heart almost went into seizure.

A Sandman.

Weaving away from a blast of the Colt forty-five, he bore down on me with frightening speed.

I ground to a halt, barely able to breathe, my lungs screaming, my heart pounding in my ears.

Frozen in horror, I stood transfixed as the gruesome spectre advanced towards me. Two, three strides and it was there, its great arms swinging, its head rotating, scanning me. In a few seconds it would have me in its grasp. Rolling away, I came back up on my knees and, with trembling hands, brought up the little black immobiliser, squeezed my eyes shut and pressed down on the button.

A loud, crackling hum followed as the thing vibrated in my hand. Then, nothing. A horrible, gaping silence, as if shrouding the entire world in a deathly quiet.

Swallowing down my fear, I opened my eyes and gasped at what I saw.

The Sandman stood inert, its arms locked in the act of attacking me.

I waited, holding my breath, wondering whether I should press the button again. I needn't have worried. As I watched, transfixed, the great figure slowly toppled forward and crashed to the ground some two feet from me, dust billowing up around it.

It had worked! The Sandman was immobilised.

I sat there, staring, an almost irresistible urge to reach out and touch it overtaking me, but then another sound brought me out of my wild, insane thoughts. I looked up to see the Hitter, his gun spraying bullets, as around him lay two more Sandmen in crumpled heaps, with fallen black-garbed robot-guards hyphenating the spaces between them. The immobiliser had done its job to perfection.

Any thoughts of celebration proved premature however as I saw, moving in a wide arc, a group of Sweepers, approaching fast. Too fast. It was only a matter of time before it was all over.

Knowing I could not wait, I ran straight to the door, not caring that I was upright. As I neared the entrance, a bodyguard appeared from outside. Already, the mainframe must have reconfigured its software, countering the immobiliser, just as I knew it would.

I had a chance. The bodyguard appeared to be concentrating on the Hitter, for he ignored me, bringing up his laser blaster to a point beyond my shoulder. It was all the chance I needed. I charged at him, head down like a bull, and butted him full in the midriff. He went down with a grunt and, although big and strong, I'd caught him off guard and he lay stunned on the ground, the blaster clattering to the ground beside him. Without a thought, I seized it, swung it towards him and released a bolt of pure, searing light into his body, slicing him in half with sickening ease.

I stood, my breath rasping, chest heaving, watching the electrical circuits spluttering and sparking, knowing the killing a cybernetic organism could never compare with taking a human life, but I had no time for moralising. I had to get away before those damned Sweepers took me apart!

"Get the fuck out, Simeon!"

I heard the voice, knew to whom it belonged.

Turning, I saw the Hitter, his bullets spent, fumbling to insert a new clip. He was slow, far too slow. Desperation caused him to spill the clip and the Sweepers were moving with the speed of hover-bikes. Not one bullet had hit them, and the immobiliser had no effect on them. The Sweepers were immune.

Their lasers shot out streaks of light, striking the Hitter across his body, one beam cutting him down from the left shoulder to his right hip, parting him in two like an over-ripe fruit, the two halves of his body peeling away to the sides.

No blood. Every artery cauterised.

His eyes boiled in his head.

Almost throwing up, I forced myself to stagger on, leaving the ghastly scene behind me, and lurched through the main entrance. Believing the stationary hover-bike to be immobilised also, and not having the luxury of time to find out, I ignored it and pressed on, breaking into a loping run.

I didn't know where I was going, which direction to take, or how far I should go. My only thought was to put the nightmare I'd just endured as far behind me as I could manage. So I did just that, racing across the road and into the open landscape beyond, moving easily over the rock hard scrubland. As unforgiving as any tarmac, it actually aided my stride and I bound across it without much hindrance. Soon, I made the rolling hills ahead of me, easing my pace, getting into the rhythm. All those hours and hours at the treadmill at home paid off. We had to do that, it was all part of the rules. Daily exercise, uncompromising, exhausting, but now proving its worth. To be out here, in the open air, running in the real world, could there be anything better? Even with the great laser blaster in my hands, it was almost dreamlike and intoxicating. I pushed the reasons why I was doing it to the back of my mind – there would be time for that later – and followed the direction of a stream meandering through the fields, crossing it without pausing, not even caring if it was deep or shallow. I only had one thought in mind – escape.

After what seemed hours, I finally stopped, my lungs bursting, the stitch in my side like a knife. I stumbled amongst a spreading mass of trees, a wood.

Cool and quiet, I slowed myself down to a walk, never stopping to wonder why no one was pursuing me, why the lasers hadn't shot past my head, why gyro-copters and hover-bikes weren't filling the air with their bee-like drone. I thought that I had out-distanced them.

Now of course, I realize that that was madness.

You simply can't outrun the Sweepers.

And the Sandmen can detect you through your chip.

All in all, I was very stupid back then.

Eleven

Hungry and cold, I came across a cave in a hillside and wandered inside. Big enough to allow me to stand upright, it offered the only shelter I could find. Despite the darkness, it felt safe and so much warmer than outside so, forcing myself to clear my mind of what had happened, I slumped down and tried to make myself as comfortable as I could.

Despite my best efforts, as I sat in the silence, the distant sound of dripping water my only companion, I went back over the dreadful events of that awful day. I never suspected in a thousand years that something like this could have happened, that everyone could use me so readily, without conscience. I was supposed to be smart, top of the class. What a load of bull that was! As I sat with my knees drawn up to my chest, I kept going through everything in my mind, trying to find some meaning to it, but always running into dead ends. Alone, confused, embittered, I was now a fugitive, fleeing from justice, with nowhere to go and no one to help me.

Twisting myself, I peered out towards the daylight, the distant mountains nothing but blurred sweeps of grey. Perhaps the altitude, together with the remoteness of this place, prevented the Sweepers or the Sandmen from finding me. Out of sheer instinct, I ran my fingers through my hair. I couldn't feel the chip in my head, but no one could, otherwise some might attempt to dig it out. Kitchen-surgery Yolanda called it. We'd all heard a rumour, promulgated on the net, about a young guy down in Swindon who had tried to gouge his out with a bread knife. The image of what it must have been like made me shudder. Of course, he died. But now, I wanted so much to feel it, to rip it out, to free myself from its control. It was the means by which the authorities controlled us, kept us under observation, found us when we went missing. Perhaps its range was limited to within the confines of the City, and would not transmit here in the open countryside. Perhaps I should have taken some comfort from those thoughts, but I didn't.

Settling back against the hard, damp rock wall, I pushed such thoughts aside and settled instead, with a whole new clarity, on Yolanda. I pictured her face smiling across at me. Those huge eyes, drawing me in, making me want to dive inside and disappear. Yolanda. We had shared so much, and now she was alone, with no means of knowing where I was, what I was doing. New fears gathered within me, fears for her safety. Would the authorities, even now, be questioning her? Torturing her? The first trail of tears ran down my cheeks as I imagined her crumbling beneath their fiery stares, their hard voices forcing every snippet of truth from her. She would be their immediate point of contact and they would bully her into revealing everything we'd ever spoken about, but most especially our last conversations about Stoker and his 'team'. Her judgement, so clouded because of her frantic concerns for my welfare, might desert her and persuade her to tell them anything they wanted to hear.

Sitting bolt upright, I smashed my fists down on the ground, frustration and anger now my masters. I shouldn't have left her, I should have realized right from the beginning what would happen – how they manipulated and coerced me, the fall guy for their insane schemes, and now abandoned me. But to put Yolanda through it was inexcusable – it was my fault, all of it and I'd involved her recklessly and without any thought of the consequences. I'd failed her. Bottom line.

I put my face in my hands. Whilst I sat there, in that dark cave, worrying about my situation, Yolanda was with them. What might she be going through at the hands of the Sweepers? If only I could contact her, reassure her, tell her that I loved her, that I was sorry. Guilt bore down on me like a massive lead weight and I squirmed as I rolled over, pulling my knees up into a foetal position. I whimpered, filled with self-loathing, feeling so alone without her, and so afraid.

I must have drifted off to sleep because when I first heard the noise, streaks of grey light were cutting through the blackness of the cave. It was morning and I sat up, rubbing my eyes, shivering with the cold.

Out of the gloom, a shape moved over me, quickly followed by another. Panicking, I scrambled to my feet, desperately trying to find the immobiliser or the laser I'd dropped somewhere. Groping around like a drunkard, I couldn't find them. Then the shapes drew closer and I knew I was lost. They were here – they'd found me!

A face moved up close to me. I could see the eyes, smell the rancid breath. There was a mild, distant curiosity in its expression, which soon drifted away as it nuzzled past me, followed by a stream of others, bleating as they went.

Goats.

The relief left me at a rush and I fell back against the wall, laughing at my stupidity as perhaps a dozen or more came into the cave, nosing around, giving me the occasional glance but otherwise totally disinterested. Which was more than I could say for what I saw standing a little way behind them. The herder. He stood to one side of the entrance, eying me intensely, the bodyguard's gyro-laser cradled lightly in his gnarled hands.

Our eyes locked. I didn't know what to say. In fact, I doubt if I could have said anything at that moment, my throat parched with fear. Quivering, I waited for him to swing the gun towards me and march me back down to the Protector's residence.

He took a step forward and I tumbled backwards, collapsing to the ground, hands splayed out, my eyes never leaving his. One my hands folded around the cool, inert blackness of the immobiliser. I'd found it, but what possible good could that do me now? I turned to him, expecting at any moment to hear the electric burn of the laser, then the solid thump of the beam hitting me, sending me into oblivion.

Something flickered across those gentle, brown, doe-eyes of his, the eyes of a man who had spent his entire, simple life amongst these hills, tending his herd, each day the same as the previous one, the same as every one would ever be. Uninterrupted, peaceful, unquestioning. Instead of threatening me, he ran a burnished hand, as cracked as untreated leather, across his mouth, no doubt wondering what he should do with me. He muttered something in a language I had never heard, then reached inside his coat and produced a canteen of water, which he threw over to me. Without a pause, I gratefully opened up the top and drank.

His eyes never left me.

And still he held onto the gun.

A slight smile fluttered at the edges of his mouth and he gestured for me to come closer. Scrambling to my feet, I stuffed the immobiliser in my belt, and took a few tentative steps towards him. He pulled around a canvas bag from his shoulder and pulled out a loaf of coarse, dark brown bread. Tearing it with his hard hands, he gave me a large hunk and I greedily wolfed it down, closing my eyes in ecstasy. It was the most wonderful food I had ever tasted. I couldn't remember when I had last eaten, and I crammed more of the bread into my greedy mouth, washing it down with the canteen water, smacking my lips, this simple food like a feast. I grinned my appreciation.

He pulled out what looked like a filthy rag, squatted down and flattened it out on the ground. To my surprise, I saw it was a map. With a short, stubby finger, he traced a line along the sketch of the mountains, looking at me for confirmation that I understood. I didn't, but I nodded nevertheless. He grunted, picked up the rag and stuffed it inside the bag together with the remainder of the bread. Striding over to the cave entrance, he jerked his head, demanding I follow.

We set off, my curious saviour and me, along a well-worn mountain pathway, meandering ever-upwards. His pace was brisk. Well used to living in this harsh landscape, years of scaling the heights had honed his body into a lean, strong physique, but soon, as we ate up the distance, my legs and lungs burned with exhaustion. I wanted to stop, rest, suck in breath and recover, if only slightly. But every time I made as if to slow down, he would snap his head around and bark some sharp, guttural words, forcing me to continue.

Minutes rolled by. Hours maybe. At some point, I looked around and, raking a shaking hand across my face, I realised the terrain was changing, the barren, dried up earth replaced by a verdant plateau of lush grass, rimmed by the distant outline of trees.

Pulling up, I strained to breathe. On the treadmill back in my apartment, I'd eaten up miles and miles, but this altitude took its toll and the breath wheezed and rattled in my chest. We were high now and, over to my right, more mountains soared higher still. I wondered not only where he was taking me, but for how much longer we needed to traverse this endless place.

He wandered over to me, mouth twisted up with impatience. Having picked up an old branch from somewhere, he tapped his leg with it, grunting, urging me to continue, words not necessary. So, with head down, I surrendered to the inevitable and tramped on.

That night we slept under the stars and when the morning came, he repeated the ritual with the water and the bread. I knew it wasn't enough to sustain me, that soon the lack of vitamins and proteins would begin to tell. I had lived a life of pills and carefully selected liquefied food. Back in the City, the water I drank was laced with chemicals, providing my body with defence against disease and sickness. I hadn't known a day's illness since… since my parents were taken. Would my body cope with this new, meagre diet, I wondered?

The goatherd sat, cross-legged, regarding me with those big, unemotional eyes. There was something like disappointment there, a faint expression of something. I wanted to question him, at least ask him his name. I had put my faith in him, unquestioning, trusting him to lead me to … to where? Freedom?

"Who are you?" I asked.

There was no reply, not even a flicker.

Beside him, the big laser lay grim and silent. Could he operate it, did he even know what it was?

"Why are you helping me?"

Springing to his feet, he hefted the bag and laser across his shoulder and, gesturing with the stick, pointed vaguely towards the mountains, which seemed no closer than they were yesterday. Sucking in a breath, I got to my feet, tired before I had even taken a single step, and moved in behind him as he struck out through the grassland.

Sometime in the afternoon, I knew I couldn't go much further. I called out to him to stop as I collapsed amongst an outcrop of hard, bare rock. Muttering under his breath, the goatherd strode up to me, pointing towards the horizon. I didn't understand what he meant but, as he clearly required me to continue, I climbed painfully to my feet and followed him.

The horizon, as things turned out, was not what it appeared. We were standing on a great ledge, the plateau ending abruptly to reveal a sprawling valley below. A cluster of buildings lay there, several broad streets dividing the area up into what I assumed was a town. Never having left the City, such a collection of buildings held nothing but mystery for me. I had travelled further in the past two days than at any other time in my entire life. Every step took me further away from the controlled world I knew and closer into the unknown. That fact alone was terrifying, but, as always, a far greater pain ate away at the very fibre of my being. Yolanda. Always hiding my true feelings for her, up until recently, the pain of guilt bore down on me, the reality of predicament making me miss her more than I could have imagined possible. A great hole in my stomach, not caused by hunger, but by a yearning to be with her once more, grew ever bigger.

I'd abandoned her.

To an uncertain, but terrifying fate.

Without wanting to, as I looked down towards the huddle of tiny buildings, I broke into body wrenching sobs. I had no way of contacting her, of reassuring her, of hearing her voice. Had she been hurt by the Sweepers, or was she even alive? With no means to find the answers, I pressed the heels of my palms into my eyes and sobbed bitterly, openly, not caring a damn if the goatherd watched me or not. With images of her lovely, smiling face looming up in my mind, I wondered if I would ever again touch her skin, feel the warmth of her lithe body, kiss those beautiful lips...

Forcing myself to drag my hands away, I wiped away the tears, sniffing loudly. The goatherd looked out across the valley, unaffected by my wretched snivelling. Did he understand, did he even care? He had brought me to this place, pointed out the town. Perhaps the town could offer the chance to communicate with Yolanda? I couldn't begin to guess what I would find down there, but there had to be something, surely – something that would help me find answers.

As I gazed into the valley, I understood with such clarity that whatever it was I found down there would probably lead me to either salvation... or incarceration.

He gave a sudden bark and, snapping my head up, I followed his outstretched hand and saw the horrors of the present overcoming all of my thoughts, my sense of loss, my anguish – everything except my fear.

Moving up the hillside, their great legs making easy going of the incline, came three Sandmen, their evil-looking heads swivelling, searching. Searching for me.

Frantic, I turned to go, but his hand clamped on my arm like a vice. I tried to pull myself free, without success.

And I knew then what the plan had been all along.

Looking into his soft, neutral, eyes I saw there was nothing there. Nothing at all. No dilation of the pupils, no blink. The ice ran through my belly. Those eyes, they held not a glimmer of humanity. How could I have been so stupid not to have recognised the signs – no food or drink passed his lips, no exertion proved too great. And, without me once questioning his motives, he had brought me to within spitting distance of the Sandmen. Only vaporisation waited for me now.

Summoning up every ounce of my strength, with a mighty jerk I managed to tear my arm free, his fingers raking the flesh. Blood sprouted. Those fingers were steel. Clutching at the wound, I took a step back and watched him unslinging the laser gun, and turn it towards me.

But he had underestimated me. Perhaps his scanner was not perfected, or the altitude disrupted his processors. I didn't care what the reason was, but when I aimed the immobiliser he had failed to identify, a tiny flicker of alarm crossed his face. He froze, momentarily at a loss, and when the device crackled, humming in my hand, he gave a few sharp, spasmodic jerks of his legs and arms, flapping like a bird in distress, then fell silently and deathly still to the ground.

Without a moment's hesitation, I took the gyro-laser and ran, heading back along pathway, putting distance between myself and the Sandmen, thinking that if I could make it to some form of cover amongst the rocks I could shelter there, perhaps even hold them off.

The first blast hit the outcrop next to me, sending up a great spray of red-hot shards of rock. I swerved, remembering the Hitter's instructions, thank God for his advice. But even as I moved, another blast struck even closer to me, a shower of jagged rock chips hitting me like bullets, spinning me round. I stumbled and fell to the hard earth, just as another bolt shot inches above my head. I gasped, the earth hard and sharp beneath me, the impact jolting the gyro laser out of my hands. Rolling over, I managed to scramble behind a large boulder but already the first Sandman loomed over me like an avenging angel, his great arms curving downwards to seize me, slice me apart. I aimed the immobiliser in his general direction, pressing down on the button with all my strength, hoping this would help deliver a more potent pulse of disruption. But I needn't have worried. Stoker's handy-work did the job and the Sandman fell backwards across the scree, all control gone, hitting his head with a tremendous crack on a jagged rock.

Silence followed.

Slowly, my body shaking with horror, I got to my feet and looked out across the plateau. The other Sandmen lay lifeless amongst the rocks, having followed their companion's fate. Allowing myself a moment to force air into my lungs, I swept up the gyro-laser, and jogged away from the path towards the distant mountains, hoping to take myself still further from the world I had rejected.

As another night crept over the mountains, the temperature plummeted and I knew I couldn't last much longer. In my rush to escape, I had left behind the water and bread from the goatherd's bag. Bits of rock, blasted by the Sandmen, peppered my side like shrapnel, causing a jolt of pain to stab into my ribs with each step. Slowing to a stagger, by now my stomach screamed with hunger, my throat as dry as sand. If I didn't find some fresh water soon, I knew I was finished.

Close to the foot of the mountains, I found another cave. Not as large as the first, but big enough to give me shelter. As I huddled down amongst the rocks, my limbs ached with the cold, my muscles screaming for rest. I wondered if I would be alive to greet the morning sun. I tried to conjure up pictures of Yolanda, to give me something worth staying alive for, but I couldn't remember her features any more. My mind was a jumble of broken, twisted memories, none of them making any sense. I was sliding into delirium. All I could see was a single image of a Sandman, relentlessly marching down the street where I used to live, seeking out those that had strayed, those that had inadvertently missed the curfew, those who were lost.

I was amongst them.

I was also lost.

I curled up, all alone, with no one to listen to my sobs, and all I could hear was the sound of the Sandman coming, the relentless pounding of his boots drawing ever closer.

Twelve

It wasn't a Sandman who woke me, but someone else.

A nutmeg brown face, bronzed from a life lived outside, framed by a ragged, congealed grey beard, loomed close to mine. I thought for an instant it was the goat man, come back to capture me or lead me into another trap. As things came into sharper focus, however, I could see it wasn't. This man was real. His eyes shone with a burning lustre, almost a childish impishness. No matter, I thought to myself, I was past caring. The world seemed to grow cloudy again and I slipped back into blackness.

The second time I woke I knew I was in a different place. Gone were the sharp, jagged stones that perforated my back, gone the cold shadows of the cave. Instead I found myself lying on a bed, with sheets and a pillow. My old clothes were gone. I felt clean, warm and safe. I'd returned home, to my safe and cosy apartment, all of it a terrible dream, a nightmare. I was back in the real world. Smiling contentedly, I turned over.

My eyes snapped open and I lay deadly still.

I hadn't dreamed anything.

Of course I hadn't.

To confirm it, I ran my hand down my side and discovered a bandage covering my wound. I winced as I pressed my fingers against the gauze. In dreams, flesh doesn't become damaged. And the waking moments push away the pain. So, I had to ask the question...

Where was I?

My last conscious thoughts before waking up were of that face. I was in the cave then, my exhaustion total, the fight drained out of me. Now, here I was with clean sheets pressing around me, soft, sensual... If I closed my eyes I could allow myself to drift off again. I bit down on my bottom lip. No, that wouldn't do – I had to remain conscious, alert, ready to defend myself. Although my side ached, I felt much stronger than before. I knew that, if I had to, I would be able to do something.

I listened for clues as to my whereabouts, a sound to help me get some bearings on where I was. All I could hear were a few birds singing outside and that was curious, for birds no longer flew into the City. So this was the countryside, or the town the goat man lured me to? Perhaps Sandmen loomed close by. Sandmen, however, don't tend wounds and put you to bed underneath clean sheets. They frazzle your brains, with no questions asked.

Slowly turning over onto my back, I sat up.

A normal room, sparsely furnished with a small dressing table and wardrobe set against the far wall, gazed back at me. Both items appeared old, but solid. The walls gleamed white, a single sash window allowing the light to flood in. Simple, clean and bright.

I rubbed my face and winced. My head hurt and I carefully felt a bump or graze on the back of my neck. It was tender and when I brought my finger around I could see a tiny speck of blood. Checking my pillow, I found more tiny spots of red. I must have tripped and fell, but I couldn't remember anything like that happening. Perhaps I was concussed. I wasn't sure, but the pounding in my head grew worse. At least it meant I was alive.

Without warning, the door swung open and the bearded man from the cave walked in. Big and threatening looking, as he stepped forward I instinctively drew back in my bed, pulling up the sheets in a pathetic attempt to protect myself.

But protect me from what, I couldn't guess.

Grinning, he held up his hand. "Don't worry," he said cheerfully, moving closer, "I'm not going to hurt you. I brought you some food."

He settled a tray of food down next to me. I saw eggs, beans, bacon, toast. My mouth hung open, drooling, and I suddenly became aware of how hungry I was. He laughed, clapped a giant paw on my knee and left without another word.

For a few seconds I eyed the food. Perhaps it was poisoned? Perhaps it was all another trick? I knew this was how all that psychological stuff worked – they lulled you into a false sense of security, made you trust your captor, believing they were good people, friends. Then, when you were fully won-over, they'd ask the questions and, because you trusted them, you'd reveal every-thing. Classic. But that food...

So ravenous that I couldn't give a damn if it was going to be my last meal on earth, I attacked the food, cramming it into my mouth, almost swooning in ecstasy as the flavours exploded across my tongue. If this was poison, then it was damned good poison!

All too soon, I stared down at the empty plate, sighing contentedly. I sat back and closed my eyes, relishing the moment. For the first time since leaving The Protector's home, I felt safe. If this was a trap, I no longer cared.

The door creaked open and I opened one eye to see the same man coming back in. He was smiling again. "Enjoy that?"

I managed a nod and he took the tray away to the dresser. He then came and sat down on the bed.

"My name's Warren. This is my home. It's not much but at least it's all paid for." Another laugh, but I wasn't in the mood for jokes. He shrugged, "I suspect you're wondering what the hell you're doing here?"

I nodded briefly, my eyes never leaving his.

He reached behind him and pulled out the immobiliser.

I gasped. The room grew cold and, without thinking, drew my knees up to my chest.

"This is some piece of technology," he said, hefting it in his hand, ignoring my reaction. "Where did you get it?" He looked straight at me, eyes hard and unblinking, waiting for my reply. I wasn't going to give him one, not until I knew a lot more about him and what he wanted. A fatalistic shrug seemed to suggest he knew that anyway. "You used this against Sandmen?" He stood up without waiting for an answer and crossed to the window, keeping his back to me. "I haven't seen a Sandman for a while, until of course I came across those three you'd finished off... With this." He held up the immobiliser as if were a red card at a football match. He still had his back to me and I couldn't see his face, but something in his voice told me he was impressed. "They have no need to come all the way out here, not usually. People like me are no threat to them, or to anyone else in the City. The authorities know that, so they keep them away. But," he turned to look at me with cold, unblinking eyes, "this little beauty will certainly make me feel a lot safer. From what I saw, it obviously works very well."

I nodded, licking my lips, gathering up the courage to speak. "Yes. It works very well."

He raised his eyebrows. "Strange that they haven't adapted to it. The Sandmen."

"I think it evolves, each time it's used. Tiny bits of reprogramming inside it, preventing them from finding defences."

"Always one step ahead? That's clever." He looked at it. "Who made it?"

I wasn't going to tell him that so I gave him my well-used shrug.

"No matter," he said. He opened the drawer of the dresser and carefully put the immobiliser inside. Closing it again, he pulled out something else from his pocket. It was small, flat and gold coloured. A chip. "This was yours."

Now I really was afraid. My hand went straight to the little bloody patch on the back of my neck. I felt my entire insides drop. My chip!

"I removed it," he said, confirming my worst fears. "But don't worry, after I've reprogrammed it, I'll slip it back in. You'll never know the difference." He paused, his eyes boring into mine. "More importantly, neither will they."

"*What*?" I gaped at him. If there was even a suggestion that my chip had been tampered with, I would be eradicated. Everyone knew that. Prime directive made it clear. "What the hell are you saying?"

"This thing was full of viruses. I've cleaned out the lot, but in so doing I also had to wipe away some of the core programming. If you were to put this back in as it is, the Sandmen or the Sweepers will vaporise you on the spot. So..." he held it up, inspecting it, "I'll make a few changes. When I've finished, no one will know anything about what you've done."

I gulped. This couldn't be real. No one had the technology to alter core-programming. Some had tried and failed and had paid with their lives for their foolishness. Despite my rising panic, his comments needed explanation, so I stuttered, "What I've done? What does that mean?"

"Don't you know?" He smiled, but this wasn't a smile of amusement. "I found your goatherd, and, like I said, the three Sandmen that you'd immobilised. That's treason, young man. And treason means death. Do you want to die?"

I was in a state of shock. I shook my head, deflated. I fell back against the headboard.

"No, didn't think you did. You have to trust me...Simeon."

I jerked upright. "How...?" Then it all came in a rush. I didn't need an answer to how he knew me. He'd scanned the chip. Not only did he know my name, he knew *everything* there was to know about me. Including my involvement in the death of the Protector. This Warren character had me right in the palm of his hand, to do with as he chose. I gazed at the foot of the bed, my mind reeling, lost and alone.

He slipped the chip back into his pocket. "I'm going for a ride this afternoon. I think it'll do you good to join me. Get some fresh air into your lungs. What do you think?"

What could I think? Whoever this man was, he was going to be the means to rebuilding my life, or…perhaps ending it. I was certain of only one thing: I had very little choice in anything anymore. So I nodded my head and he went out without another word.

For a long time I sat, face pressed into my hands, wondering why life was so full of shit. If I hadn't taken that wrong turning, none of this would have happened. If those damned rebels, or agitators, or whoever they were, hadn't pressed me into doing their dirty work, I'd be home right now, rolling around the floor with Yolanda and…

Blowing out my breath, I swung my legs from under the sheets and stood up. I wore a pair of old shorts, which weren't mine. Jesus, he'd undressed me…

Across the room were a pile of neatly ironed jeans and t-shirts. Picking up a shirt, I pressed it against my nose and breathed in the glorious aroma of freshly laundered clothing. It reminded me of a simpler, happier time, when Mum would do the washing, always on a Tuesday, the kitchen full of steam and the smell of clean clothes. I stood, the memories swirling around in my head and, not for the first time since I'd left the dead Protector's house, I cried.

His motorbike was an amazing piece of machinery. At least fifty years old, but so well looked after that it appeared like new, the chrome gleaming, reflecting the sunlight with the intensity of a mirror. Revving up the engine, Warren motioned me to get on board. I sat behind him, clinging on for dear life as he instantly roared down the winding, empty road. The engine gave off a deep, throaty growl that was wildly intoxicating and, despite the speed, I felt safe and secure. I actually found myself enjoying the exhilaration of being out on the open road, the wind in my hair, the vast expanse of nothingness all around, urging us to continue, to discover something new.

The countryside flashed past, but I took the time to take in its features. Rolling hills and sparse bits of woodland, interjected with clusters of broken down ruined buildings. Animals grazed in the fields, animals which I had only ever seen on holographic screens. Cows, sheep and the ubiquitous goats. How could so many things survive in this mad, desolate world?

Eventually he slowed, taking the bike down a narrow, rutted lane which led to a village, the like of which I had never seen before. Not even in images, because we were not allowed many images of the past, only the authorised ones. But this was undoubtedly from the past.

We stopped, the silence falling like a heavy blanket. My ears were ringing from the roar of the bike's engine and now, with that gone, all that remained was the rush of air down my ears. Shaking my head, I slipped off the seat and stretched my back.

Warren remained astride the bike, waiting, as if expecting something, or someone, to appear from one of the many small grey stoned buildings grouped around the square. A square dominated by a central stone monument, words inscribed on the face, a bronze soldier standing on top, one arm outstretched, the other holding a rifle. Frowning, I studied the figure, recalling something like it from our history lessons. Not a modern soldier. A warrior from an earlier time.

"This place hasn't been lived in for many lifetimes," Warren said.

On the far side stood an old fountain, long since dried up, with little steps around it where once, years before, people could have sat and watched the world go by. Wandering across to it, I did just that.

After a few moments, Warren joined me on the cold step, stretching out his legs in front of him. "Pretty place," he said in a distant voice, his eyes roaming the empty buildings, the silent streets.

"Once maybe."

"Yes. Years ago, before the bombs, before all the killing... I suspect there were many places like this, where people lived out their lives quietly, peacefully."

"Did you?"

"Me?" He thought for a long moment, as if he had never considered the question of living peacefully before. He shrugged. "I think I *tried*, which is not quite the same thing. Then the wars came and nothing was to be ever the same again, of course."

"I don't remember much about it. I was too young, I suppose."

"You don't remember anything?"

I stared down at the ground, fragments of memory dancing across my mind. "Bits and pieces. Sirens, running to the bomb shelters. But I was too young. My earliest memories are of the Sweepers."

"They came after peace was signed, as the State struggled to rebuild what was left. The wars changed everything."

"It wasn't the wars that changed much for me, that was down to the Sandmen."

I felt his eyes boring into me. "I'm going to be honest with you, Simeon. I learned a lot about you from your chip."

Yes, my chip. Scanned for everything of any relevance. My suspicions had once more proved correct. The question now was, what was he going to do with all that knowledge?

"How is Yolanda?"

I tensed at the sound of her name and tried not to look at him, despite his eyes piercing through me.

"You haven't been in touch with her?"

I shook my head. He must have known that I hadn't. So what was he doing, testing my honesty?

"Perhaps you should."

"And how will I do that? Out here, in the middle of nowhere?"

"I have the technology." He smiled as I gaped at him. "Yes, even out here, Simeon, there are some of us who have embraced the new technologies. Does that surprise you?"

"Nothing much surprises me anymore. Perhaps what surprises me most is why you haven't taken me to the Sandmen."

"Maybe I don't want to." He slapped his knees and stood up, stretching his arms out wide, "It's good to be so *free*, Simeon. Don't you want to be free?"

"I don't know what being 'free' means."

"No more worries, no more concerns. You and Yolanda…you have feelings for each other. You could live a good life, Simeon. A life without fear."

"You think? And how am I supposed to do that, knowing what I know, seeing what I've seen? As soon as I set foot back in the City, the Sandmen will vaporise me…if they don't torture me first."

"And why would they do that?"

"To find out what I know…about Stoker."

He frowned. "Is that his name? Stoker?"

I felt the first tingling of fear, a few icy fingers tickling at my neck. I looked at him, his face half covered by that tangled beard, the thick, wire-wool hair.

69

I wish I'd taken more notice. "Didn't you know? I thought you'd scanned my chip thoroughly."

"Yes. But your Mister Stoker...he was very thorough himself. Quite a man when it comes to programming. I tried to find more about him, but he'd put in place enough defences to deflect even the most determined attack. Nothing I tried could break through." He looked out across the square towards the still, silent houses, grey walls blank and expressionless. Houses without people. Just stone. No life. Dead. "Stoker," he said, his voice sounding distant. Without warning he clapped his hands together, bringing us both out of deep, meaningful thoughts. "But, to get back to your question, Simeon. I've erased the details of your little visit to the Protector, so the Sandmen won't recognise you as a threat – or a renegade."

"I've never thought of myself as that."

"No, well you wouldn't – because you've never been involved in killing before."

"I didn't kill anyone," I protested, a little feebly.

"You think not? You helped in the assassination of the Protector, Simeon. You're an accomplice."

"I had no idea that he was going to be killed."

"Really? And what did you think it was all for, you visiting him like that?"

"I...I don't know. He was expecting me. He wanted me to...I..." I put my face in my hands, "I don't know."

"He was expecting you because your mister Stoker had broken into the mainframe and allowed you access. You were set-up, Simeon. They used you to get inside, to frame you for his death. A simple plan and you, *simple* Simeon," he gave a little laugh at his own joke, "you swallowed it."

"How do you know all this?" I was growing more and more anxious, my anger brewing up, covering my fear. "Who are you? Why did you help me? How did you know I was in that cave?"

"Lots of questions, Simeon. Perhaps it's time for us to head back, before it gets dark."

Nonchalantly, he swaggered over to his bike and ran a loving hand across its petrol tank. "A thing of beauty, don't you think? It's a classic two-thousand and four Sportster. Fifty years old. They don't make them like this anymore."

I strode over to him. Despite his size, I wasn't going to be intimidated, or ignored by this man. "I want you to answer me."

"There'll be time enough for answers, Simeon. Look at this place," he swept his hand across the village vista, "a quiet, rural scene. Picture postcard, they used to call it. Now it's dead. In twenty years time, it will be overgrown and forgotten. Do you know what the population of this country is now, Simeon? No? Fifteen million. *Fifteen* million. Before the wars, there were nearly eighty million people living in this land."

"But they weren't all killed in the wars, were they?" I breathed hard. "How many disappeared like my parents? How many million mothers and fathers simply vanished?"

He chewed his lip in thought. "Ooh...lots. But that was deemed to be necessary, Simeon. To save us all from each other."

Straddling his bike, he turned the ignition and the engine rumbled into life. He revved it a few times, laughing at the growl. "What a fabulous sound that is! Come on, we need to get going."

"Who *are* you?"

He smiled thinly. "Oh, just someone who cares. Now, let's go, then you can tell me all about the night your Mum and Dad disappeared."

Thirteen

But we didn't get to talk about anything that night.

Instead, as we rode back through the burgeoning dusk with the streaks of auburn threading through a purple sky, I caught him looking sideways. He slowed the bike and I followed his gaze. We both sat in silence, scanning the hills, searching for something. Something he'd seen. Something I'd seen.

Figures. Moving. Across the green of the hills.

But how could that be?

Not here, not now. Everything was dead.

Or so we thought.

I saw the first of them loping down the other side of the hill. We were in a small valley, with nothing to protect us from prying eyes.

As I looked, more of them appeared over the ridge, small specs of black gradually growing larger. Not Sandmen, not Sweepers.

People. Brandishing spears.

More fanned out across the road, making escape impossible.

He turned to me, his face grim. "We're in trouble," he said simply.

It was enough.

I was running from the bike even before he told me. I was used to running now; I'd done enough of it over the past few days. The difference was, in the past, I had known what I was running from. The Sandmen. Something to fear, something to dread. But this was different. This was unknown, and infinitely more terrifying.

Bounding over the low hills, I veered off to the left and rolled down a small dip. A pain like that from a knife ripped into my side and, crying out, I managed to scramble behind a clump of rocks, desperate to get out of sight, hoping our pursuers would concentrate on my biker friend. I didn't care what they did to him, if they caught him. I only cared for myself.

Dreadful thoughts.

Dreadful mind processes.

Dreadful.

As I lay there, in the damp, filthy earth, I gingerly pulled up my shirt and inspected the bandage. A red smudge grew as I looked. Groaning, I fell back, staring at the sky, praying the pain would go, that they wouldn't find me. Dare I look up, chance a glance? How dangerous would that be?

Curiosity is a powerful fault.

Pushing my body up with my hands flat on the earth, I peered over the rocks.

Warren hadn't moved, standing rigid as they swarmed around him like ants. I watched as the lead one hit him in the stomach with the end of his spear. I heard the outrush of his breath as he doubled up and winced when a second blow, a vicious uppercut, lifted him off his feet.

I didn't wait any longer. I sprang up, ready to turn and run, but my chance had gone. They were there. Several of them, their wild faces split into maniacal grins, bodies naked, rippling with muscles, hands holding spears.

It was over.

But not quite yet.

I dodged the first one's lunge and, keeping low, hit him in the solar plexus with my shoulder. He fell down with a grunt. Taking up his spear, I swung it, cracking the second attacker across the side of the head, then rammed the end into the third's guts. The pain in my side hit me like a sledgehammer and I buckled, stumbling backwards, sucking in my breath, knowing my wound was open and bleeding. Through tear-filled eyes, I saw the first one recovering. Summoning up my dwindling strength, I kicked him hard in the head and turned, sprinting over the hill, not daring to look behind me.

Reaching the next rise I noted the changing surroundings, no longer barren, bereft of life, but one as alien to me as this world is to the planet Mercury.

Before me, hewn out of the living rock, stretched a community of crags, tiny caves, and larger, gaping caverns. And around them, marking the entrances to these subterranean dwellings, were tiny, carved wooden statues of warriors holding spears. At once grotesque and also strangely beautiful, these manikins, swathed in strips of hessian and sealed over with tar, stood guard, silent and vigilant, perhaps imbued with supernatural powers by the people who worshipped them.

Those people were here now, swarming across the rocks like so many black beetles. Men, women, children. Primitives. Survivors from the wars, who had returned to the lessons of the dim and distant past in order to eke out an existence.

I fell to my knees and let out a wail of despair.

The footfall came close. I squeezed my eyes shut and waited.

It didn't help.

Something hard and heavy smacked into the back of my head, slamming me face-first into the earth. Mouth filled with grit, hot blood oozing from my skull, I surrendered to their strong arms, lifting me like a trophy.

A sacrifice.

Fourteen

They were singing. Chanting to be more accurate. I could hear them from the deep, dark hole into which they bundled me, tightly bound, unable to move. They had swooped around me as I reeled about, my head cracked open like an egg, urgent hands clawing at my body, overpowering me, dragging me off as I struggled and squirmed in a desperate bid to escape. They were too many and too strong and as my resistance ebbed, so their chanting grew louder. Without ceremony, one of them lashed leather cords around my wrists, then threw me into the pit in which I now lay.

I craned my neck to try to catch a glimpse of the world outside through the opening, not much more than a tiny hole from which I could see the night sky. But nothing more. I was totally exhausted and jagged rocks dug into my back as my skull pounded. I tried to wriggle around, but the last remnants of my strength ebbed away, and I allowed myself to drift into a swirling pit of semi-unconsciousness.

Sometime later I grew aware of that distant chant. "Warren?" I strained to sit up, my side splitting, head aching. Blinking, I looked around me, the blackness complete, Warren nowhere to be seen. A thought flashed through my mind. What if he were dead? What if they had already killed him, slit his throat, and threw him down here with me? I shivered, forcing the image from my mind, to replace it with something less horrid. Something beautiful.

Yolanda.

I wondered, once again, where she was, what she was doing. Was she thinking of me? Would she be worried? What would she do if she were? If, as I suspected, she had already tried to get in touch with me, gone round to my apartment, checked with school, found I was missing, she might then contact the authorities. But they, of course, would already have contacted her, taken her to one of their cells, forced her to tell them what she knew – which wasn't very much. Whatever they wanted, she would give them – anything, to stop the pain.

Because they would inflict pain.

Shaking my head, I squeezed my eyes shut and tried to force away the picture of her suffering. If I ever got out of this, would she ever forgive me? When this was all over, could I make her understand?

When this was all over?

What was I thinking? Here I was, trussed up like a prize turkey, listening to a bunch of lunatics singing death-songs, re-enacting some ancient North American Indian ritual, adding their own particular brand of hatred, preparing to…to do what? I shuddered to think.

I don't know how long they kept me down there. At some point, I must have drifted off to sleep because I wasn't aware of anyone else in the hole until rough hands lifted me up by the shoulders. Blinking my eyes open, I registered nothing except the stench of their sweat invading my nostrils. Ahead, some brandished torches, whilst others dragged me along a cramped tunnel which snaked upwards towards the night, the toes of my shoes making trails in the broken ground.

Reaching the top, they threw me to the ground, knocking the wind out of me. Instinctively, I curled up into a tight ball, which proved a pathetic attempt to protect myself from attack as first a kick slammed into my side, followed by more rough hands taking hold of me. From somewhere came the sound of yelling, but by now my senses were in disarray, pain engulfing my body, blood seeping from my head and side. Through blurred eyes I caught sight of figures silhouetted against the dark sky, gyrating wildly before me. All around, fires crackled and spat, turning the night blood orange, the air filled with the steady beat of drums. Hundreds of black, shadowy shapes danced, arms thrown up, legs kicking out, voices raised as one, chanting in a series of high-pitched squeals which sent a shiver down my back. The noise, the commotion, the pressing heat of the fires, all mixed together to create something akin to a mad scene from a painting by Hieronymus Bosch. Semi-naked bodies writhed before me, some on the ground, others leaping like mad demons, cackling and screaming, each nightmare scene designed to instil fear.

My legs folded beneath me as the strength drained from my body and I crumpled to my knees, blubbering. It was an insane, desperate world they had brought me to, one that would soon see me stripped and sliced up, ready for the pot. I wanted to cry out, to bring some end to the lunacy, but nothing worked, my throat dry and constricted, my eyes wet and blurry. All I could do was wait, wait for the end, hoping it would be swift and painless.

They dragged me across the piece the dirt towards a line of posts set into the earth, large bales of compacted straw stacked up at their base. Something stirred in my whirling mind, a memory of history, of how witches, or religious zealots and heretics ended their lives tied to such stakes, and burned. Was this to be my fate, burned alive, roasted on the spit, then my flesh consumed? I threw up my head and howled at the night time sky, bejewelled with a trillion stars, and they slammed me against the post, lashing my body to it with leather thongs. I stood limp, resigned to my fate, and watched them without speaking or complaining.

Pleased with their efforts, cackling like demented hyenas, mouths salivating, eyes wide with perverted glee, I turned and gasped. Warren hung there, against another post, head down, hair covering his face, clearly unconscious. He was the lucky one, I mused, free from witnessing the lurid scenes all around. Would his be a quiet acceptance of our fate, or a mad attempt at escape?

I turned away, not caring about anything anymore, and focused on the fearsome bunch in front of me. Naked bodies streaked in dirt, lank hair hanging free, they danced as if possessed, careless, consumed by their lusts. I couldn't see a single female. Despite my growing distress, I wondered if they might have returned to the caves, taking their children with them, well out of earshot of the horrors yet to come. But they would have heard the drums, their pounding filling the night air, louder even than the chants. Such a mass of sound must have taken whole ranks of drums, beaten upon by a small army of men, and yet I could not see any evidence of them.

Shaking my head, I forced myself to study these strange, jerking figures and the more I peered at them the more unnerved I grew. There was no random stomping of feet or throwing up of hands, but a controlled, repetitive movement, as if they followed a strict pattern, well rehearsed, without error or fluctuation. I counted the beat, crazy as that may seem, and I realised they repeated this pattern over and over.

And there was more.

At first I wasn't sure, but flicking my eyes from one group to the next, it struck me with startling certainty.

Each group appeared duplicated repeatedly throughout the press of bodies. Soon, I could pick out individual figures, noting their features, and checked with others on either side. They were identical.

Holding my breath, I struggled to make some sense of this. But even as an answer formulated in my brain, some drew closer from out of the red and black night, their faces set in ghastly grimaces, sheened in sweat. They feigned jabs and prods with their spears, jumping from one leg to the other, making strange whooping sounds whilst behind them, others waved their torches, turning in small circles.

It was obvious the end was drawing close.

Their plan to burn us alive.

Fifteen

I took a deep breath and shouted, "*Warren*!" He didn't flinch, so I used the name I'd secretly christened him with, "Biker – Biker, wake up!"

If the sound of my voice had worked in rousing him, it may have stopped one of the wild men rushing forward to strike me across the face with the back of his hand. The blow stung my eyes and I snapped my head towards him, glaring. This close up I could smell his stinking breath, peer into those twisted, gnarled features – a face of someone sub-human, without conscience, a primitive. I recoiled at the sight.

Beside me, Warren groaned. I turned to him and, not wishing to receive another blow, waited for him to raise his head and look at me. He grinned.

"Having fun?"

I sneered, "Who the hell are these people?"

"Remnants. Survivors. Call them what you like. They're the refuge of humanity, Simeon. And they're cannibals."

So, with my thoughts confirmed, I struggled with the notion we would become food for these *primitives*. I gulped, strained against my bonds, and rasped, "We've got to get out of here."

"Have we?" Smiling, he shook his. "And how do you propose we do that? Appeal to their better nature, maybe?"

"We can't just stand here and be...burned to death!"

"I don't see we've got much choice. You didn't know they existed, these people?"

"No, never. I didn't know people like *you* existed. All I've ever known is the City." I wriggled against the post, in a pathetic attempt to loosen the leather thongs. It was useless. "I don't want to die like this."

79

"Would you have preferred dying at the Protector's home? Helping your friend?"

"I told you – I wasn't helping him."

"So why did you allow them to recruit you, Simeon? Why did you agree to go to the Protector's home?"

I balked at his even, searching questions. This was no time for a cosy, fireside chat. "Are you mad? Why the hell are you asking me all of this now? Look at them, prancing around, getting ready to cook us to a cinder and all you're worried about is..." I frowned and gave him a searching look. "You should know the answers to all of this. You scanned my chip."

"Yes. Most of it. But I told you – your friend Stoker, he'd put too many blocks on the damned thing. When I searched too far, it crashed, erasing all of the data. I need you to tell me where their hideout was."

Despite the flames' suffocating heat, the press of stinking bodies, the swirling mass of maniacal monsters all around, my blood ran cold. This wasn't right – his calmness, his matter-of-fact manner. Slowly, I formed the words, "But you said you could reprogram it. That the Sandmen would have no knowledge of me, or what I'd done."

He raised his eyebrows. "I thought you said you had nothing to do with it?"

"You know what I mean – have you or haven't you recreated my personal profile on that chip?"

"Yes. No worries there, little friend. Just tell me why he recruited you and where."

"I can't remember – I took a wrong turning, a random, accidental event."

"Just one, big coincidence?"

"Yes."

He laughed and turned towards the writhing bunch of wild men. "Problem is, Simeon, I don't believe in coincidences."

"So what do you call finding me in that damned cave?"

With that damned smile set frozen on his face, he slowly turned and viewed me for a moment too long. "Exactly."

Before I could respond, a sudden cry rang out from one of the men standing a little way off from the main group. Everything stopped, the music ending abruptly, and an eerie silence followed, the only audible sound the heavy drawing in of breath from their fetid lungs. I glimpsed towards Warren, who shrugged his shoulders.

"All good things come to an end," he muttered softly.

I had no idea what that was supposed to mean, but almost as soon as the words left his mouth, the first Sandman came over the rise, the beam from beneath his jockey cap cutting through the night. Striding forward on his great legs, his arms slashed this way and that, sending the wild men screaming in every direction.

But the Sandmen had cut off their retreat.

More of them appeared, light beams striking individuals with terrifying accuracy, vaporising them as they ran. Those that ventured too close were caught in the cruel claws, sliced and dissected, human bodies shredded by the merciless mincing machines that were the Sandmen.

The screams grew in volume, curdling my blood, the sounds like the squeals of terrified pigs collected for the slaughter. I wanted to block my ears, retreat from the mayhem, but all I could do was turn my face away from the butchery, a blood orgy which left me feeling sick and ashamed. Yes, these men would have killed me without a thought, but this senseless massacre was beyond reasoning. Were these people of no consequence at all, to be swatted and stricken down like flies? Was that what they were, their humanity completely lost?

It was the legacy of my world.

Life, individual life, was of no consequence anymore. No one cared. No one stopped to think. Mine was a soulless, thoughtless world, controlled by faceless people who viewed us as nothing more than pests, to be exterminated at will.

"Simeon." Warren's voice broke over the cacophony of screaming and yelling, "We have to get out of here."

He was stepping down from the post, rubbing his wrists. A saw the flash of steel in his hand, and then he was next to me, the blade slicing through the leather as if it were paper.

"How...?"

He clapped me on the arm as I pulled myself free. "They never thought to search me, Simeon. Too drunk on the thought of eating me for their supper! Come on, we can make it to the bike and get away from this."

My wrists were red raw where the leather had cut into the flesh, but I didn't care, my only concern to follow him back over the low hills towards where they first caught us.

Running hard, at the brow I stopped and looked back. There weren't many of the wild men left now. One or two were putting up some sort of defence, striking at the Sandmen with their primitive spears. It was useless and pitiful and I watched them die, slaughtered with sickening ease.

Warren's voice shook me alert. "Simeon!"

It was the only reminder I needed to get me running again.

Sixteen

From the moment the bike accelerated down the dirt track, I knew something had changed. Not just with Warren, but with everything. The air itself had a different smell about it, the mountains and hills seemed unreal, the half-light casting them in deep shadow, all features smudged.

Pressing my head against the reassuring solidness of Warren's back, I tried to bring some order to my thoughts. I had so many questions swirling around in my head I felt dizzy. What had the past few hours all been about? Where had those wild men come from, and why had the Sandmen suddenly arrived to save us.

Save us?

Now there was a contradiction in terms.

The Sandmen were supposedly there for our protection, keeping us safe at night from the terrors that lurked outside. We all knew, with grim certainty, that their *real* purpose was to keep us under control.

We rode through the night and I clung onto him, my eyes closed, head swimming. I had no answers, only more questions. Why had Warren interrogated me the way he had. Didn't he know the answers? His explanation of Stoker putting in blocks may be true but somehow I didn't believe it. Warren had scanned my chip after removing the damned thing from my brain – if he possessed the ability to do that, then surely he would have the necessary know-how to bypass any sort of defense, no matter how sophisticated. Warren... my saviour, or my inquisitor?

As the bike decelerated, I looked around. Dawn was breaking all around, the surroundings coming into gradual focus. We were lumbering along the track which led to his home. The engine roared and I clung on. He was going too fast. Like my brain.

It was all becoming too much to take in.

We ate silently, a thin gruel he'd conjured up, my thoughts elsewhere, lost in images and ragged memories of this insane night.

Sitting at an old, cracked and warped table, wood sizzling in the open fireplace, I took in my surroundings. Plain and simple. No trappings of modern society. Not even a computer. Not one that I could see. Perhaps he owned a hand-held device, which were not allowed in the City. We could only use traditional desktop machines with large interactive monitors, monitors through which they watched us. Laboratory mice. Rats caught in a trap.

My wrists hurt, the welts running around them throbbing. Putting my spoon down, I rubbed the chaffed skin, hissing with the pain. Without a word, Warren came over and spread ointment over the swelling. I smiled my thanks as instant relief washed over me.

"You feeling better?"

"A little."

"You shouldn't worry so much." He sat down opposite me. "It was nothing really."

"Is that what you call it? They were getting ready to cook us for dinner."

"I always knew we'd get out. Didn't you?"

"All I knew was paralyzing terror – how could you know we'd get out? Who *are* you?"

He picked up the bowl and crossed to the sink and washed it. Returning, he settled a glass full of water in front of me before he sat down. "You need to drink. It's important to keep yourself hydrated."

Running my finger around the rim of the glass, I grew confused, arching a single eyebrow. "This is water? We don't drink water anymore."

"We do here. It's fresh, from a spring. Try it."

I did and it tasted sharp and clean. Like nothing I'd tasted before. "My Dad used to tell me that when he was young you could *buy* water from shops. Shops! I've never been to a shop, let alone bought water."

"Your father lived in a world that was still normal, Simeon. A simpler, safer world where people could live ordinary lives. Before it changed."

"Changed? You mean the Sandmen?"

"More than them. The wars devastated everything, leaving our world nothing more than a refuse dump. Radiation levels were high, cities were strewn with dead and broken buildings. A few good people managed to salvage some remnants of civilization and rebuilt everything. It took a long time, but eventually order was restored. But it was very different from what had gone on before."

I gaped at him. His depth of knowledge astounded me, but also frightened me. "But why did it change? Was it just the wars?"

"Wars always change things. But those wars...they changed *everything*. With the United States and China virtually destroyed, Europe had to take charge. Which it always has done. The crucible of civilization."

"I learned that in school. That we were the first people to civilize ourselves, build cities, create laws."

"Yes. And that is true, Simeon. We were the first, the Europeans. The Asian and African people came later. Much later. We taught them you see, after we discovered them – taught them everything we knew. But, like the impatient children that they were, they rose up and tried to become greater than we were. They turned on us."

"I've never seen an Asian."

"No. and you never will. They're all dead."

My mind reeled at the thought. "All dead..."

"The world has returned to almost how it was. Before other species of human were created, before we had need of them. When there was a need, we had to create them, you see. In the great laboratories of the south and the east. We produced them by the million. A conveyer belt of humanity."

"I had no idea...I just assumed..."

"Never *assume, Simeon*. There are huge gaps in your understanding because schools have not taught our children particularly well. Did you know, for instance, that the United States invented writing?"

"Writing? You mean—"

"Before we had keyboards and interactive screens, people used pens. Some still do. The people of the United States first laid writing down over a hundred years ago, as a record of our world. All that we know of their time is due to those first writings. The thoughts of an ancient and venerable people. They put their words down in books, Simeon, not data-bases. They used words, not machine-code. Have you ever read a book, Simeon?"

"I'm sure I saw one in the virtual library. I seem to remember..."

"No matter. I have one or two you could borrow. Priceless now. But that was how people learned about the world, before information was downloaded."

"But how could they believe it? If someone had written these things down, how could the facts be verified?"

"Our governments verified them, Simeon. And we can always trust our government. That is one of the great fundamental truths of society. Trust in those that govern."

I nodded. He seemed so wise, so full of understanding and truth. I was slowly realizing how incredibly fortunate I'd been to be rescued by him. How privileged.

"So much has changed in this world, so much created through our advanced technologies – so much that is good and pure. For instance, Simeon, have you ever thought about how people travelled in the past?" He glanced outside. "My bike, Simeon. A wonder of the ancients. Again, the people of the United States invented machines that could travel on roads, across the skies, over the oceans."

"Oceans..." I followed his gaze through the window. The morning sun shone reflected off the chrome of his motor-bike. I'd travelled on that machine, experienced its raw brute power, and yet I had never stopped to think where it might have come from, who had built it, and why. The thought that the same people had also built machines that could travel across oceans... something else beyond my experience, only ever viewed on the interactive screens.

"We owe so much to those noble people," Warren continued, almost as if to himself. He put his chin on his hand, shaking his head. "Such wonders, such awe-inspiring creations. Pyramids in Africa, built to give thanks to the universe, vast rail networks to link the cities of the world, electricity and, of course..." He raised his glass, "The purification of water. We owe them a huge debt of gratitude."

I couldn't help but laugh at that. "But those... *cannibals*...they weren't pure..."

"Pure in their purpose, Simeon. Simple people, scared mentally, desperate to eke out any form of existence. Society always has room for people with purpose."

"But they would have killed us."

"Because they knew no better – they had escaped to the outside in the hope of finding some form of salvation, instead all they really found was despair. A return to a baser life, without all of the advantages you have, Simeon. You and all those other fortunates like you. You have the truth inside you, Simeon. All they have is a twisted, perverted notion of what life should be like. The Ancients had the same beliefs, and that was their downfall."

My brain was hurting with all of this. We'd had a few history lessons in virtual school, but not very many. Such knowledge was deemed less important than mathematical theory and quantum physics. What was the point in learning about the past when we had so much to do in the present?

"There's so much I don't know," I put my face in my hands, feeling the dreadful weight of my fears overwhelming me. "So, when the wars were over, and we came out of it…

"The Sandmen came."

"The Sandmen changed everything. More than the wars I think."

"Yes, they did." His eyes narrowed, boring into me with a frightening intensity. "But you understand why they had to be created, don't you, Simeon? To protect you."

His voice changing, so cold now, so hard. I gulped, shifting in my seat, uncomfortable under his gaze. "Protect me…protect me from what?"

He played with his tangled beard. "Wild men, like the ones that tried to kill us. And others. Renegades. Agitators. Anyone who is a threat to our – *your* safety…"

"Parents."

His smile was humourless. "Yes. Those most of all."

The day moved on and I spent my time browsing through the bookcase he showed me, dipping into well-thumbed volumes, some so old the pages fell to the floor from cracked, broken spines. Warren brought me food and hot tea. Cautiously I sipped at it, relishing the sweetness, the aroma of mint filling my nostrils, causing my head to clear so quickly it span. He laughed, floating in and out of the room and I heard him outside tinkering with his bike.

In a small backroom I came across an old computer monitor and, making sure he wasn't close, I switched it on and sat down to read the reams of code.

In the night, one of the coldest I'd known, I snuggled beneath the covers, remembering other nights much like that one. Despite my youth, or perhaps because of it, the memories were vivid, like scenes from a film played out before me. I remembered huddling on the sofa, well wrapped in an eiderdown quilt, Nan making me a hot drink in the kitchen on an ancient gas stove. The electricity had long since died, and there was no heating. We were so poor, but somehow we managed.

I closed my eyes, the years returning, the curtain pulled back once more as I recalled that awful, terrifying night so long ago …

The shouting woke me up. I sat up in my bed, mouth open, breath held, straining to listen. Throwing back the cover, I padded downstairs and found Mum and Nan in the kitchen, voices raised, faces strained with terror. Mum caught sight of me and rushed forward, hugging me close, her urgent kisses smothering my cheeks and mouth. Shocked and breathless I didn't have time to question what was happening until she said in a hushed, frightened voice, "Your dad hasn't come home."

"He's missing," added Nan.

I learned about it all much later, of course. When I could understand a little more. Before they took Nan away as well.

Mum sat me down and told me the story of that night.

Dad hadn't come home at his usual time. This was a frightening thought, because the Sandmen patrolled the streets after curfew. Theirs was the domain of the night. The Sweepers took charge in the day. There was a comforting certainty about the Sweepers. People knew the Sweepers, knew that they were human beings. That they could be spoken to, perhaps even pleaded with. Not so the Sandmen. They were half machine, half genetically re-engineered people. They never spoke. Only killed. And they killed anyone out after curfew.

Dad had not come home.

The curfew bells tolled and Mum grew frantic. Gripping my arms so tightly her nail dug into my flesh, she looked at me with tear-filled eyes. "My sweet boy."

She leapt up. "I'm going to find him."

"You can't!" I stood up, trying to pull her down. "You can't, Mum."

Nan joined in, pleading, begging her not to go, at one point breaking apart, the tears tumbling down her cheeks. "*Please.*"

But Mum was determined. "I have to go and look for him."

Nan and I exchanged a look, both of us realizing at that point no power was going to prevent Mum from venturing out into the lonely streets to find the man she loved.

She had an old hover bike stuck in the under stair storage area. I don't think she'd ridden it for about a year, but that didn't concern her now as she brought it out and fiddled around with the ignition. It spluttered, then hummed into life, gently easing itself off the ground.

Nan clawed at her arm, the words nothing more than a jumbled, desperate mess. But Mum had such an expression of determination on her face she looked like someone else. Not my Mum at all, more like a stranger, afraid, angered, all of that and more. She pushed Nan away, gave me one last look, then swished through the main house entrance and out into the night. I ran to watch her go, Nan calling me, her fingers brushing over my arm, failing to grab me.

As I reached the door I pulled up sharp and Nan screamed.

A Sandman.

How did they move so quickly? How could they sense that one little boy planned to step out into the night when he should have been tucked up in bed? But they did, and they were always there, and they didn't bring anyone any dreams, only death from their beam or their long, lashing claws of steel.

Nan hauled me back from him and pressed the button and the heavy the metal door closed with a resolving slam. Shaking, she held me close, so close I could feel her heartbeat pounding against my ears. Like the pounding of the Sandmen as they marched down the street, night after night after night.

And Mum was out there. And Dad too.

I never saw either of them again.

Sighing deeply, Warren pushed himself back in his chair. Disturbed by my dreams, I'd wandered into the main room and found him sitting in silence by the fire. He motioned me to sit beside him. "Tell me your story, Simeon."

So I did. And now, with it finished, I stared into the flames and fought back my tears.

"I'm sorry, Simeon."

"It happened a long time ago. I've sort of…come to terms with it."

"Sort of…I'm not so sure."

Shrugging, I sniffed and wiped my eyes with my sleeve.

"Your Nan? What happened to her?"

"The Central Directive. The day all remaining parents, grandparents, uncles and aunties were herded into local stadiums and…" I bit my lip, determined not to cry. The pain of that memory was such that my whole body shook as the visions came into my mind.

"You need to sleep, Simeon. Tomorrow, I'll try and give you some answers."

Sleep.

I did my best, but the memories returned. The Central Directive … Dear God …

I dreamed I was a little boy once more, Dad taking me down to the promenade to watch the hover boat trials. Thousands of people were there, all baying and screaming in the wonderful, festival like atmosphere. I even saw street vendors selling things like hotdogs and ice creams from Italy. Our country no longer produced ice cream and they cost a small fortune to buy, but Dad nevertheless handed one over to me. I could almost taste it once more in my dream, the years just melting away, just as the ice cream did, dribbling down my fingers in the summer heat.

Everyone was happy. Banners fluttered, klaxons bleated, children shouted in glee.

Then it all changed.

Far out in the bay one of the hover boats suddenly reared up, as if it had been yanked backwards by a huge, invisible string. For a moment there was an anguished silence from the crowd as everyone watched in mounting horror as the boat flipped onto its back and erupted into a great ball of yellow flame. The sound of the explosion hit us moments later, everyone ducking instinctively. A different screaming broke out now. Screams of panic and fear, all sense of enjoyment and fun gone. Another boat tried to veer away from the flames. I caught a glimpse of the driver grappling with the controls, trying to engage the boosters, but too late, his boat moving too fast, human reactions too slow. Onboard computers should have kicked in, but this was a competition, man and machine. No virtual or artificial intelligences at work here. The second boat clipped the first, still engulfed in flames, and banked over on its side, skimming through the water, lifting too far, pitching right over. It hit the water once, twice, three times then began an awful summersault before it broke up and it too burst into a massive explosion.

People broke and ran in panic. Taking me by the hand, Dad quickly swept me up, holding me to him as the swarm of people rushed madly by, pushing and shoving, like one huge snarling beast, individuality blurred, the only thought escape.

A woman in front of me fell. Pressing my face into Dad's chest, I knew what was going to happen. As Dad tried to move us away, I chanced another look, my suspicions proving so horribly correct. Others stumbled across her, tumbling and tripping over outstretched arms and legs, knocking each other down in their furious desire to get away. Her mouth opened in a silent scream, chest crushed, lungs unable to work. She died like that, as did so many others.

"We need to get away," shouted Dad, forcing his way over to the left through the press of humanity. A big man bashed into us and Dad nearly lost his footing. Somehow he managed to stay upright. Teeth clenched with determination to get us away, I knew he would not succumb. As another man tried to push us forward, Dad struck him in the jaw with his elbow. The man went down, swiftly engulfed in a rush of heaving, heavy bodies.

Using all his strength to cut us a pathway through the press, we made it to the far side, and the concrete wall separating us from the marina beyond. Some people were pinned right up against it and I watched in horror as a man's face went white, his eyes rolling up into his head. Again I saw how a human being died, right in front of me, his chest so pressed inwards by the mass of people that he couldn't breathe.

Dad did a terrible thing then, a thing which I never believed him capable of. With me in his arms, he used this man, lodged upright against the concrete, as a sort of step-ladder, climbing over him, Dad's right foot pressing down on the poor man's head to lever us onto the top of the wall. Standing up, I gazed out across the sea of people, gazing at them fighting each other, arms raised, some unable to move, most wailing in terror, whilst behind them, the rescue boats were already clearing up the debris.

Then came the public address and a loud, frighteningly close klaxon sounded the alarm. From out of the clear blue sky, hover bikes swarmed like insects, Sweepers dismounting at a run, lasers and blasters carving great pathways through the surge.

I felt Dad tense, then gasp. Looking up I saw him pressing his hand against his mouth in terror. Despite my youth, I knew this was wrong. Why were the Sweepers killing people? What possible good could that do?

Later I was to learn, of course, that the Sweepers had orchestrated the entire incident. The 'accident' out at sea, the crowd panicking. All of it staged to allow the authorities to ban future public gatherings of any kind, for fear of renegade terrorist acts. We all knew the truth, of course, although nobody ever mentioned it.

Dad managed to bundle me over onto the other side of the wall where we remained, huddled together, until it was all over. I don't how long we stayed like that. An hour? Perhaps more. It felt like days and I remember wondering if I would ever again know calmness or peace. By the time the noise had stopped and we finally stood up, the scene before us was like something from the aftermath of a medieval battle scene. Bodies and limbs were everywhere, the ground drenched in blood, many of the wounded and broken, groaning pitifully. The Sweepers threaded their way through the corpses, vaporising those people close to death, directing those merely bruised and battered towards the far corner of the area, where other Sweepers scanned individuals and checked them against their records. A deathly quiet descended as the survivors shuffled silently along, bemused, shattered.

"Now then," said the soft, almost kindly voice of the Sweeper as he came up to us, "either of you hurt?"

"No sir," said Dad, straightening up.

The Sweeper scanned him, then me. He grunted. "Father and son," he said quietly. "You were lucky."

"Yes sir."

"Did you see the incident?"

"Yes sir. Boat blew up, sir."

"Blew up, you say? How did it blow up?"

Dad shrugged slightly and I could sense the Sweeper tensing. Quickly, Dad continued, not wishing to sound in any way antagonistic, "Sorry sir – I meant, I don't know, sir. It was just riding along then it pulled up on its stern, going into a sort of cartwheel."

"Stern? You know about water vessels?"

"Only what I've seen on telecasts, sir. Nothing real, sir."

"Mind you don't learn too much." The Sweeper looked down at me and tussled my hair. "Bright man, your Dad. Are you a bright boy, Simeon?"

"Yes sir."

He nodded. "I'll check you out at the academy, when you get there. Now, make your way home, all transport is cancelled from this point, so you had better move on quickly. The Sandmen will be abroad before long."

"Yes sir, thank you, sir."

We moved away without another word, Dad pulling me along by the hand, breaking into a half-trot. I looked back and saw the Sweeper still looking after us. It was one of the most terrifying sights I had ever seen.

Over breakfast, I recounted my memory to Warren, who listened in silence, pondering my words. He slowly sipped his coffee. "This was all a dream, Simeon?"

"No, More of a memory. But I dreamt it."

"So it did happen?"

"Oh yes. I think so. My mind ... Yes, it happened, exactly as I've said."

"Rare for a dream to be so...vivid."

"Perhaps it's because you still haven't replaced my chip. Perhaps it's that which has given me a greater grasp on reality."

Pressing his lips together, Warren looked grim. "I re-fitted it some time ago, Simeon. Whilst you slept."

Instinctively, my hand went to the tiny welt under the hairline on my neck. It was there all right. "Why didn't you tell me?"

He shrugged, fending off the question, "So perhaps it is the *chip* which has given you a greater sense of reality, Simeon." He finished his coffee and stood up. "You're a complex lad, Simeon. Not usual at all. Your chip gives no clue as to your insightfulness, but it's there all right. You are top of your class, Simeon. In every subject."

"Who the hell cares about that?"

"The Sweepers, the authorities. They won't vaporise you, not a boy of your ability. That one who said he'd see you at the Academy. He'd already ear-marked you for greatness."

"But...but I never finish my assignments, I'm always late—"

"Potential, Simeon – you have the potential for greatness. Right now, society is reeling with the death of the Protector. These will be dangerous times, perhaps more dangerous than at any point since the Protector took charge. Back then, the riots that engulfed every city and major town in this country, Simeon, almost destroyed our very civilisation. In the years before your birth, Simeon, this was a dreadful place to be. After the wars, people were dying by the thousand. Before there was order, before the Sandmen. There was no control, you see. People could wander around the streets, burning, looting, murdering. There was no justice, no consequences. That dream of yours was a memory you have stored away deep inside your sub-conscious, so deep that even the chip cannot reconfigure it. That is quite remarkable."

"I once thought my memories were nothing more than distorted, jumbled up pieces of news reports I'd seen. I never fully understood...They showed pictures, of course. Said it was the act of agitators, faceless people bent on destroying order and..." My voice trailed away as I suddenly began to realize that all I was doing was regurgitating what I had heard all those years ago from the authorities.

Warren reached across and squeezed my shoulder. "Oh yes, it happened. What is even more remarkable is that you knew, even then, that it was not the act of terrorists. You see, the official history clearly states that the whole event was sabotaged by malcontents. But you, Simeon, you knew the truth. That instinctive ability to weed out fact from fiction that makes you unique. It also makes you very valuable – and very dangerous."

Seventeen

Later, we took the bike and cut across the countryside, heading down an empty highway, seemingly the only vehicle left in the entire world. Neither of us had spoken since Warren's parting shot about me being 'dangerous'. I still didn't know what that meant. Perhaps I wasn't supposed to.

The road snaked on through green, featureless hills, leaving the bleak and blasted area of the wild men far behind. I couldn't help wondering how far the Sandmen would go to destroy their enclave. Would it mean the deaths of the women and children, huddled in the scooped out caves within the mountainside? I knew Sandmen didn't have any conscience, that their sole purpose was to destroy, crush resistance, sweep away any malcontents. The wild men were different – a separate society, based on freedom, a rejection of the modern world, and they would die, eradicated by the merciless Sandmen.

With the wind whistling past my face, I drew my mind back to the strange incantations of those people. Where had they learned them, what were they for? Had something, in some wholly unfathomable way, controlled them, taught them what to do? The way little groups repeated the same movements over and over, only a mere handful being truly individualistic in what they did, almost as if...

The sprawl of the City loomed up before us, breaking my reverie. A thick pall hung over the blackened high-rise buildings, which, from the distance, looked like rotting teeth, in sharp contrast to the clear, clean air of the countryside. Funny how my ideas of 'normal' had changed so quickly. The thought of returning to those grim streets, of my apartment, my computer, pills...it turned my stomach and I clung onto Warren's back, burying my face into the thick material of his jacket.

Perhaps the one part of returning 'home' which brought any sense of joy was the thought of seeing Yolanda again. In what state I would find her, I had no idea. My only hope was that she was well, that her ordeal had not been so very awful and that she could find a way, in time, to forgive me for everything I had put her through. For I knew, without a doubt, they would have interrogated her, forcing her to reveal *everything*.

Warren brought the Harley Davidson to a stop and turned to give me a nod. I clambered off, stretching my back. The ride had been long, my muscles stiffening up, and I let out a long moan as joints cracked and feeling returned.

Looking across the plain before me, I noted how the green grass gave way to scorched shingle. I was within walking distance of the city limits.

Warren pushed up the visor of his helmet and studied me for a moment. "Promise me something, Simeon."

I arched an eyebrow. "That depends."

He laughed. "I like you, Simeon. You're pure, untainted by everything that you've lived through, still retaining your sense of self. A throwback. I admire that." He gestured towards the shadowy outline of the City, "They'll scan your chip, but they won't see anything out of the ordinary. The death of the Protector may not be common knowledge yet, but I'm sure it soon will be. When that happens," he looked at me again, "remember what I told you. You have the truth, in here," he patted the left side of his jacket, "in your heart. Just, be careful, Simeon. Don't give too much of it away. Trust no one, Simeon. *No one.*"

"I don't understand," I said, looking at the grim silhouette of the City's spires, "I don't understand what you mean that I 'have the truth'." I frowned, turning to him, "What truth?"

He didn't answer straight away, perhaps mulling over how best to put his thoughts into words. Or, more accurately, to give his words more power, more weight. "You've questioned things, Simeon. Things that no one else has ever done since the coming of the Sandmen. No one wonders the way you do. In the early days, any glitches in the chips were ignored, but then, gradually, those individuals who revealed certain *traits* were... well, let's use the word, 'removed'. In fact, they were reconditioned, reprogrammed. Some of them became Sweepers, others..." Something dark crossed his face and he ran his tongue over his top lip. "Some simply ceased to be. But you," his voice sparked again, "you have a quite remarkable ability to overcome the programming of the chip, not just through a fault in the software, but an innate, natural ability to think for yourself."

"That still doesn't answer the question, Warren. About me knowing 'the truth'."

"You know, Simeon. Didn't you get an insight when you watched the primitives dancing? Didn't you note the way so many appeared the same?" He grinned, "And don't you know why the Sandmen never vaporised you, or why the Sweepers let you go after The Protector's death?" He brought down the visor with a loud snap. Pressing the ignition button, he revved up the bike unnecessarily and said something over the roar, something I couldn't catch. I leaned closer, cupping my ear, almost touching his visor. His words were a jumbled mess as the revs became louder still. The only word I heard was 'destiny', before he slewed the great machine around and roared off. I stood and watched the dust trail as he rapidly disappeared into the distance and I can honestly say I felt sadness. He had saved my life, more than once, and he had given me insights into why we lived in the world we did. But who he was, and why he had helped me, I still had no idea.

As always, the main thoroughfare was empty. No one had access to private vehicles anymore. Only the occasional bus floated passed. I saw the same grim faces pressed against windows, their eyes unblinking, unfocused. Lifeless.

In the main square, where sometimes little groups of intellects gathered to discuss the latest advances in cyber-technology, there was no one. Not even a Sweeper. I crossed the slate grey paving, streaked with the filth of a dozen years, and veered left towards Yolanda's apartment block.

I'd decided from the outset that the only sensible thing to do was to go to her first, explain things, try and make her understand. I had no idea how I'd find her – upset, ecstatic, terrified, or just plain angry. Running through all the possible permutations, I'd rehearsed my opening lines over and over, but in the end, I needn't have bothered.

As I came towards her apartment block, there she was. Her face finely chiselled, her ebony skin glowing, her mouth so perfect, so full. She just stood there, in the doorway and her great eyes bulged. Suddenly, with no warning, without a single word, she broke into a run and threw herself at me, and I caught her and held on, tighter than ever before, and she responded, hugging me so tightly I thought she'd never let go.

Lost in a glorious rush of emotion, we kissed, those smooth lips, the smell of her, the touch of her skin causing the strength to drain from my legs and my mind to swirl.

At last, she pulled back, gasping, and she held me at arm's length again, studying me with a fiery intensity in her saucer-sized eyes. "Where the hell have you been?" she said, her voice tiny and fragile. Before I could answer, she took me by the hand, pulled me inside the main entrance to the apartment block and shut the door with a slam.

We went up the stairs in silence, her hand still clamped around mine. I could see the outline of her body through the thin, cream cotton one-piece dress she wore and I longed to be close to her once again. At the door to her apartment I swung her round and now it was my turn to kiss her. Our mouths folded over each another, the softness of her lips like liquid velvet, her perfume heady. I was close to losing control, yearning for her, every fibre of my body aching, demanding to meld with hers. Again she drew back, looked at me through the smoke of her eyes, then pushed open the door. She led me to the couch, holding my hand like a mother would, and sat me down. She snuggled up next to me and, after a tiny pause, she broke into tears, not loud, but tiny jolts, like electric shocks coursing through her body, the tears silver trails against the mahogany sheen of her flesh. I didn't know what to say, so I simply put my arms around her and held her close.

They were the only words I needed.

Later, after we had made love, we stood on the veranda and gazed out across the city, watching the occasional hover bike cut across the grey sky. Leaning into me, I slipped my arm around her waist, feeling the solidness of her toned body against mine, revelling in the wonder of her, this moment pure Heaven.

"Where did all the people go, Yollie? After the Central Directive?"

"Our parents, you mean? I don't know. I can't remember."

"I can remember their faces. Can you?" She shook her head. "I can hear their voices, recall their words, our conversations, the things we did."

"I haven't got anything like that, Simeon. Are you sure your memories aren't just dreams? You want so much to have a past that perhaps you have invented all of this, to give yourself comfort?"

"Comfort? No, not that. You don't get comfort from knowing your parents disappeared in the night, or from the look of terror on my mother's face as she went out searching for my dad. She never came back. I lie awake, thinking about what might have happened, where they went."

"Well, I don't know anything about any of that. All I know is that I'm happy with the now. Why worry about the past?"

I didn't pursue the point, recalling Warren's assertion – that in some fantastic way, beyond my understanding, I was indeed unique. Yolanda was perfect, but her perfection had as much to do with the programming in her chip as it did with the loveliness of her body.

I peered across the silent streets towards the main entrance to the City, to what I knew lay beyond – the rolling hills, mountains, the cleanliness of the air. "But why doesn't anybody go outside anymore?"

"Outside the City?" I nodded. "Well, we have everything we need inside. And, besides, you must be sick of being outside, Simeon. You look as though you've spent the last few days under a tropical sun."

I gave a little laugh. Yes, I must have looked very different from when I had left. Replacing my usual ghastly pallor was a new, healthy looking tan. To emphasis the change, I put my hand next to hers and laughed as I compared our complexions. She squeezed my hand and looked at me. "Tell me now – where have you been?"

How much to tell her? How much did she already know? The crazy thing is, in all of this, I had no clear understanding of how long I had been away. I knew it was days, but how many I couldn't be sure. Enough for the authorities to make their investigations, to question, to seek out and destroy. They must have contacted Yolanda, so she had to have some knowledge of what had happened. How to shield her from everything, that was the dilemma facing me, because the more I told her, the more danger she could be in once the Sweepers came knocking, knowing I was back. Did she need to know *everything*? The less the better, I decided. Besides, perhaps the authorities had yet to announce anything. Even if they had, it was bound to be lies. The Protector's death might result in panic.

So, where to start? It was my turn to lead, so I took her hand and I gently sat her down.

So many questions.

So much confusion and self-doubt.

Despite all of my fears, and those I felt for her, I pitched straight in, laying it all out in a rush. The accidental meeting with Stoker, the Hitter, the visits to the Protector, the second time finding him dead, the fight with the Sweepers, the escape, the goat man…the only thing I didn't tell her, and I'm not sure why, was how Warren had helped me, repaired my chip, brought me back from the brink. The lessons he'd given me, about the history of our world, I touched upon none of it. I even omitted the scene with the Wild Men. It just didn't seem relevant. Or perhaps something, something in the way she cocked her head to one side and looked at me, swallowing me up with those eyes, as if drinking in every single word, storing it…Perhaps that was what held me back from giving away every snippet of information.

She remained listening to my words in silence. Finally, I finished. For a moment she sat, allowing it all to sink in until gradually, her features changed, and I had an awful feeling a curtain was pulling down, not just on my story, but on Yolanda's feelings for me. I held my breath, not daring to ask what was wrong. Her hardened features told me everything I needed to know.

Slowly, her eyes narrowed, bottom lip quivering, her stoicism crumbling, and a single tear rolled down her cheek. I wanted to reach out and touch her, hold her face, to give her some comfort, but before I could, from her mouth came the words I never believed she could say, "You murderer, Simeon."

"*What?*" Left speechless at this sudden, unexpected transformation, I sank within myself, gaping at her.

Nostrils flaring and shoulders tensing, she pushed me hard in the chest with the flat of her hand. "Get away from me," she shrieked, scrambling to her feet, stepping back from the sofa. "You, you deliberately took it upon yourself to do all that they wanted and you never once stopped to *think*?"

I stood up, hands spread out, pleading. "But Yollie, you knew that I had no choice. What Stoker said he would do, his threats – haven't you listened to anything I've said?"

With her face twisting into a mask of fury, she spat out her words like a snake would its venom. "You liar! You *killed* the Protector. The only good thing in this whole, stinking world and you killed him – you're a *murderer*, Simeon. *You.*"

"I didn't, I didn't kill him – he was already dead. I told you, it was the Hitter —"

"*Liar!*" She pushed me in the chest again and I staggered back, hitting the edge of the sofa and fell into it with a grunt. Before I knew what was happening, she came at me like a mad beast, lips drawn back, teeth bared, hands outstretched like the claws of a wild cat. I threw up my arms as she charged forward, instinctively trying my best to protect myself.

Dashing away my pathetic defences, her punch landed on my jaw, jarring my head back, rattling my cage. I felt my brain flip, senses spinning, a vague notion of falling overcoming me. The softness of the sofa cushioned my landing, and I rolled over onto the floor, watching, stupefied, as the blood dripped from my shattered nose. Pushing myself up on my hands and knees, I tried to focus on the spots of blood, forcing myself to regain an inkling of where I was, and stop the horrible spinning in my head.

"You murderer, Simeon."

"No…" I reached out, pawing at her. Where had her strength come from, this animal like ability to swat me like some insect? I groaned, tendrils of fear gripping me, tightening around my throat. "No…"

She took me by the collar, yanked my head back and lifted me off the ground with frightening ease. I stared into her face, that lovely, smooth, beautiful face. The face I dreamed of, the one I longed to kiss. "Yollie…" She punched me again, a swinging right into the side of my head. The lights danced in front of my eyes. She held me there, like a rag doll, the strength leaking from my muscles, the pain spreading over me. Her knee came up into my gut and I retched, folding forward. She still held me by the collar and I hung in her grip limply, trying to speak, to plead with her to stop. But nothing came out from my lips but a pathetic gurgle. I wanted to tell her I loved her, that I was sorry for everything I'd done, that nothing like this would ever happen again. All I wanted was her, nothing else. Nothing else mattered. *Yolanda, Yolanda please.* Her fist swung upwards and cracked into my nose. Pain like a lance speared through me, tears spouting, and I fell back, the ceiling spinning around. I could feel the blood erupting from my nose but that was nothing to what I was feeling inside. All I wanted was her, the touch of her hands on my body, those lips pressing against mine. It was only moments ago that we had melted into one another, and now everything, every single thing had been turned on its head and all because of me and my inability to explain.

"Get out," came her voice from a long way away, "Get out, Simeon and don't ever come back! If you do, it will be the Sweepers who take you away, I promise you."

I lay on the floor, gazing at the ceiling, her face nothing more than a spectre, lacking form and substance. I lifted a finger and tenderly touched my nose, instantly winced and brought my hand back to see the blood. Sucking in air, I rolled over, trying to refocus, not just my eyes but my thoughts as well. She'd become like something possessed, out of control, her aggression unimaginable, and nothing like the Yollie I knew and loved. One moment loving and kind, then a savage animal. Of course, I knew why. It was so obvious.

Standing, I reeled like a drunkard, taking in great, ragged breaths. I pressed my fingers against my nostrils, trying to staunch the flow of blood, biting back the tears, holding on as the pain raced through my face, certain every bone in my head was broken, the power of her blows so frightening, so … *superhuman.*

"I said get out."

With my legs like rubber, all the strength gone, I looked at her through eyes filled with despair and anguish. She stood, eyes blazing, hair standing out at weird angles, hunched and taut, fists still clenched, ready to spring.

I wanted to say something, something that might bring a change of heart, sweep away this creature she now was. But I had nothing to give, nothing to convince her of my innocence. Holding my nose, I slowly walked to the door and pulled it open with an effort. Defeated, I turned for one last, desperate plea, "Yollie—"

"Out, or I'll kill you now, you bastard!"

The door slammed full in my face, cutting off my words. Cutting off my life.

For a long time I sat in the stairwell, head on my knees, trying to clear away the drunken debris that my messed up brain had become. The pain had eased and the blood had stopped, but I knew I looked a mess, the front of my shirt streaked with spots of red, my face battered and bruised – but I didn't care. My whole world had changed, my only true friend, the only person I cared for, was now lost to me. An enemy. Hate-filled, angry, full of disgust and loathing… how was I to come back from this, regain any semblance of a life worth living?

The ferocity of her attack left me reeling. I had no idea she could be like that, turn in a single moment from a sweet, loving girl into a wild fury. She was no longer the girl I thought I knew. And yet, as I sat, overwhelmed with sadness and shame, I had the strangest feeling that everything would all come good in the end. Somehow, some way, Yolanda would learn the truth and we could rebuild our life together. Call it naivety if you like, I felt it was realism. All I needed was patience. She needed space, time to come to terms with what had happened, time to realize my innocence, that I was simply in the wrong place at the wrong time.

That last thought brought me up sharply, clearing my head better than any analgesic. Who was I trying to fool? I'd been set up, by Stoker and Hitter, the very moment when, in that stinking room, they put me in that chair and forced me to do their bidding. Primed and parcelled and sent off for delivery into the arms of the Sweepers. I knew everything was an elaborate plan to frame me for the murder of The Protector. Warren had showed me how corrupt it all was. Yolanda had yet to realize it, but I hoped that one day soon, she would.

Not yet, however.

What happened to Yolanda in that whirlwind of violence was beyond imagining. It was all too clear, too apparent to me the reason – they'd gotten to her, tampered with her chip, altering her personality. As soon as the truth fell from my own lips, she'd snapped, gone into some sort of over-drive. Perhaps my admission was the switch, the trigger that caused her chip to overload and change her into an uncontrollable banshee. And would she, even now, be informing them, contacting the Sweepers, telling them that the plan had worked, that I'd done exactly what they'd predicted – confessed. They knew me, always had and I, like the fool I was, I'd fallen into their trap as easily and as readily as I'd succumbed to Stoker's threats only this time, Yolanda was the key, my love for her my undoing. They'd manipulated her, and I wondered if the day would ever come when she understood the truth about everything.

As things turned out, that day was to come much sooner than I could ever have imagined.

Eighteen

Standing in the doorway to my apartment, everything appeared just the same as the day I left it. And yet, there was something...A coldness. Unfriendly, unwelcoming. Taking a breath, I stepped over the threshold.

The house computer welcomed me with its usual sterile voice, asking me if I had eaten. I flopped down on the sofa and answered that I had, which was a lie, but I didn't care if it realised or not. Before me, across the wall, the hologram screen flickered into life and I waved my hand to select the channel I always watched at that time.

My interest in history had been a constant source of amusement for Yolanda. However, my interest in ancient sport horrified her, believing it to be 'counter-productive', whatever that meant. Why did I find it necessary to watch grown men kicking a ball around a grass pitch? Couldn't I spend a more productive day studying, completing the pile of backed-up assignments that snarled up my school files? Dad had always gone on about the 'glory days' when he was young, how *his* dad had taken him to real outdoor stadiums to watch real people playing a game. Everyone had to wear protective clothing of course. The simple truth was, the 'glory days' were nothing of the sort. For everyone, one's personal past always seemed golden, so wonderful, the Sun forever shining, people everywhere so full of fun, smiling, laughing. As for me, if I tried hard enough, I could rustle up a memory of something similar – a few glimmers of a time when we would sit around the table, a close-knit family, sharing the sheer joy of living.

I sat up, rubbing my face, as the house-computer hovered close, a glass of liquid minerals appearing as if by magic at my side. "You have vitamin deficiency," it said, the LED array flickering across its surface, forever changing hue, tone and colour, not unlike the cuttle-fish I'd seen on any number of nature telecasts. "I can also detect –"

I waved it away, not caring what it could or could not detect. I drank from the glass, winced a little as the thick, alkaline liquid hit me. Curious how quickly one's reactions changed, how our bodies adapted to a new set of intrusions. My intrusions with Warren had been of the natural variety – fruit, bread, water, things I hadn't tasted, not since... since my childhood.

The original chips were designed to suppress all such memories, to keep us subdued, free from emotions. My chip, through some happy stroke of fate, had a glitch and I had been due to have it reprogrammed just around the time I met up with Stoker and his compatriots. Now, it seemed that whatever Warren had done with the new chip, I still retained vestiges of nostalgia. That uniqueness which made me, so Warren had intimated, in some inexplicable way, 'special'.

We never saw Mum and Dad again after that terrible night when she went out looking for Dad. She never returned. For a number of days, Nan tried to keep things as 'normal' as she possibly could. She served me meals, got me up for school, did her level best to run the household in the time-honoured way. In the quiet of night. I could hear her sobbing gently to herself. Curiously, I became reclusive, retreating deep within myself, training myself not to ponder on what had happened or, perhaps more importantly, *why* it had happened. Nan would sit, stroking my hair, her eyes never leaving my face. We hardly ever spoke. My existence became a curious half-world, almost dream-like, locked between the mundane, day-to-day tread-mill, and a burgeoning feeling that something massive was about to occur. Every day I would wake and sit up, the thought pressing down on me, wrapping itself around my chest like a lead waistcoat, that a monumental transformation of everyone's life was going to happen. Then, many months later, perhaps even years after my parents had disappeared, we received the notification to attend a citizens' meeting in the City Park.

The last time we had gone there, the Sandmen had first been introduced. This night, they were already there, standing silent all around the great field as people slowly filtered in, heads down, shuffling quietly forward, no one looking at anyone else. The all pervading atmosphere of dread so real you could pick it up, actually taste it at the back of your throat. When everyone had finally assembled, the Protector stood on the rostrum as before, flanked by Sweepers. He told us, in his soft, caring voice, that our parents had been resettled, that they were safe, that we would see them again soon. We were entering, he told us, a 'new dawn', the beginning of a way of life that was completely different from anything that had gone before. He grinned when he declared that our parents were 'wonderful people', that they had shaped who we had become, but even so, they were 'imperfect', they made mistakes.

"Children are the most valuable resource we have," he said, his voice liquid smooth, melting our hearts, filling our stomachs with a warm glow, "Because of that, mistakes cannot be tolerated. Some of you have grown true and straight, but others…" He shook his head and for the first time, the grin slipped away. "So, from now on, the State will look after you all. We will provide for your every need, from the food on your plate, to the education you receive at school and college. We will nurture you, equip you with the tools and skills to become fully functional members of our new society. There shall be no wastage, no mistakes. Each and every one of you will thrive, becoming essential cogs in the machine. An exciting era has dawned, one which is free from fear, free from want. And, most importantly, the bonds that restrict you, the bonds of affection which stifle you, will be forever removed. Then, and only then, can you fully embrace the new era and become fully integrated into our brave and wonderful society."

He turned to the Sweepers and nodded. Slowly, they came down amongst us, smiling, patting out heads, everything so calm, so acceptable. There was no panic. They moved through the crowd, separating the people into groups, the children being moved off to what were called 'conditioning areas', whilst our grandparents – the only 'family' any of us had left by then – were taken to another field way over on the far side. "Everything is perfectly fine," the Protector told us, "You will be reunited with your loved ones in an hour or so. You will see them all again soon."

We never did.

I hugged my Nan and she kissed me on the top of the head, telling me to be a 'strong boy'. Then, giving me a final smile of encouragement, she tramped off with all the rest. I stood, watching her as she moved off into the distance, swallowed up by the others who all obediently did as they were bid, sheep herded away. She didn't look back, and I felt a stab of regret about that, a spear in my heart. I bit back my tears as best I could. To find some help, I turned, looking desperately for a friendly face.

It was then that I saw Yolanda.

She came over to me, her own face wet with tears. We didn't say anything, just stared into one another's eyes. Then a large Sweeper came over to us, placing his hands on our shoulders, "Everything will be fine," he said in a gentle, reassuring voice. He smiled down at us and firmly guided us towards the conditioning area.

We were fitted with the chips that evening and then taken to large dormitory units where we were looked after by white-coated technicians, who sat us down in black-backed chairs. We trailed into a large white room, so white that I had to screw up my eyes, and some curious device was pressed over my head. I turned to see Yolanda sitting next to me. She winked, gave a smile and I felt my heart lurch, all of my anxiety flying away like some escaped bird, gone forever. All I wanted was to look into that face for the rest of my life. I didn't even notice the technicians configuring this and that on the device, barely flinched when the first surge swept through my brain, didn't give a thought when images leapt into my subconscious. Time became blurred. I can't recall if we stayed there a day, a week, a year or even three or five. All I can remember was that at sometime later, we were shown to our own, personal apartments and that when I walked through the deserted streets, I had my hand in Yolanda's. That was so long ago… I think.

The memories became vague, like the old, grey images of the past that I studied. Our studies began almost immediately on our placement in the apartments. I hardly gave a thought to my old house, my old life. My parents and Nan, they became nothing but ephemeral shapes, lost in a cloud of unknowing. Sometimes these images were clear, other times blurred. And, like them, I would gaze at my study units dancing before me, nothing making sense. Detached from everything around me, I wandered through life in a sort of half-daze, my memories like part of someone else's past. It's a struggle for me to remind myself of the events that happened, that they were real. Throughout that initial honeymoon period, I never questioned any of it, just sat like a sponge and soaked it all in, never once stopping to question why. Gradually, however, my mind would turn more and more to the past. Distant memories became much more resolute and concrete. Often I would cry in the night, my head under the sheets, recalling how it once was.

I grew bitter, full of anger … and gradually, the question surfaced, the one which forged who I now was.

Why?

I often ask myself that question. Not out loud, of course. Central Control would pick up such an utterance and a Sweeper would arrive, to interrogate me. No, this, together with others, is the main question I ask myself. Why did any of this have to happen? Why was it necessary to take away our parents, our grandparents, everyone who had ever loved or cared for us, to replace everything we treasured with the fear of the Sandmen?

After Brazil had lifted the last World Cup to be played in the real world, I told the computer to close down the screen and I sat and allowed my mind to drift. After an age, I gathered myself and went over to my desk computer. It hummed into life and told me I had messages from various people. None of them were particularly interesting, except for one, well down on the list. I ran my hand over the interactive screen and a face came up. It was a face I thought I recognised, but the more I looked the less certain I became.

"Simeon!" I craned my neck forward. The face was in deep shadow, but his voice was clear, despite it being so low. "Simeon. We need to talk."

It went blank. A little like my brain. Not recognising it, the voice sounded bright, unthreatening and yet I couldn't help but wonder if it had been disguised in some way. The slight inflection was vaguely familiar, but who it was, and why did we 'need to talk'? I ran a locality scan but nothing came up. It was from an undefined destination. The voice recognition programme failed to come up with anything either. And why hadn't the anti-viral protection software blocked it, or challenged it in some way? Could it be possibly the sender had the ability to bypass the Central Controls?

Racking my brains, I wandered over to the kitchen and found a pile of pills assembled and waiting for me. I'd missed my medication for a number of days now, hence my feelings, my paranoia. I wolfed them, chasing them with another glass of minerals supplied by the house-robot. Immediately, a sense of euphoria coursed through my body.

It was going to be all right.

* * *

I must have dozed off, for something forced me to jerk upright, senses alert. For a moment, I felt a rush of panic, not knowing where I was. Looking about, I half-expected the goatherd to reappear out of the gloom, or Warren. Or a Wild Man. It was dark and cold but as I sat, I slowly realised where I was.

Rubbing my eyes, I shivered and said aloud, "Computer – lights," Startled at how loud my voice sounded in the quiet confines of the room, I waited until a subtle, ambient glow simmered around the corners and slowly the familiar surroundings of my apartment came into focus. Taking a moment to stretch, I became aware of voices outside, beyond my front door. A low, steady hum. It was night. Curfew was in force. Immediately I assumed that something terrible had happened – a fire or a radiation leak. Rubbing my eyes again, as if that might in some way help me identify to whom the voices belonged, I went over to the door and pulled it open.

The harsh corridor lights stung my eyes, blinding me momentarily with their intensity. Forced to look away, when I turned again I could make out two figures at the far end of the hallway. They were arguing, despite their low voices. I could see anger in their twisted faces, the red glow on their cheeks. I shouldn't have stood there, feeling like an unwanted witness, but I was chewed up with curiosity and couldn't tear myself away.

There was a boy, about a year younger than me but much taller, and a girl, a shock of red hair sprouting from her head, making her appear wild, almost out of control. She had blood on her t-shirt and she had him by the shoulders, shaking him. The boy, reacting, gripped her by the arms and as she tried to wrestle free, she screamed. A piercing, hellish sound. He took her wrists in one hand whilst the other moved to the back of his trousers. I saw it then. The knife. He brought it round, the blade snapping out, its blade glinting evilly in the false light of the hallway. She froze, her struggling ceasing. Time became suspended, a moment captured in still-life, and she turned her face to me. Monck's Scream. I felt my stomach turn to mush, not daring to believe what I was witnessing. The painting at The Protector's home, now real, stepping out from the canvas to seize me by the throat. I staggered back against the wall, my legs like jelly, no strength to hold me up. Then she screamed again, mouth a black cavern, the sound louder than even the air raid sirens which still roared out every month or so across the City.

Agog, I watched in fascination as the boy raised his knife. A knife? Nobody carried knives. There was no need to. Warren had one, I recalled with instant clarity. Warren...

In my daydreaming, I missed the fact that both of them had ceased their struggle, that their faces were turned to me, noticing my presence for the first time. They stood, wide-eyed, glaring at me, features burning with hatred. Suddenly I felt afraid, and for good reason.

The boy, dropping the girl's wrists, now rounded on me and charged. Frozen to the spot by the sheer intensity of his attack, all I could do was raised my arms in a pathetic attempt to ward him off.

The girl screamed again and he hit me, driving me through my door, to land on the floor. Desperately, I tried to raise myself, but he was all over me, his strong legs gripping my sides, pressing my head down with one hand whilst raising his knife with the other. I thrashed under him, but he was too strong, too insensed with rage. "*Informer!*" he screeched, the blade flashing, the hand coming back, preparing to strike.

I closed my eyes and waited for the heat of the knife to sink into my flesh. Was this how it was all to end, murdered in my own home by an unknown. I should never have stepped outside. Curfew. Curfew meant the Sandman should have come to my aid. But they were not here – they had abandoned me, sacrificing me to this mad attacker. Perhaps this was also part of the plan. Crying out, I squeezed my eyes shut and waited.

The piercing of my flesh never came; instead I felt the heat from the edge of a streak of light which flashed bright even though my eyes were clamped shut. I gasped, the weight the boy's body on top of me disappearing in an instant and I chanced a look. For a moment I thought I'd made a mistake, that I too was going to be engulfed by that beam, but no. A single instant of blinding light, then nothing. The boy, the one with the knife, had simply vanished.

A rough hand pulled me to my feet and I stared in disbelief towards the Sweeper filling my vision. His eyes narrowed. "Hurt?"

I took a moment, eyes darting around my room. There was the couch where I'd fallen asleep, the door still standing open. It appeared as it had before. "Er- no, sir. I don't think so."

He scanned me before he drew himself up to his full height. "Just a domestic," he said lightly, putting his vaporiser back under his coat. "Nothing to worry about, Simeon. Try and rest. Rise early and catch up with your school-work."

"Yes, sir. Thank you very much, sir."

He touched his helmet in a kind of salute and went out. I followed him and peered into the corridor. Two more Sweepers were with the girl, who was crying. They administered a pill of some description. Almost at once she broke into laughter. One of the Sweepers took her to what I assumed was her apartment.

I started as I realised the Sweeper who had helped me was staring straight at me. I forced a smile. "Get some rest, Simeon," he said.

Without another word, I went back inside and pressed my door shut. Leaning backwards, I stared around my room. There was nothing to indicate what had happened. Not even a smudge of memory. One moment the boy had been there, the next nothing. A human life simply eradicated, without a moment's thought. I bent down, felt the carpet where we'd struggled. A slight warmth passed through my palm, the only clue. Nothing else.

And who would know? Who would care? Would anyone mourn him, or question why the attack had come, with such ferocity?

Feeling heavy, my body shaking, I fell into the couch, the red-headed girl's face looming before my eyes. Who was she? Why had they argued?

I closed my eyes and tried to clear my mind. Music, soft and mellow, came on, easing my anxiety. The house-robot provided me with a pill, which I took without hesitation, and soon, very soon, all my fears and confusion subsided. Together with the memory.

But not completely.

I stirred from my slumber, my head stuffed with kapok. I padded into the bathroom, stood under the shower and waited for hot the water to revitalise me.

It didn't.

I passed through the air dryer and went out into the main lounge, my head thumping, and ordered a glass of hydrate to stimulate my dulled emotions.

A memory trickled back. The eruption of violence, the gut-wrenching terror of being so close to death. What had pitched the boy over the edge, caused him to attack me? Was it a problem with his chip... surely the Sweepers would have known long before he had gone berserk?

I stood in front of the window and looked out at the dark, brooding outlines of high-rise buildings dominating the horizon. Beyond, as I now knew, was another world, simple, untainted, yet holding its own dangers. Wild Men. Goatherds. Bikers. Returning home, my argument with Yolanda, and now the attack in the corridor. None of it fitted together, everything unrelated, or so I assumed. Random instances, that's all they were. Then, the message on the computer. The voice, the dark face.

The face of someone I must know. I pressed my fingers into my eyes and shook my head. It was all such a blur, such a jumble of mis-matched images and happenings.

A surge of determination, an iron rod in my spine, brought a new resolve. I went out, strode down the corridor, not even thinking for a moment that a Sandman would come. I was beyond that now, all of my intentions set on one simple desire – to find out why it had happened.

I pounded on the red-head's door and waited, my forehead pressed against the cold metal. I heard something stirring within, and I slammed my fist against the door again. It opened and there she stood, hair in disarray, eyes round and wide, full of questions. I stopped, not knowing what to say, how to begin. Then, she reached forward, the back of her hand stroking my cheek. I stood transfixed, hardly able to breathe. "Answer the call, Simeon." Then she stepped back, a flutter of a smile on her face, and closed the door.

Something moved far below and I raced by to my apartment, pressing the door closed, and stood there, shaking, thinking of nothing but her words. *Answer the call, Simeon.*

From the window, I could see the smudge of dawn playing around the edges of the sky. Morning. The computer told me I had another message, but I should access it at first light because now it was still sleep time. Ignoring the computer's dark warning, I settled myself in front of the screen and waited. The face came up, the voice the same as it was before. Enough time had lapsed for me to work it out, to realize who it was. Disguised or not, the really was no mistake. Taking two protein pills and the one item I knew I'd need, I gathered myself and went out into the city streets.

I went to find Stoker.

Nineteen

Crossing the main street, moving from doorway to doorway, I finally found a piece of flattened land and an old dilapidated hut which I fell into and waited until the light completed its victory over night and the morning dawned proper. With curfew over, I moved on, keeping my head down, hands in pockets, avoiding eye contact with the few people who were wandering around. A hover bike glided by and I hunched my shoulders in a pathetic attempt to keep myself small. I gasped as it swished to a halt, the Sweepers stepping out to block my path.

"Simeon," the first one said, whilst the other scanned the street. They seemed on guard, as if expecting something, but what I had no idea.

"Yes, sir," my eyes were downcast, my heart pounding, my mind full of uncertainties.

He touched me on the shoulder, "Out for a stroll?"

He was scanning me, so any lies would be instantly picked up. "Bit confused, sir," I said. "Had a few bad days, sir."

"Yes. I understand, Simeon. That incident in the corridor…nasty."

I nodded. "Bit troubled by that, sir. Wondering why he attacked me, sir."

"Nothing to worry about, Simeon. You know we're always here, watching over you." He patted my arm and for the first time I looked up at him. Beneath his helmet, I could see the glimmer of his eyes, human eyes. Perhaps he had been a father once, with a son like me. Then, he titled his head and said the most curious thing I had heard from a Sweeper. "You will be careful, won't you, Simeon?"

His gaze held mine and I felt such a glow creeping through my body that I had a sudden urge to hug him. He smiled, warm and wide as his hand cupped my chin and gently pulled my face upwards. "Yes, sir," I mumbled, "Thank you very much, sir."

"You're a good boy, Simeon." He tapped my pocket. "You won't need that...hopefully."

I gawped at him, waiting for the tug of his grip, the wrench as they both grabbed me, lifted me into the hover bike and swept me off for reconditioning. But none of it happened. He simply turned away without another word. Then they were gone, the bike banking off to the right and arcing up into the sky where it was lost amongst the high-rise buildings, some of which had lights on. A new day. Things to be done. That brought me back to reality. I had to keep moving.

Not so long afterwards, I found the place, my memory serving me well. The old battered door stood closed, its frame rotten, the panelling warped. Without hesitation, I put my shoulder against it and pushed.

It was dark inside, just as I remembered, the stench of must, dry rot, decay invading my nostrils. Swallowing hard, I pressed my palm against the door, closing it, instantly blocking out the last vestiges of light. Pulling out the torch from my pocket I switched it on and trained its intensive beam around the interior.

Soon I picked out the debris, the detritus of past lives, the ghosts of previous occupation. Old chairs, tables, some burned out electrical devices, but of Stoker's bank of computer equipment, there remained nothing. I felt that somewhere there had be a clue, a tiny remnant that would indicate that everything I had seen and experienced was real. I had to find something, anything that would give me some answers, so I moved further into the building, paying particular attention to the corners.

Over at the far side there was a mound of rubbish. It seemed to be just papers and bits of old material. I stooped down, hoping there would be something, and rooted through. I found it. Tiny and insignificant, but perhaps, just perhaps... I slipped it into my pocket and then continued my search for any further evidence.

There was nothing else of any significance and I stood up, training the torch beam towards the rear of the building. An old set of stairs loomed out of the darkness and as I drew closer I could clearly see that they were close to collapse, the wood blackened and splintered, as if it had been set on fire. Even as I reached out and touched the balustrade, it groaned dangerously. I knew it couldn't take my weight, but I had to chance it anyway. Curiosity was burning inside. I had to find Stoker, confront him, tell him that his plan had failed.

Of course, he knew all of that already. But to tell him to his face, that was my innermost desire now.

My first step on the stairway brought with it what I expected. It gave way as soon as I put pressure on it and my foot went straight through the rotten timbers as if they were made from thin balsa. I cursed, pulled my foot out with a yank and rubbed my ankle roughly. It hurt like anything and I cursed again. It was then I heard the noise.

The softest of footfalls.

I whirled round, the torch coming up to try and pick out the intruder. Before I could react, a black shape fell over me, knocking the torch out of my hand and strong, steel fingers took me by the throat and slammed me against the balustrade. The whole rotten edifice gave way with the force of my body as I smashed into it and I fell down amongst the broken, splintered timberwork.

Lying there, pinned amongst the shattered remains of the staircase, I could barely make out the figure looming over me. It was a man, I knew that much, and he was strong. His hand still held me and I knew it was useless to try to break free from his grip. I whimpered as he exerted more pressure, feeling my head begin to swell, my eyes boil. I dug my nails into his flesh, kicked out, tried to wriggle free. I couldn't breathe and then, as my eyes almost burst from my skull, he released the pressure, ever so slightly. Such relief came over me I almost cried out in gratitude. Then a new wave of fear came as he moved his face closer to mine. "You got my message, then?"

I managed a frown. Confused, I tried to make out his features. So, he was the man who had left the message on my computer. I had believed it was Stoker, that he had somehow managed to find a way of breaking through the security systems of the central computers to deliver his message. But this man was not Stoker and real fear kicked in then, fear of the unknown. Who was he, how had he delivered the message, how could he know I would come here, to this place? How could he...Unless he'd been following me. Of course, that had to be it. He must have been observing as soon as I had returned to the City, waiting for this moment. And yet, as I thought this through, I realized that this couldn't be the case. Any adult, lurking in the streets, would immediately be picked up by the Sweepers. Very few adults remained now and those that did, the childless ones, were constantly harassed and interrogated. There was no way he could have avoided being picked up. So the question ate away at me – how could he know I would return to this derelict building? At no point in his strange, clipped messages had he mentioned a meeting place. Therefore, he had to have some way of working it all out.

Again, I tried a swallow, but his grip, although somewhat relaxed, still remained tight. My mind was cascading around, trying to make some sense of all of this. The simple truth was, there was no sense to it, no sense at all. The more I tried to think, to grope around for an answer or even a tiny clue, the more confused I became.

"I'm glad you came, Simeon," he hissed. "You're a good boy, Simeon."

My heart stopped and I stared at him, wide-eyed. I wanted to cry out. His words echoed those of the Sweeper who had stopped me just a few moments before. Could it be just a coincidence? What was it Warren had said, '*Don't trust anyone.*' Prophesies seemed to be having a habit of coming true.

He hauled me to my feet and let me go. I gagged, coughing hoarsely, rubbing my throat, wishing I had some water. As if reading my mind, from nowhere he thrust a canteen into my hand. "Drink it." I gazed at it, wondering if I should, Warren's words ringing the warning bell inside my head. Necessity, however, overcame my suspicions. If he had wanted to kill me, he would have done so already, this mysterious stranger. So I took a sip, waited, then drank some more. Whatever it was, the pain in my throat vanished, and I instantly felt refreshed, the strength returning to my limbs, restoring my senses.

"My name's Corrigan," he said, taking a sip from the canteen himself. "I'm here to ask you some questions, Simeon. Questions which I need answering."

I waited, not knowing what to say. I still couldn't make out his face in that pervading gloom, but I suspected that perhaps he was one of the other men who had been in this room all that time ago, along with Stoker and Hitter. Who else could he be, I asked myself? The idea didn't make me feel any less threatened.

"I need to know what happened at the Protector's."

That pulled me up short and another rush of cold fear coursed through me. I had to cough, to clear my throat, before I answered, "He...he was dead when I got there."

"You're sure of that?"

No hesitation this time: "Positive. I saw his body."

"And Carling?"

"Carling?" I instantly answered my own question. Carling, the man who I'd christened 'the Hitter'. That must have been his name. I shrugged, "He helped me get away."

"Yes, but what happened to him?"

Those pictures reared up again, the way his body jerked as the lasers hit him. "Sweepers killed him."

"You're sure?"

Why was he questioning everything I said? I pulled in a breath, anger at the edge of my voice. "Yes. I saw him die."

The bluntness of my reply seemed to send a shock wave through him. He reached out, fumbling for something to keep him upright and for a moment I thought he was going to fall down. He managed to press his hand against the wall, steadying himself. "That wasn't supposed to happen." He stood there, silent, the only sound his breathing as he sucked in the air.

"He saved my life," I said, by way of explanation.

Without any warning, he flicked out his hand and hit me across the face. I fell back, tripping over the broken staircase timbers and cried out as jagged splinters stabbed me in the small of my back. Almost at once, I scrambled to my feet. "Why does everyone hit me," I yelled. "What am I, some sort of human punch bag?" I'd had enough, anger laced with humiliation giving me a new kind of courage. I bunched my fists, "Hit me again," I hissed as I pressed a forearm against my mouth, "and I'll——"

"You'll do nothing." Corrigan turned away, his voice sounding tired, and he took another drink from the canteen. "You make me sick! One simple thing you were asked to do, one simple, stupid thing, and you cock it all up. Now we've lost a damned good man, and it's your fault!" He glared at me. Even in that dim light I could see the whites of his eyes, piercing me with their fury.

But my fury was building too. "My fault? You *used* me to get in there. If I hadn't..." My breathing came in short gasps, anger clouding my judgement. What was the point? He wouldn't listen, he was too bound up with his sense of loss, or failure. I couldn't care which it was, I was just sick to the back teeth of people using me, thinking they could do what the hell they liked. All of my nervousness, my fear, swiftly disappeared in the bleakness of the moment. "Where is Stoker?"

"Stoker?" He swung around, facing me. "You think I'm going to tell you that? After what you've done? Why do you want to know where he is anyway?"

"I need to tell him that his plan was flawed from the beginning – they knew everything. I was let in, Corrigan. The Protector knew I was coming, he was expecting me."

"Because Stoker had infiltrated their security systems, you idiot! The Protector had been informed by his own computers that you were on your way. *Stoker had programmed it that way.*"

"Then…" I knew that of course, I always had. The same way Sweepers had scanned my chip several times and not found any hint of treason there. But that still didn't explain why everything had gone wrong on the second visit. "Then why did Carling have to die? Why couldn't Stoker have done something to stop that?"

"That's what I need you to tell *me*, Simeon. The answer's simple – you betrayed him, betrayed us."

"How could I do that? I had no way of informing anyone. Besides, you told me that if I did, you'd shop me to the Sandmen."

"How did you get away, Simeon?"

"I told you. Carling helped me. He kept the Sweepers at bay whilst I got out."

"But why didn't they follow you, Simeon?"

"They did. But I lost them."

"You lost them? Sweepers?" His voice took on an almost bored tone. "With the most sophisticated scanning devices ever invented, with a vast range, so sensitive they can differentiate between a grasshopper and a cricket at a thousand metres? Their brains are neurologically linked to massive mainframe computers that instantly guide them to their quarry. Are you taking me for a fool?"

I gaped at him, his words cutting through all the fog. Words of truth. Everything he said was so matter-of-fact, so obviously true… and the inference that I had in some way managed to bypass the security systems, or maybe even conspired with the Sweepers…It was clear that they must have let me escape. And yet…I turned away, rubbing my head with my fingers, the pain from his blow forgotten now, a new throb pulsing away at my temples taking all of my attention. The goat man? What about him, why give him the opportunity to hand me over to the Sandmen? Why not capture me straight after the Protector's murder? Why allow me to get away and…

"The Biker," I whispered, the awful truth now revealed as clear as a summer's day.

"Who?"

I whirled around, words spilling out. "A man, a man on a motorbike. He rescued me, helped me against the Sandmen, brought me back to...He wiped my chip, reprogrammed it."

"He did *what*? Are you completely insane? Who was he?"

"I...I don't know. Just a man. He lived out in the country, free from surveillance and control. No Sweepers, no Sandmen. Just green grass and—"

"And the ability to reprogram chips? Not many people can do that, Simeon. I've only ever met one."

"Stoker."

He gnawed away at his bottom lip for a moment, deciding over the validity of my words more than likely. "If you're lying to me, Simeon, I swear I'll—"

"I'm not lying, Corrigan. On my mother's life!"

He took in some sharp breaths, struggling against the enormity of what I had revealed. "So now we have another programmer." He hit his hip with his fist. "We have to find him. You have to take me to him."

"W-when?"

"Tomorrow. You'll meet me at the old monorail station. Seven o'clock." His hand shot out and he grabbed me by the collar and pulled me close to him. "Don't be late. If you are, I'll come looking for you...and I'll kill you."

Twenty

The streets were as empty as a desert as I stepped outside. Glancing left and right, giving myself a moment to adjust to the light, I cut across the main thoroughfare, my head filled with concern over what had happened between Corrigan and me. Once again, I'd become an unwilling pawn in whatever game was being played out by these people. Now, however, the pressure had been racked up. No longer satisfied with shopping me to the Sandmen, the threat of death now hung over me, crushing me. I had no doubt that Corrigan would carry through this threat, no doubt at all. Caught in the web of intrigue, what hope was there of me ever breaking free?

Walking along, another concern began to take dominance. An uneasy stillness that seeped out from the fabric of every building I passed pressed in all around me. As I rounded the first corner, the great klaxons blasted forth their terrifying drone, telling the citizens that curfew was about to begin. My heart almost stopped. It couldn't be! I entered the central computer through my chip, a simple mind-meld skill we'd been taught at virtual-school, and the time came up in my mind, showing me that there were hours to go before we had to lock ourselves away in our homes. Could it be wrong? The readout was linked with the central atomic clock at the Citizen Central Hall, so it couldn't be wrong!

I blinked it out. There was no mistaking that awful sound. Like a bleating hog, skewered through the brain, it shrieked its warning. I broke into a run, not daring to linger for a moment longer. It gave two warnings, the first giving people five minutes to get inside, the second allowing them two minutes to bolt the doors and pull down the blinds. As soon as those two minutes had lapsed, the Sandmen appeared, roaming the streets, searching out those who had not made it in time. The idea of them, those great legs, the blinding beam of their lasers cutting through flesh and bone, the great scissor claws dismembering those that tallied. I gave out a cry and dug deep, pumping my legs. Five minutes and counting.

The second klaxon hooted as I ran up the steps that led from the river. I'd never make it; my chest burned, sweat stinging my eyes, a pain like a tear in my muscles lancing through my side. My pace slackened, but there was nothing I could do. Running through the countryside was one thing, moving freely up hillsides, the Sun on my back, taking in that good, clean air... this, this was a race against fear, and fear debilitated, slowed you down, made your limbs as heavy as lead, muscles as unresponsive as if they'd been atrophied. In this state, how could I hope to outrun the Sandmen?

I couldn't.

They came around the next corner, their long legs eating up the metres at a phenomenal pace as they ran me down. I'd made the last street; ahead of me was my apartment block. It had never looked so welcoming, but it may as well have been a dozen miles away. I fell into a deserted shop doorway and cowered there, the air rushing in and out of my scorched lungs, heart thumping impossibly loud. What possible good was it going to be, me huddled there, legs curled up against my chest, eyes closed, hoping ostrich-like that they hadn't noticed me.

The first one towered over me. I could feel it and I chanced a glance upwards. Its great blank face peered down at me, scanning me as I pressed myself into an even tinier ball, mumbling a prayer that I had conjured up from my memory. My life was about to end.

The Sandmen did not wait for excuses, reasons or explanations.

They just vaporised.

I have often wondered what it would be like to die like this. Alone, forgotten, my life snubbed out with no more thought as one would give to squashing a bug. Useless. Pointless. A life lived, then blanked out. Recently, it had become something of a recurring nightmare.

I held my breath and waited.

The last time this had happened I was with Dad. We'd been coming home late after visiting one of Dad's old friends. The evening had disappeared as I'd watched and played on the gigantic model railway layout I'd gone to see. Entranced, neither of us noticed the time until the klaxon sounded. Rushing full-pelt through the darkened streets we almost collided into a Sandman, looking out from nowhere. Dad stood up to him and, amazingly, it stepped back, allowing us to continue. Grinning as if he had achieved some sort of tiny victory, Dad held my hand and within a few short steps we were home. That was the last time we were together. The following day he disappeared. But that memory clinged to me like a second skin. I couldn't rid myself of it.

My father. My blood. My life.

And now, here I was, trembling with the dread of the moment, waiting for the inevitable, mumbling the ancient words that somehow had come into my head, "Our Father, who art in Heaven, hallowed be Thy name..."

I opened my eyes.

For a moment I couldn't believe what I was seeing. There was nothing there – the Sandman had gone and I was alone.

After scanning me, he had moved on, no doubt looking for other hapless souls who had strayed beyond the confines of their pitiful homes, running the gauntlet of death that was the curfew. Feeling lost, unable to understand the Sandman's reaction, I pulled myself to my feet. I felt weak, legs wobbly, my stomach churning, breath catching in a windpipe made from roughly sawn wood. I needed another mouthful of Corrigan's magic water.

Setting off towards my apartment, as I neared it, I became aware of other outrageous happenings. There were people in the street. Children, of all ages, gathering in small groups on street corners, jabbering to each other, their eyes wide with fear and uncertainty. This shouldn't have been happening – the curfew had sounded, that meant everyone was supposed to be indoors, despite it not being yet night. Nothing made sense and I slowed, crossing over to one group, who initially shrank away but then, as they recognised me, they seemed to relax.

"What's happening?" I asked no one in particular. A big teenager, whom I had passed a few times in my block, shrugged his solid shoulders and jerked his chin in the direction of the main square. "We got the message through the hologram screens. Weren't you there?" I chose to ignore him, not wishing to get into a long explanation of why I'd missed the message, and followed his gaze. Gathered in the square were Sweepers and Sandmen, waiting, but for what exactly I had no way of knowing.

Gradually, more and more young people emerged from their homes. Some were half-dressed, hair tousled, rubbing their eyes, woken from a nap, others were fully dressed. Everyone appeared dazed and confused. What emergency had brought them outside, the curfew klaxon designed to urge people inside, not to gather outside. This sort of thing was unprecedented, to call the curfew then assemble people in the streets in the daytime. Nighttime lent such gatherings an air of uncertainty and dread that the sunlight tended to dispel.

But not so today.

Fear oozed from everyone's pores, so thick you could taste it, certainly smell it. I stepped away from the group and it was then that I saw her, gliding through the crowd like a vision from some religious happening. Yolanda. She was dressed all in white, the material contrasting starkly with the colour of her skin. People followed her, aghast. I could see boys' jaws dropping. I couldn't blame them. She looked totally gorgeous.

She came straight up to me and kissed me full on the lips. I looked at her, astonished, hardly daring to breathe lest I broke the spell. I had to be in a dream. Only hours ago she was adamant she didn't want anything more to do with me. Closing my eyes, I shook my head to rid myself of this hallucination, but when I opened them again, she was still there.

"Simeon," her voice was low, friendly. I couldn't work it out. "Simeon, I'm sorry. I judged you too harshly, too quickly." She held me in her arms, pressing her face into my shoulder. Was that a sob? She stepped back. The truth was in the wetness around her yes. "Can you forgive me?"

My loins buzzed with desire. "Of course I can – I can forgive you anything." Sense reeling at the extraordinary sight of her, so ravishing, so completely luscious, I panicked when I saw her bottom lip trembling. Quickly, I took hold of her, kissing her very softly on the lips. I yearned to do more, but not here, not in the open. "It's okay, Yollie. I forgive you, I promise."

"Are you sure?"

"Yes. I'm sure." I smiled, allowing myself a moment to swim in the liquid gold pools of her eyes. Taking her by the hand, I led her away from the gawping expressions of those around us to the old, disused fountain in the centre of the square. I sat her down on the grey, broken steps and held her hand in mine. "Do you know what's happening?"

"Oh, Simeon. Haven't you been home?"

I looked at her and frowned. She had that patient tone in her voice again, the one she used when she scolded me, as if she were talking to a very small child; the voice she took on whenever she chastised me about something totally trivial. This time, however, it was different. The whole world was out on the streets and the curfew had sounded. So it certainly wasn't trivial.

"Yolanda, just tell me what's happening."

"Not here," she said, standing up. "I've a feeling things are going to get…" She bit her lip, almost as if she didn't want to commit her thoughts into words. "Ugly," she said at last.

Frowning deeply, I searched her face for some sign she had knowledge of what was about to happen. Why would she say *things are going to get ugly?* Around us, at least a hundred Sweepers and half as many Sandmen gathered, whilst people continued to spew out into the streets, perhaps thousands of them, converging on the square from every area of the City. The meetings in the park sprang to mind, and what followed there. I shuddered at the memory, my blood running cold. "Something big has happened, hasn't it? And you know what it is."

As I held her eyes, a scream shattered all our thoughts. I span around to see the redheaded girl from my corridor being frog-marched out into the street by two burly Sweepers. She was struggling like a fish out of water, body jack-knifing in a pathetic attempt to free herself. On reaching the centre of the square, they threw her to the ground where she lay, squirming and sobbing like a tiny, frightened child.

Yolanda seized my hand and pulled me away, but. I didn't want to go – I needed to see what would happen next. Yolanda's voice sizzled with urgency as she hissed, "Come on, we have to get to my place." I tore my face from the redhead and looked at Yolanda, her face etched with terror. This was no time to argue. With my hand in hers, she led me to her apartment.

Twenty-One

We both stood in front of the holographic screen, watching the news as it played itself out, sombre music whispering in the background, the commentator's voice low, serious. And throughout, scenes of the life of the Protector. Much cheering and applauding from gathered groups of wide-eyed children. Steady ranks of Sweepers, making their cross-chest salute. Thousands of drone infiltrators and hover-bikes swarming across the sky like black flies. It was all very impressive and all very solemn.

"Our glorious leader, the Protector, is dead," rang out the voice, over and over, letting the news sink in, telling us all that 'undesirables', who must be rooted out and stopped, had assassinated him. "Until such time, emergency laws are in force and everyone has to remain in their homes from eight o'clock this evening."

"But the curfew was called early," I mumbled.

"No. The announcements were made to accompany the curfew call. But you weren't at home to hear them, were you, Simeon?"

I caught the edge in her voice, the accusing tone. I chose to ignore it. Best not give her any opportunity to question me about my whereabouts. "No. No, I wasn't."

She sighed deeply, "We were told to assemble in the street, to receive instructions."

"So why did you bring me back here?"

"I thought it was safer. Like I said, I think it's going to get ugly. That girl... the redhead. Who is she?"

Before I could give an answer, the news announcer did it for me, his voice blaring out, "In Sector Fifteen, the first of many such agitators will be summarily executed before an assembled crowd, to show our resolve in weeding out those who would attempt to undermine the order of our society." The face of the red-headed girl invaded the screen. She looked younger, much fresher, eager, that shock of red hair neatly coiffed. A model picture.

"My God," I muttered.

"Don't *say that!*" Yolanda gripped me by the arm and turned me to face her. "Who is she?"

"She lives on my floor, that's all I know. Her flatmate, or a friend, I don't know what, he... I saw them arguing. He attacked me. The Sweepers came, vaporised him before he could..." I shook my head, closing my eyes for a moment as the memory welled up. She, that girl, she had done nothing. Not to me at least. Now, she was being trussed up ready for the execution. Who the hell was she? Just an agitator, or something more?

"You were attacked by an agitator? Simeon, why would they do that?"

"None of this makes any sense, Yollie. Why would anyone——"

My sentence was finished for me by the first explosion, a massive blast coming from way off on the far side of the City but powerful enough to set our building shuddering with the after-shock. Another quickly followed, the soft crump of bombs falling, the crash of falling masonry. Then came the screaming, distant but no mistaking the terror it was thick with. I stared open-mouthed at Yolanda who simply held me with those big, saucer eyes.

"What the hell is happening?"

She gave no answer so I crossed over to the window and looked down towards the square. People were scattering in every direction like rats whilst beyond them, from between the towering black shapes of buildings at the City limits, plumes of black smoke trailed upwards into the sky. The steady pounding of heavy guns accompanied the smoke, with the crunch of lasers arcing through the air.

Yolanda came up behind me, snaking her arms around my waist, and pressed her cheek against my back. "It's some sort of attack," I said, my voice sounding as if it were detached from me. I could hardly believe what I was saying. Attack from where, from whom?

"It's too dangerous for you to go back outside," she said, turning me around. She reached out to brush my face and the thrill raced through me. "You heard the announcer. Curfew. You'll have to stay."

She smiled, took my hand, and guided me to her bed.

We made love with the sound of gunfire and explosions filling the night, drowning out our cries. Rolling off her, staring up through the darkness, I could hear Sandmen stomping down the streets. Occasionally I picked out the rapid running of human feet, swiftly followed by a piercing scream. As the night drew on, such sounds became less and less until eventually, silence fell like a blanket over the City until now, with the morning arriving grey, everything would be as it had always been. Sterile. I couldn't sleep however, and I lay there, my mind racing with all sorts of confused thoughts. Of one thing I was certain. The redhead. I'd been set up. All of it was a ruse, to lure me out into the street, to meet up with Corrigan. She was part of it, and she lived on my floor. That couldn't be a coincidence. I squeezed my eyes tight shut, blocking out her face. She would be dead now, either sliced up by the claws of the Sandmen, or vaporised by lasers. Either way, the assembled crowd would have seen it, the lesson learned.

I turned and gazed at Yolanda, sleeping like a baby, the sheen on her peer-less skin visible even in that eerie half-light. We'd hardly spoken all night, apart from the cries of our lust. Spent, she'd offered me a night time pill, which I'd accepted, but then put under my tongue whilst she took hers. Within two minutes she had fallen asleep, leaving me to try and figure everything out. Needless to say, I failed, and my head pulsed with pain as the sun began to break through the bleak looking sky.

I got out of bed, crossed to the balcony door and stepped out into the early morning chill. It was unusual for anyone to step onto their balcony, hence it not being connected to the computer. Everyone was wary about spending too much time outside, even during the day. Certainly nobody who had any sense would sit on a balcony for more than five minutes without protective eyeglasses or a cap. What was rarer still was for anyone to be awake so early, certainly after the experiences of the previous day. I caught the attention of two Sandmen down below who were still patrolling the deathly quiet streets. I stood and allowed them to scan me and then they went on their way. I watched them marching rhythmically into the distance, wondering what malevolent mind had created such things. In old nursery stories, the Sandman was supposed to come and get you ready for bed, make sure you were safe and sound. These monstrosities were designed to simply keep everyone in check. Any deviation would result in immediate death.

I rubbed my face, feeling tired and very old, having witnessed so much in such a short space of time. My life had changed out of all recognition from what it had been such a short time ago. I was barely eighteen, but had already lived an entire lifetime. Eighteen? Would I *ever* see nineteen?

I turned and again looked at Yolanda, sleeping soundly, all swathed amongst the sheets, one ebony arm draped over the edge of the bed. She'd hardly stirred all night, the pills doing their job as they always did. I went over and slipped in beside her, propping myself up on my elbow, tracing the curve of her luxurious body with my fingertips. Not a murmur left her lips. It was a deliciously erotic few moments, one of the few times I was in complete control of her. What would she make of my plan with Corrigan, I wondered. How did she see my part in the sorry tale of the Protector's death? And if she suspected that I had conspired in it in some way, would she betray me? Perhaps, just perhaps, she believed that because I hadn't been interrogated that I was innocent of any real crime. Was it this that had changed her mind about me? But then she had no knowledge of the alterations to my chip.

Sitting up, I touched the still tender ridge beneath my hairline, wondering again what changes Warren had made to the chip. I looked at my fingertip, saw the thin film of yellow puss there, and knew any Sweeper with half a gig of processing power would detect such a problem. I blew out my breath. Everything was a mess, and could only get worse. Corrigan's plan was to meet me at seven. Plenty of time until then, so I dressed, patted my pocket to check the piece of technology from the old hideout was there and, resigned to my fate, waited for Yolanda to wake.

Twenty-Two

Sometime later, stepping out of the shower, my eyes met Yolanda, standing in the bathroom doorway, rubbing her eyes, looking dishevelled but beautiful.

"You're up early," she said through a yawn and padded over to the washbasin and waited whilst a fine mist drenched her perfect face. Instantly refreshed, she turned and flashed me a smile. "I thought we could get some work done."

"Work?"

"Yes. All that schoolwork that you've backed-up – remember school, Simeon? That thing we're supposed to do?"

"But I've got things to do, Yollie – I can't…"

She came over and snaked her arms around me. My stomach did a flip as she wriggled her pelvis against mine. "Work, Simeon. If you don't catch up they'll come for you and they'll take you to Finishing School. No one comes back from there… unchanged. And I don't want you to change, Simeon. I want you to be just like you are now, forever." She stretched upwards, kissing me lightly. "And, as a reward, if you do all of your assignments, I'll take you to a place you've never been to before… Heaven."

Alive with desire, I closed my eyes, her body pressing against me, feeling so good, those well-toned limbs, taut, firm. My mouth fell open and I suddenly found it hard to breathe. I groaned inside, not daring to believe what I was going to say. "Yollie, I've got to go and meet someone. But I won't be long."

"*Meet* someone?" She tensed and stepped back, her eyes hardening, the vixen returning, devouring the soft-doe she had only just been. "This isn't more of these stupid games you've been indulging in, Simeon? You heard what the announcer said – about everyone remaining indoors. The Sweepers will vaporise you."

"No, they won't." How to make her believe me without revealing the secret of my tampered chip? I couldn't reveal the truth. If I did, then she would be in as much danger as I was. Struggling to force down my desire for her, I gripped her arms, felt her biceps bulging. "Listen, Yollie, I've just got to go out. Only for a short while, I promise. When I get back, then I'll do the school work, all of it." I forced a smile. "I swear to you, I'll never go out again after this."

Tiny pools collected underneath her bottom eyelid. "You're up to no good, Simeon. I can sense it."

"No you can't, Yollie – you only *think* you can. It's not as bad as all that, I swear, but I need to go and talk to someone. It's nothing sinister." I marvelled at how easily the lies came. Something, some doubt prevented me from trusting her.

"Is it something to do with what you told me about?" It was as if she were reading my mind. "Is it something to do with the Protector, about what happened when you went to see him?"

"No, no, it's something to do with – *school.* I've made contact with an old student. He said he would help me." Startled by my invention, I had to see it through, even if I didn't know in which direction my lies would take me.

"An old student?" Her mouth formed the words slowly, as if savouring them as part of an untried meal. "Simeon... if you're lying to me..."

"I'm not," I lied. "Look, I'll be back before you know it."

I kissed the top of her head and pulled on some clothes and rushed out, knowing she didn't believe a single word I'd said.

Twenty-Three

The old monorail station was a vast, empty space now, broken and deserted, its past glories ghostly shadows. Breaking through a side door, I followed the path of an ancient service tunnel until I reached the far end, barred to me by a flimsy, rotting door, as thin as rice paper. One push from my palm and it fell open and I stepped out into the huge, cavernous void.

Craning my neck. I gasped as I peered upwards towards the great ceiling, an enormous dome, glass panels clouded with grime, some broken, shards crunching underfoot as I wandered deeper inside this cathedral to a dead world. Rusted and decaying escalators linked the different levels, where once whole armies of passengers had come to take the monorails to every part of the country, the arteries of the old days, conveying the lifeblood of society to conduct their business and keep everything running smoothly.

Nothing remained of it now, save this derelict, forgotten amphitheatre, replaced by the clinical, sterilised age of controlled youth.

"*Simeon.*"

The sound of my own name made me start. I span round to find Corrigan coming towards me, laughing.

"Sorry," he snorted as he drew close. "I didn't mean to make you jump. You're early."

I breathed a sigh. "No point in hanging around." Our voices sounded thin and metallic in that great void.

"No, I suppose not. You no doubt heard the latest, last night, on the news? The death of the Protector"

"Yes. They made no mention of suspects."

"Well there wouldn't be any, would there. Haven't you realised how things work, Simeon? Lies, deceit…you should know all about that."

I frowned. "What do you mean?"

"You and Yolanda. Why do you keep lying to her, Simeon? Afraid that she'll denounce you? Afraid that she'll turn her back on you, again?"

Taking me by the shoulder, he guided me to the far side of the forecourt, our footsteps echoing eerily in that massive space. He sat me down on a plastic bench and patted my knee like one would to reassure a child.

"Why are we here?" I asked, looking down at his hand resting on my knee.

"Here? The monorail station?" His eyes swivelled, taking in the yawning space."We can still use the tracks, to take us out beyond the City boundaries. No scanners here, no Sweepers, no Sandmen…"

"You mean we're safe?"

"As safe as we can be."

"I thought that when I was in the countryside. I was proved wrong." Rubbing my face, I suppressed the urge to scream, frustration mixing with rising anxiety. "What were those explosions last night?"

"Explosions? I didn't hear any explosions, Simeon."

"Are you mad? They were everywhere – people screaming, buildings collapsing. It was like the City was under attack."

"Simeon," he craned his head around to look at me, "you worry too much. Just accept that almost all you hear and see is lies. Most of what you experience are computer generated images, to keep you, and everybody else, under control." He smiled, noting my shocked expression. "Enough eulogising…" He fished inside his coat and brought out a small package and pressed it into my hand.

"What's this?"

"I have another task for you, Simeon."

"No," I bit down on my bottom lip. "No, I've been used too many times. I'm not going to—"

"You'll do as you're told Simeon – you're in too deep to back out now."

"Back out? Back out from what?"

He smiled. "This is what I want you to do…"

* * *

Yolanda was waving her hand across the interactive screen when returned. She wore a thin cotton t-shirt and skimpy blue shorts, her slim legs rippling, shiny with perspiration. She'd been exercising. She forced a smile. "You weren't long."

"Told you I wouldn't be."

She grunted and crossed to her desk. "I took a little break, did a workout." She ran a hand through her hair, ballooning her cheeks. "Seismic geology and agriculture. I'm sick to death of it, but I have to get through."

I took her in my arms and kissed her, her lips so full, so soft. I moaned.

"I have to get on," she insisted, pushing me away. "I'm needed. Well, not just me, *all* of us. I have to pass, Simeon. To help us understand how we can increase crop yields."

"Yollie, the government will do all that – experts. You don't need—"

"No, Simeon. We're the experts – the experts of the future. We must find new ways to feed our people. It's our duty, Simeon. Our reason for being."

"My Dad told me all reason had died when we went to war. Billions were killed." I glanced away, looking into the past, remembering my dad telling me how the only thing we had to look forward to was fear.

"What are you thinking about?"

I shrugged and went into the bathroom, misting my face, trying to bring some life back into my weary body. "Stuff," I said.

"Well, if it's 'stuff' you want, you'd better get over here and do some work. The college wants to know where your assignments are."

"The college?" I came back in and watched her playing around with the screen, her hands taking up bits of information and downloading them into her chip. "How did the college know I was here?"

Without pausing for an instant, she simply said, "I told them."

I smirked. So like Yolanda, unable to trust me to do anything for myself when it came to education. Crossing to her I called up her assignments and glanced through them. "You're good."

She smiled at me, "I know," she said. "Now, you settle yourself down here," she motioned to the couch, "I'll get you some refreshment, and then you can start in."

"Thanks."

"Simeon," that tone again, the patient school-ma'am, ignoring my sarcasm. "This has to be done, you understand? If you don't get this finished by today, they'll come for you. Why don't you ever access your messages?"

"I don't know." Instinctively I ran a finger along the ridge under my hairline. "There's a glitch I think. With my chip."

"Really?" She sat down next to me, face ashen, tiny creases appearing around her eyes, worried. She ran her fingers through my hair. She took in a sharp breath. Then he pulled my head down, and parted my hair to gaze at where the chip sat just beneath the skin. "That looks sore, Simeon. What the hell have you been doing?"

I pulled away from her, "Nothing. It's just – it doesn't seem to be functioning properly." I looked into her eyes. "Yollie, you think I should take it out?"

"*What?*" She stood up, suddenly looking scared, "Are you completely out of your mind? You know that is strictly against the rules, Simeon. A Sandman would be here within thirty seconds."

"Okay," I held up both my hands in surrender, "it was just a thought. It hurts like anything."

"Then we should go to Programming Central. They'll fix it. We'll wander down as soon as you've done your assignments."

I groaned again. She was like…what was it Dad used to say… '*A dog with a bone*'. That was it. Not that I'd ever seen a dog. Not a *real* one, at least. But it seemed to sum up Yolanda's relentless desire to get me to finish my schoolwork.

She went out to get me the refreshment, and I keyed in my password. The screen immediately filled with a mass of screaming messages and I sat back, closed my eyes, and wondered for how long I would have to sit in that damned chair.

In the quiet of the following morning, I brought out the processor I had picked up in Stoker's hideout, and knew instantly what it was. It didn't take long to rig up a workable adaptor and soon I had it plugged into the hard drive of the house computer, having quickly suppressed the security protocols that would alert Central Processing. I reckoned I probably had five minutes before someone, somewhere picked up on what I was doing. Time enough to look through the information the processor contained. Time enough to feel the slab of ice in the pit of my stomach expand, my skin pucker, and the hairs stand up on end as I scanned through the images. Truth had once again made itself felt.

Twenty-Four

The Intensifier's face loomed across the wall. He was the chief administrator of my school-college and, as far as I knew, one of only two human beings on the staff. He broke into a broad smile when he saw me.

"Ah, Simeon," he wheezed, that sickly monotone voice causing me to squirm. He reminded me of a plump, white witchetty grub, all pasty and slow moving. I could barely force myself to look at him. "So, you've finally completed your tasks. Well done. Total score for this semester, Simeon is ninety-eight point three seven five, which is below your usual but still puts you in the top one percent of your year. How does that make you feel?"

"Marvellous."

"I hope that's not a note of sarcasm I can hear there, Simeon. Humour really doesn't become you. Or anyone, for that matter."

"I've noticed."

"Good. It's not one of your more over-stated attributes, Simeon. *Noticing*. Why haven't you been at your desk these past few days?"

"Sick."

"Poppycock!"

"Poppy-*what*?"

"I would have thought an historian as well read as you, Simeon, would have known the meaning of that archaic phrase? But never mind, no doubt your mind has been elsewhere. Talking of which, how is Yolanda?"

"Yolanda? What's she got to do with anything?"

"I think you know the answer to that one, Simeon. Look, I'm not in the business of apportioning blame, but I'm not quite sure if this relationship is beneficial."

"It's not a '*relationship*' – we're just friends."

"Yes. And I'm the Queen of Sheba." He grinned, the grooves in his fat cheeks growing deeper. Then, suddenly, his expression grew serious. "Look, just be careful. You're a star pupil, the finest we have ever had. You are destined for the Academy. Nothing must jeopardise that, and certainly not your nightly romps with that gorgeous girl."

"Nightly romps – how the hell—"

"Don't interrupt me." He took in a gurgling breath, steadying himself. "We're all in a bit of a turmoil with the news last night, Simeon."

"News? You mean the death of the Protector?"

"What else?"

I almost asked him about the attacks, but then I remembered Corrigan's explanations. Computer aided graphics. Were those explosions, like everything else, a mirage, a heap of lies?

"Things are going to be changing fairly fast," he continued, "and the one thing, the *only* constant in this quickly changing world is the need for educated future leaders, Simeon. Do you understand the magnitude of what I'm saying to you?"

I wasn't sure if I did. Trawling through the words, he seemed to be making a suggestion that was mind-blowing in its enormity. I sat, dumbstruck. Had he actually said what I thought he'd said? *Future leaders*? I shook my head, "I don't think I do understand."

"Well, my advice to you is to be careful, Simeon. Very careful. Don't trust anyone."

"I've heard that before. From others."

"Have you? And what else have you *heard*, Simeon."

"Lots."

He raised one eyebrow, "Most of what you hear are lies, Simeon."

I frowned. The exact same sentiments I'd heard from Corrigan. "Then how do I know what is the truth?"

"Ah…" His finger appeared, waggling in front of him, "that's the trick, Simeon. How to tell the difference."

And with that, the wall went blank.

I sat gaping at the screen. More images of the Protector in a series of suitably heroic poses flickered before me. I couldn't help but think that everyone knew where all this was leading. Everyone, that is, except me.

Don't trust anyone.

The same phrase used by many different people. Was it all a conspiracy, and if so, to what purpose? I was eighteen years of age, with the brain the size of an elephant's – or so some said – with not a single clue about anything.

Chomping down on a mango fruit, juice trawling down the corner of her mouth, Yolanda wandered in. "Mmm, I got one of these from Rupert on the fifth floor. Do you know his father used to own…" Yolanda's voice seeped away into the atmosphere as she sensed my mood. "What's the matter?"

"What score did you get?"

"What?"

"Score. In the finals – what score did you get?"

"Oh…er, not very good really. Sixty-three percent. How about you?"

Around us, the house-robot floated by, sending a fine mist of perfumed water over Yolanda's hands, cleaning up the juice.

"Ninety-eight."

"*What?*" She nearly choked on the glass of liquid minerals the maid gave her, and went into a fit of coughing. I jumped up to slap her back. She spluttered, face red, and flopped down into the couch. "But – but that's amazing, Simeon. You only completed it all this morning."

I kept my voice flat, neutral. "I know. Interesting, isn't it? There's you, banging your head against computer screens and holograph walls for the best part of two months, and here I am, in just a few hours, getting into the top one-percent of all students in the country."

"Just make me feel pathetic, why don't you?"

"No – I didn't mean it like that. I meant…Oh, I don't know. It just seems too…too convenient, that's all."

"What, that you're a genius?"

"I'm not a genius, Yollie – I'm a waster."

"That's wastrel, Simeon. And you're certainly not one of those. Everyone knows you're brilliant – why do you think all the girls want to meet you?"

"What are you talking about? I've never met any girls – except you."

"That's because I'm insanely jealous. Want to see your message board on '*Friendlies*'?"

"Not particularly."

"Well, I think you should."

She waved a hand through the air. "Friendlies," she said, the only social site sanctioned by government. Highly monitored, it still proved immensely popular, especially after curfew.

The screen flickered and the site came up. Yolanda fiddled around, redirecting the portal to my home page. *My home page!* I had never created one, but there it was, my name and everything about me, together with a very clear photograph of my good self, beaming out towards my secret admirers. I gawped as swirling images of hundreds – literally *hundreds* – of smiling, jabbering girls jostled for screen space, imploring me to contact them. I rubbed my eyes and turned to Yolanda. "God, Yollie, that's insane."

Snapping her fingers, the screen went blank, and she leaned towards me. "You never go on, do you?"

"No."

"Why not?"

"Well, I…" I felt my cheeks burning and I tried to say something meaningful, but all that came out was a non-committal grunt.

"Why don't you go on the site, Simeon?"

I stared into those eyes, the thrill buzzing through my lower abdomen. That perfect face, those full, soft lips, consuming me. My words came softly, "Because I've got you."

"*Got* me, what does that mean?"

"You know what it means."

"No, I don't." She held my face, those eyes holding me, no escape possible. "Tell me."

I swallowed hard. "I love you."

* * *

The robot-maid served us some carefully prepared nibbles for lunch. I'd asked for a glass of orange juice, but Yolanda's credit rating did not stretch to such a 'luxury item'. "I need a change of clothes, Yollie," I said, munching down the last of my high-fibre snacks. "I'll pack some things then come back."

"You promise?"

"Of course." I kissed her before crossing to the door. I waved my hand over the sensor, but it didn't budge. I shot her a questioning look. Sighing, she went tried it herself. The result was the same.

"Computer," she said, a note of tension creeping into her voice, "open this door, please."

"I am unable to," it said, sounding as friendly as it ever did. "We are under imminent attack."

We exchanged another worried look. "Imminent attack?" I echoed. "Attack from whom?"

"Central Control has recommended everyone stay at home."

"But why?" Yolanda crossed to the large screen and flashed her hand over the channel changer. "What's happening?"

The screen remained blank.

"Computer," I demanded, going to the window to look outside, "give us a full report." There was only silence. "*Computer – respond!*"

In a world dominated by technology to be suddenly denied access of any kind was like being taken from the arms of a loving parent, and I knew all about that.

We fell into one another's arms, desperate for mutual comfort.

We heard it first as a low rumbling sound in the distance, a throb, pulsating through the City. Tearing myself from her embrace, I peered out of the window, searching the sky.

I saw them, swooping low in large, black waves. Black, evil looking aircraft, slicked back wings, slicing through the air, engines whirring high-pitched, sounding like grotesque mechanical mosquitoes. As I stood, mesmerised, I saw the first missiles streaking from beneath their fuselage, to dart through the air and strike the surrounding buildings. Swinging around, I dived towards Yolanda, flattening her to the ground, despite her struggles, despite her screams, covering her with my body.

Explosions blasted through the still air, the crump of bombs hitting the ground, windows shattering, masonry falling.

I held onto her trembling body, her face buried in my chest. I dared not breathe, struggling not to whimper. Yolanda needed me to be brave, so I held on, pressing her face closer still.

Being in the middle of the high-rise block may have saved us, as the first missiles smashed into the top storeys, the massive blast causing everything not well tied down to fall and smash to the ground.

The screaming began soon afterwards.

Close and becoming closer.

Beyond the apartment door, a mad stampede of terrified occupants thundered past.

"We need to get out here," I said, sitting up as high above a horrible groaning and creaking of shattered masonry filled the air.

"We should stay here," she said, voice quaking, face crumpling in terror.

A horrible, acrid smell of burning drifted under the front door. I shook her by the shoulders, "Yollie, we have to get out. The block's in flames. If we stay here, we'll die."

I stood up, feeling like a passenger on a storm-tossed ship as the apartment block leaned horribly to the right. I took her by the hand and went to the door.

Of course, it remained locked.

Trails of grey smoke snaked beneath the door. Frantic now, I screamed at the house computer to let us out, but it remained silent, all systems down, destroyed by the rocket attacks.

Yolanda took to pounding on the door, in the hope that a passer-by might rip it open from the outside. But no one did. Their only instinct was their own survival.

"Where's the over-ride?" I blurted, running to her desk, pulling out drawers, sifting through papers. "The over-ride, Yollie – where is it?"

She looked at me, body locked in terror as yet another missile smashed into the building, tipping her over the edge. Falling to her knees, she tore at her hair, screaming. The window shattered, air like ice blasting around us, and I stumbled to her bureau, her files once so neatly stacked, now a mess of swirling, jumbled up papers as the wind roared through her apartment.

I found it. A flat, black button under the first shelf. I pressed it firmly and the screen flickered to life. The keyboard came up. "Yollie," I yelled, "what's the code? Yollie, *for God's sake!*"

She sat, statue-like, eyes locked on something far, far away. I dropped in front of her, gripping her by the shoulders. "Yollie, I need the code. What is the code?"

Mouth dropping open, she pointed to something beyond me, something outside. I turned and groaned as my life pitched into a living nightmare. Before me was some insane image from an unknown world. Floating down from a hundred hover-copters were paratroopers, thousands of them, training their vaporisers into the mass of people running amok below. As if in a dream, I staggered over to the gaping gash of the window and watched the paratroopers hitting the ground, spewing out death and destruction at every point. Tiny figures dropped, sizzled and disappeared, a Bosch image of hell, here on earth. Except this was no imagined painting – this was real.

Twenty-Five

"Okay," I said, stepping away from the window, turning my back on the many scenes of carnage playing out below. Pulling in a breath, I knew I had no choice but to continue with the façade of being in control, if only to give me time to retrieve the code from her. If she panicked now, we'd be lost. Forever. "Yollie," I said again very slowly, "I need the code. Think, please. It's very important. Once we have the code, we can get out."

Shaking her head, a glazed expression crossed her eyes. I leaned into her and kissed her gently on the lips, "Yollie. Please. Just think."

"It's you," she said distantly.

"What? What do you mean?"

"You. You're the code."

It took a moment for me to register the meaning of her words, then I grinned and kissed her again, turned quickly to the keyboard and stamped out my name. The screen flickered to reveal a long list of possibilities and I chose the command for opening the doors. The reassuring clunk of bolts drawing back from the front door made both of us to cry out in relief. Taking her by the hand, I pulled her towards the door and wrenched it open.

People were running, many of them screaming, pushing, punching, desperate to escape, smoke and fumes filling the corridor. I never guessed so many inhabited the tower block, all of them spending the best parts of their lives locked inside the confines of their apartments, swallowing the lies, refusing to accept the truth.

The truth we were like so many laboratory mice. Every one of us.

A terrible whooshing noise engulfed us, and I whirled around as yet another missile came straight through the window, hurtled inches past my head and slapped into the wall opposite. I caught the horrified scream of a girl close beside me before the rocket erupted into a huge, blinding flash of white light. Then nothing.

* * *

The room was black, blacker than night. As black as a deep cavern.
I was dead.
Nothing remained.
From the distance, I heard steady, rhythmical breathing.
My own.
In an instant, it all changed.
I snapped my eyes open as scorching lights erupted all around me. Too strong, too bright, I squeezed my eyes shut again and twisted away. I tried to blink them open, but blue spots danced before me, as if I'd peered into the Sun. Shaking my head, I sat up. A hand rested on my chest, gently pushing me back.
"Yolanda?"
A kindly face loomed closer, a woman's face. This wasn't real. Truly, I had passed over into whatever realm awaits us when we leave this mortal one behind. We didn't have women in our society. No need. No need for mothers.
Rubbing my eyes, disbelieving, confused, speechless, I looked and she remained standing there. Dressed in pristine white, her face framed by raven hair, eyes wide and bright, so intensely blue and inviting, the urge to reach out and touch her overwhelming. The desire became so powerful that I reached out, my fingers brushing against her skin, and I stroked her cheek. She smiled. "Simeon," she said, her own hand now smoothing the hair from my forehead. "Simeon, you're safe. Try and sleep." Her voice, so mellow and soothing, cocooned me in soft, velvet pillows. Whatever it wanted me to do, I couldn't argue, I wouldn't want to. My hand, so heavy, fell away and I allowed my eyes to close as I drifted away, happier than I had been for years.

For how long I slept, I have no idea. It may have been an hour, it may have been a week. All I can remember, with any clarity, was sitting up one bright, sunny morning feeling refreshed, safe and alive.
Looking around me, I took in the details of a bright, sparsely furnished room with a small, white table in the corner and, next to it, a cupboard or wardrobe also in white. I lay in a single bed, the sheets crisp and clean. I was alone.

I swung my legs out from beneath the covers and sat, taking a moment to get my bearings. All of the numbing exhaustion that had haunted me for the past few days now gone, I stretched my arms and went to stand up. A profusion of cables and tubes attached to my chest and arms prevented me from taking a single step. I wanted to swat them away, thought better of it, slumped back onto the bed and stared out of the window.

In the distance, tower blocks, like jagged fingers, pointed towards a sky streaked with hues of grey. Plumes of smoke poured from between the building and some, in the further distance, were ablaze. Occasionally, a single black interceptor flashed across the sky. But there were no more screams. Only silence. For that I was grateful.

I wondered if the lack of noise was due to the room being soundproofed, the window triple glazed. Was this perhaps where conspirators ended their days, brains smoothed, personalities made blank? I dragged a trembling hand across my brow. Was this my end too?

Before my fears took hold, the door swung open and a very large Sweeper stepped into the room to glare down at me. "Feeling better?"

I'd survived the blast, the attack, the missile, but would I survive what was to happen next.

The Sweeper was scanning me and he frowned.

"Simeon," he made some sort of report through his helmet. They used neurological communication, but it was always obvious when as their eyes rolled up into the back of their heads. It was disconcerting the first time you saw it. Now it made me feel strangely reassured. Life was still going on, as normal as it ever was.

His eyes came back. "You're going to have to go to Re-programming, Simeon. As soon as you're able. Your chip is malfunctioning. You can't be released whilst it's like that. The Sandmen will kill you."

I didn't say anything. So, the Sandmen, the Sweepers, they'd all survived the attack. Not that I doubted it for a single moment. The paratroopers that I'd seen dropping down from the hover-copters were drones, not human beings. They wouldn't have stood a chance, not against the technologically superior Sweepers.

At least, that was what I believed.

At first.

The door swished open and the woman came in again, clicking her tongue impatiently at the sight of the Sweeper. I gasped in disbelief as I saw her push him aside. That in itself was remarkable, but nothing to what she then said, "Get out, you great oaf!"

I sat and stared in amazement as the Sweeper, without a word or backward glance, did as commanded. I gaped and all she did was smile, sitting down next to me, stroking my forehead. "I was worried about you, Simeon. You took a nasty tumble. If you hadn't been found when you were, then..." She shrugged her slim shoulders and smiled again, "But you were top priority, naturally. Nothing was going to get in our way."

"I don't understand."

"No, of course you don't. Try not to worry; everything will become clearer when you start to feel a little more...human."

"But..." I squeezed fingers into my eyes, "what about Yolanda?"

Her eyes closed, like shutters coming down on my concerns. "When you're better," she cooed, stroking my forehead again, "then you'll understand. Now, you rest and I'll come back later."

Rest? By ignoring my question I could only assume one thing – Yolanda was dead.

* * *

When next I opened my eyes, most of the tubes had gone. There was only one, a thin wire running from my arm to a tiny monitor beside the bed, bleeping hypnotically. I felt myself slipping away into unconsciousness again, but I fought against it this time. At least I thought I did. I snapped my eyes open with a start, catching myself falling asleep as I often did, thinking I had slipped off a kerb, or stumbled in a crack on the road, and she was there again.

She eased me forward, puffing up the pillows behind my head to make me more comfortable. Then she unexpectedly felt behind my head at the raised area where my chip was situated. I winced.

"It's very infected," she said. "It wasn't inserted at Programming Central, was it?"

The look in my eyes must have revealed more than I had wished. She shook her head. "It's a wonder you survived at all, Simeon." She reached inside her white coat pocket and pulled out the processor. The one I had found at Stoker's old hideout. "And what is this?"

I shook my head. What was I to say? How much did she already know? Who was she?

"You're a woman," I said pathetically. I felt pathetic, as well as sounding it.

A smile then a little laugh. "Well done," she scoffed. "You must be getting better."

"No, I mean...how? I've never seen a woman, not since...Not since Nan was taken."

"Taken? You mean reassigned, surely."

For some reason, her easy dismissal of my words brought the bile to my throat. I snapped, "I mean '*taken*'! They were all taken. I know that much."

"Simeon," she looked at me with a serious glint in her eyes, "you've been told a lot of things which simply aren't true. No one was *taken*. Society simply had to be...realigned. That was all. Your parents, everyone's parents were resettled in the east. Where there was more food, Simeon. More arable land. There was nothing sinister in anything that happened. I'm proof of that, Simeon."

"But..." Something in her soft, simmering eyes made me so want to believe her. And yet... "We were told all about it, at school." I closed my eyes to recount the mantra burnished within our minds, '*Our duty is to uphold the safety of the children of our world, to protect and comfort and guide. We have no need of fathers or mothers. We only have need of our beloved...*' My voice trailed away and I opened my eyes to find her staring at me with what looked like controlled fury.

"Finish it," she spat, all of sudden becoming angry, her features hardening.

I swallowed hard, "...'*We only have need of our beloved Protector.*'"

"What a pity you didn't recite that before you killed him, Simeon."

I cowered away from her blazing, accusing eyes. "I didn't. You know I didn't."

"Do I? Convince me – tell me what happened, Simeon. Tell me *everything*."

So I did. And this time, unlike my confession to Yolanda, I told her it all. Every single thing from the moment I wandered into Stoker's hideout to my last meeting with Corrigan. I left nothing out, not even the parts about Warren tampering with my chip. Or what I had seen with the processor I had managed to link into my own computer. By the time I'd finished I was breathless, but felt as if I had been relieved of a massive burden, the wave of relief surging through me making me want to cry out, jump up and down, reach forward and hug her close. Controlling myself, I stared into her stunningly beautiful face, empty of emotion, or reaction to my words. She was silent, but tense, listening to every word, dissecting every nuance, each inflection, gauging every syllable for truth or lie. When my soliloquy ended, she stepped away, smoothed down her white coat, and looked down at me with the air of a school principle. "A pity you couldn't have told us all of that earlier." She then whirled around and was gone, replacing my sense of relief with one of acute anxiety.

I knew, without any doubt, that my confession was the biggest mistake of my short life.

Twenty-Six

There were three men in my room now. Two of them were running diagnostics having scanned my chip, whilst the third was busy setting up a tray of surgical tools. I didn't like the look of them. They were small, silver and sharp. It all seemed a bit primitive to me. No one had invasive surgery nowadays. There simply wasn't any need. No one ever got ill.

They were discussing some finer points about my chip when the door opened and she came in again. The men immediately stopped and stood rigidly to attention. She gave them a scolding glance and they all scurried out. She hadn't said a word. To command such respect, such power, bedazzled me. Feeling that perhaps I should come to attention too, I sat up.

"Simeon, I have something to tell you," she said, an edge to her voice, a slight uncertainty to its usual assuredness. She sat down on my bed and gazed at her own hands. "It's about Yolanda."

This was the moment I'd been dreading. I looked at her, trying to read her features, but she was a blank canvas, her fine features revealing nothing. I waited, waited with all the patience I could muster to hear the words that I knew were about to come.

Quite unexpectedly her hand came out and she touched my forehead, then her fingers gently brushed down the side of my cheek and she held my chin, tipping my face up slightly as she gazed straight into my eyes. "She was badly injured in the attack," she said quietly. "Much worse than yourself."

"Is she...?" Before I could finish my sentence, she pressed a slim finger against my lips.

"She's very badly shaken, Simeon. The missile... We had to operate."

"Operate? You mean – she is alive though, isn't she?" I could feel myself coming apart at the seams, and I gripped the side of the bed, any remaining strength, or fortitude, giving way to blind panic.

Taking me in her arms, she held me as the shaking took over my entire body. At last, when I managed to take some semblance of control, she held me at arm's length, her voice acting like cool droplets of spring water, easing my pain, calming my soul. "She's alive, Simeon. Barely. We had to remove her spleen. Her body was broken and she has suffered some bad scarring. The shrapnel from the missile, you see – some of it hit her in the lower back, and across her legs. There's a chance she may never walk again. We nearly lost her."

Unable to come to terms with this devastating news, my eyes filled up and she held me once again. I so wanted to run away and find Yolanda, take her in my arms, check she really was all right, but sitting there, in that warm, comforting embrace, all I managed was a pathetic, "But she will be okay?"

She drew back, a slight smile on her face, and brushed the hair from my brow, softly, gently. Over and over, she caressed me, absorbed in what she was doing. I didn't want her to stop. As my eyes grew heavy, I felt slipping away to a far and distant place where everything was good and clean. I closed my eyes and all I could see was her face.

I awoke suddenly and sat up, instantly regretting it as a stab of pain raced across my forehead. My whole skull ached as if I had been repeatedly hit with a mallet. As I kneaded my temples, I realised this was a very different pain to the ones I experienced before. Before she came to comfort me. As I allowed my fingers creep to the back of my neck, I understood why. The ridge of swollen flesh was much less now, the tenderness not nearly so great. My chip. I could feel where they had removed, cleaned and replaced it. I'd been reprogrammed.

For a long time I stood and stared into the ivory gleam of the washbasin. I ran my hand over the sensor and washed my face, the water reviving me a little. I stared in to the mirror, my face streaming wet, and checked my features. Simeon Allis. It was me, all right, the same eyes, the high cheekbones, the little dimple in my chin. But something wasn't the same. I looked older. There were deep creases at the corners of my eyes, across the ridge of my nose, furrows across my forehead. I hadn't noticed them before and, when I ran my hand across my chin, I felt the beginning of stubble. Dad had always needed to shave twice a day he was so dark, but not me...

I pulled myself up straight, grinning, relief rushing over me. Thoughts of Dad, my mum, Nan, they all came flooding through my consciousness and I became so giddy I wanted to cry out with the joy of it. I still had memories. The chip, if they had replaced it, was still not doing its job, even now. Memories. My past. Not erased, not even subdued. I really was one-in-a-million.

"Genetically," the man was saying, his voice droning on, "it is baffling. We simply don't understand it."

Nodding her head, she folded her arms across her chest and looked at me as one might do a naughty child. Which, to her, I probably was.

"Simeon," she said, "you are what is termed 'a problem'." Flicking her hand towards the technician, she dismissed him with the gesture. Sighing deeply, she moved behind me and rested her slim hands on my shoulders. "I was hopeful that it was your chip that was causing the inconsistencies in your behaviour. I realise now that I was wrong. It's you. Your... ego."

I sat in a hard-backed chair, a tangle of wires running all around me. They had probed, pinched, pulled and played with me but, from what she had said, it was clear they had found no answers. Her fingers gently massaged my aching muscles and I moaned. "Ego? What's that?"

"Your sense of self, of how you perceive yourself to be. In your case, it is so powerful, so strong, that it can overcome the processing capabilities of the chip. You're going to have to go to Central Programming and be completely investigated."

I groaned, my head slumped down on my chest and for the first time in so very long, I gave one, shuddering cry and watched as a single tear fell to the floor with a tiny splash.

Fully clothed, I sat on my bed, the tubes and wires removed, a tiny holdall, no bigger than a litre bottle, beside me. "You're going back to your apartment," a white-coated attendant announced, breezing into the room not an hour before. "You need to get ready."

I waited. Waited for so long until finally she came in, to stand in the corner, arms folded in her customary pose, watching me like a hawk.

"What's going on? I thought I was going home."

"Plans have changed."

"Why, what's happened?"

She shrugged and the bile rose up into my throat. "I want to see Yollie," I said, as forcibly as I could manage.

"Well you can't."

I snapped my head up sharply at that. "Who the hell are you? You come in here, giving your orders, telling me what I can and cannot do, well I won't have it – you hear me! I'm sick to death of being controlled, of having all my free-will sucked out of me by your damn, bloody reprogramming." It poured out of me – the anger, confusion, grief. "If Yolanda is still alive, then I needed the proof. I've lost everything and everyone and I don't believe anything you, or anyone else has said to me about my parents and what happened. It's not the truth. The State has murdered them, as they have countless millions of others, removing them as a barrier to their desire to create a new, so-called 'better' society. One for only the young." Looking at her now, this harbinger of cruel deception, I honestly think she was stunned by my outburst. I forged ahead, hoping to knock her down. "So…just tell me – who are you?"

If she had been affected by my words, she soon recovered. Very slowly she walked over to me, her face even and unfathomable. A slight smile played at her mouth. "I'm the Protector's wife," she said, and I reeled backwards. It was she who had delivered the knockout blow.

It was madness. No one got married anymore. There was no need. Nobody had children.

Or so we were told.

But, then again, they'd told us so much and if there was one thing I'd learned about our society over the course of the last days, it was that virtually everything was built on a foundation of lies.

So now, the question had to be asked, could she be believed?

Trust no one.

My eyes narrowed. "The Protector's wife?" I repeated, saying each syllable with heavy emphasis. "I don't believe it."

"Why? Because you're the authority on truth? Is that what your friends told you, Simeon? The friends who forced you into this mess? Because let me tell you, it was *they* who lied. Have you ever considered that?"

"Of course – I'm not an idiot. I realised what a fool I'd been as soon as I played the processor I found through the graphic accelerator back at my apartment."

"What did you see, Simeon?"

"The Wild Men, the countryside, the green grass. It was a huge computer programme, conjured up to trap me. The Wild Men were holographic images, projected onto…onto what? Where was I exactly?"

"Outside, beyond the City walls. That much at least was true. The things you thought you saw, however…" For a second a tiny flicker of something like sadness flickered across her eyes. "The countryside does not exist, Simeon. Everything is a wasteland, devastated by the Wars. Nothing good remains outside."

"I sensed it. I knew all along."

"Really?" She gave a cynical, dismissive laugh. "So, you stumble into an unknown house, are threatened and intimidated into doing the most despicable act imaginable, and then you ride off into the sunset with some bearded fanatic? Not really the actions of someone who is supposed to be studious and intelligent. Then they spoon-fed you lies, Simeon. And you've swallowed them all, haven't you. How's your knowledge of history, Simeon?"

"My knowledge of what?"

"History. What was it you were told…let me see…that we were the cradle of civilisation, wasn't it? That we – the United States, I think it was – they invented writing, isn't that so? They created the people from Asia and Africa to serve us. You listened to all of it and you believed every word."

I frowned at her. My mind felt like it was being pulled in any number of different directions, but two were holding my attention the most. Was she telling me that all those things Warren had said were lies? And, by far the most frightening thing of all…how did she *know* what I had been told?"

She seemed to be reading my mind, not for the first time. "Lies, Simeon. All lies. Civilisation *began* in those places, thousands upon thousands of years ago. In the mists of time, people from the East invented writing, the wheel, built cities, founded civilisations whilst we here, in this pitiful land, we lived in caves and gnawed on the raw bones of wild beasts."

"No! No, that can't be! Thousands of years, that's – that's just stupid. At school, we have been told——"

She reached out and touched my cheek, so gently I almost swooned. "It's time for a history lesson, Simeon. One which is true."

Without a word from her, the door opened and men came in. Not the same as before, although they were dressed in a similar fashion. They pulled my head down sharply and I felt something jolt in the back of my head. When I looked up again, they'd wheeled in a trolley and on it sat a large, flat monitor, like something out of a museum. A light flashed, then throbbed and I felt the jolt again. They'd linked me up to it through my chip.

The screen flared into life. I sat back and watched.

Watched it all.

The history of the world. Before the dawn of time, the rise of ape-like creatures in Africa, how mankind evolved and spread across the globe. The development of civilisation. From Ancient Sumer, Egypt, the Indus Valley, through wars and conflicts and developments in technology, right up to how our present world came into being, the Protector, Sweepers, Sandmen... All of it, finally ending with the attacks from the drones only a few days ago. Every detail described succinctly, without embroidery.

As the screen blinked out, I closed my eyes for a moment, allowing the most prominent, memorable images to linger there, in the forefront of my mind. Everything I'd seen was in sharp contrast to the teaching I had received at school, the things that Stoker and Warren had told me. I was numb.

"You're shocked," she said simply.

"How do I know that *this* is truth," I said, jabbing my finger at the now silent monitor. "How can I be sure?"

"Yours is the generation of ignorance, Simeon. You take it all in and you never stop to question. You never have the opportunity, or the inclination to *check* the facts. They are given to you through your chip, video screens and computers and you believe them. That is the tragedy of our age, Simeon – *your* age."

"But it was all provided for us. We've never had to ask or want for anything – we had no need. Not even for love."

"*Not even for love...* You believe that? Then why did you believe the lies of Stoker and the others?

"You said it before – I was *forced*."

"That's nothing buy an excuse. For your information, I wasn't forced to love my husband. I respected him immensely, was loyal and supportive throughout the years we had together, and then you took him from me – from *us*, the whole of society. And for what, so you wouldn't be D-merited?"

"I – I wasn't thinking straight. I was frightened, confused. And a D-merit is a major thing, if you didn't already know. They could have taken me to Cambridge."

"Ah yes, Cambridge. I thought about that. Where is Cambridge, by the way?"

"What?" I blinked, so registering the point of her question. "How should I know where Cambridge is? It's just some place where you're – altered. Changed. You come back different, that's all I know."

"And do you actually know anyone who has come back, changed or oth-erwise?"

I scoured my memory, checking, re-checking. "Well, not exactly, but——"

"Precisely – you can't think of anyone because there isn't anyone. More lies, more stories that you've swallowed. You really are a fool, Simeon."

"What about Damien Bridges? He fell behind, didn't do his course work, got D-merited and was sent off to Cambridge. No one's ever seen him since."

"Damien Bridges."

"Yes! He was…a sort of friend. Yollie knew him – we *all* knew him."

"All?"

"Yes. What's the matter with you? Everyone from school of course."

"How many people do you know from school, Simeon?"

I stopped, forcing myself to swallow, my throat so dry. I tried to think, to find some flicker, a face, a name. We never met one another. Lessons, brought to us through our chip, and if we had problems we simply hooked up to our tutor. Virtual tutors. Virtual lessons. I put a finger and thumb in my eyes; the pain building. She'd forced me onto the back foot, her revelations, secrets, lies or truth. I didn't know anything anymore. "I know a few," I said, voice strained, my throat raw now. "Not from school, but mainly from the band. And Yollie, of course."

"The band? The band you play the cornet for? Mr Piperson is the man in charge, yes?"

I frowned. She obviously knew all the answers, so why was she playing me like this? Where was all this leading? "You're going to tell me they're not real, they're all holograms or AIs?"

"Oh, they're real, Simeon. Very real. You don't live in a virtual world, you live in a real one. Although your so-called friend Damien Bridges lived in a virtual world. Injured himself, missed school, fell behind. Moved to…Cambridge…"

She brought out a small, multi-functional display and spoke into it very softly. Suddenly the far wall began to shimmer, various images dancing across it. I couldn't make them out at first, but there was a lot of desolation. Destroyed, ruined buildings, overgrown by weeds and wild flowers. Burned out vehicles, filth floating down the river. It was a bombsite. A massive one.

"This is Cambridge," she said quietly, pointing to the images. "Or, what re-mains of it. It was destroyed during the Second Thermo-War. As a seat of learn-ing, it was a prime target you see. And the government had offices there, having left London in the First War. Just under a million people died in Cambridge, Simeon. It is off-limits now. Hugely contaminated." She looked at me over her shoulder, "So, you see, Damien Bridges couldn't have gone there. No one can. It's deadly."

"No, no. This …" Confusion gained the ascendency. Trapped, desperate for a way out, I fought to find something, a shred of evidence which would enable me to make some sense of her words. I rubbed my head. It was hurting again. It shouldn't have been hurting that much. Something wasn't right. "I'm confused," I mumbled, squeezing my eyes tight shut, trying to get through the pain. "It doesn't make sense. Nothing makes sense."

"Well, you're not an *idiot*, Simeon." I shot her a look, a look that reflected my growing anger and frustration. She smiled, turning to me, "Work it out."

I shook my head. "Lies. What you've told me, what you've shown me…"

She nodded, still smiling. "All lies."

"But why? What's the point?"

"To make you think. To force you to pick out the scraps of truth. To remind you not to trust anyone, Simeon. Don't trust anyone or *anything*."

A shadow fell over me, and as I turned towards something hot pushed against the nape of my neck, a finely focused point of pressure and pain. Nothing registered after that.

Twenty-Seven

Anonymous white corridors meandered ahead of me, exits doorways on both left and right giving no clue as to which way I should go. There was no one about, not even the sound of anyone, just the soft hum from the strip lights above. They bathed everything in a harsh, sterilised glare. Letting instinct guide me, I tried to continue on my way, to find Yolanda and some sort of truth.

I'd woken up, a pounding in my head, tongue thick and dry in a mouth tasting of something foul. Drugged, confused, dehydrated, I had no idea where I was or for how long I'd lay in that cold, featureless corridor. Sitting up, I rubbed my eyes, and touched my neck to first find the entrance point of the injection, then my chip.

There was no evidence of either.

I wandered those empty hallways, my body aching, legs heavy. For how long, I have no way of telling. Time seemed to blur. All I was aware of was an intense throbbing behind my eyes, which refused to budge. I felt sure it had something to do with the re-programmed chip under my skin. I kept touching the area, in the vain hope that I could flick it out, relieve the ache, return some sense of order to my scrambled brain. But I couldn't. The swelling was gone. I was whole again.

Behind me a door opened. I turned quickly, not knowing whether to run or hide. In the end, I did neither, waited and watched as a white coat came out of a room and padded quietly across in the opposite direction. Without thinking, I went towards the door he had come through and went inside.

There she was.

Yolanda.

Laying on her back, beneath the crisp white sheets, her breathing came shallow and steady. I crept closer and gazed down at her loveliness. She seemed at peace, no sign of pain or anguish on her features and, slowly leaning forward, I pressed my lips upon her forehead. Her eyes sprang open instantly.

"Simeon!" She sat up, gripping my arms with surprising strength. "Simeon, you're alive!"

Unable to contain my own joy at finding her so well, so *alive,* I pulled her to me, kissing her mouth, face, head. "Oh Yollie, Yollie, I thought I'd lost you."

We stayed like that, holding one another, feeling the warmth between us blossom. "Simeon, I've missed you so much."

I pulled back, my eyes blurry with tears. "They told me they'd ... " Her eyes, so huge, stared at me with the same child-like anticipation that had first drawn me to her all those centuries ago. "Are you all right?"

"I think so." She forced a smile, a tiny wince creasing her forehead. "Back hurts."

"They said you'd been hit by shrapnel."

"Yes. My leg too. They said I'll always walk with a limp."

"Oh my God," I held her close and she groaned. I quickly let her go. "Yollie, I'm sorry. Are you in pain, can you stand?"

"Stand? I – I don't know. What are you thinking, Simeon?" She gave me that old, familiar look.

"I think we should leave."

"Leave?" A note of panic came into her voice. "Where are we supposed to go?"

"I don't know. But this place, it's not – Yollie, I think it's a trap of some sort."

"Oh no, Simeon. Not more of this. No more of your stories, your theories. They brought me here to make me well, not to do me harm – not to *trap* us. They saved my life."

"Yes. But why? Why would they bother to do that?" My hand rubbed the back of my neck as if of their own volition. "And they drugged me, dumped me in this corridor, right outside your room. Yollie, they're planning something. *She* is planning something. The Protector's wife."

Perhaps she could see my reasoning. Perhaps not. She sighed deeply. "Perhaps it was to lure you...to give you a reason...to carry on?" She shook her head, wincing a little. "I can't make any sense of anything anymore, Simeon. I thought I understood, I thought I knew what life was all about."

"You *do*, Yollie." I gripped her shoulders harder. "I want you to try and think, really hard. About your mother."

Her eyes softened, almost as soon as the word left my lips. "My mother?"

"Yes, Yollie. Can you remember anything about her? Her face, the sound of her voice, the things you used to do together?"

For moments that seemed to stretch out into forever, I watched her struggle with what I had asked. As I watched, I understood, perhaps for the first time, the difference between us. And she saw it too as her face cleared, the heavy veil of unknowing firmly pulled away. "Simeon... you can see them? Your parents?" I nodded and she gaped, taking a moment for the realisation to sink in. "Then, then all of this has really been some elaborate plan, to trap you?"

"That's exactly what it's been. All of it."

"But ... your involvement in the Protector's death ... All of it nothing more than ..." Looking down, she shook her head. "It's so hard to accept, Simeon. I knew you couldn't be capable, but ... Why?"

"They seem to think I have the key to something." I tapped my head. "My chip, it's never functioned as it should. Not like everyone else's. I remember things, Yollie. Things about my family, about the world *before* the Sandmen. But..." I reached inside my trouser pocket and pulled out the tiny processor I'd found at Stoker's old place. "This. This is something. And Corrigan gave me this..." I pulled out the paper Corrigan had given to me.

"What is it?"

"A map. We have to find this place, Yollie. We have to try and get to the bottom of all this."

"All what? Simeon, you need to calm down. You're taking things too fast." With her face in her hands, her body convulsed in a single sob. "It's too much for me."

I held her to me, pressing my face against hers, the smoothness of her face, so warm. So comforting. I kissed away her tears and spoke to her as gently as I could. "I'm not going too fast, Yollie. If anything, I've been going too slowly. We have to act decisively from now on – no more hesitating. So come on, get dressed, we're going to get to the bottom of all of this."

Twenty-Eight

Winding our way along the eerily quiet maze of featureless corridors, we finally managed to reach the hospital exit. We stood before the huge entrance, looking out across a scene of total devastation. It seemed as if every surrounding building was flattened, huge piles of rubble, twisted, mangled protrusions of rusted metal sprouting through the broken concrete like skeletal fingers. Tiny plumes of ink-black smoke spiralled skywards from the ruins and, amongst them, spread across the ground, the grotesque remains of human bodies. Not vaporised. Sliced in half by lasers. No one had cleaned up and I wondered why.

Exchanging a quick glance, I took her hand and we ran across the open square. Looking back I noted that the hospital had not remained unscathed. Great black holes and blast marks dotted its high-rise surface. One or two lights still burned like beacons as the night slowly encroached. Late evening. It would be curfew soon.

We ran as fast as we could, but Yollie struggled, the wounds in her legs forcing her to stagger and when she stumbled and fell, I quickly went to her and held her close. "Jesus, Yollie, I forgot you were so badly hurt."

"Don't blaspheme, Simeon."

I smiled at her then stopped.

For a moment, everything ceased. The world, the night, the fear. And awful, horrible black cloud fell over me, deeper and darker than anything I had experienced before or since.

"What's the matter Simeon? Don't worry about me – I'm fine. I just need a moment or two, that's all."

She sat up. I wanted to scream, but held it in. This was Yollie. I could see her, touch her. This was not a dream, and yet... And yet, it didn't seem *real*.

We continued, much more carefully now, Yollie doing her best, never complaining. She was the only constant in a rapidly changing world, where truth and lies had become fused as one. I was now at the point of doubting everything and anything that I had seen or heard. Except for Yolanda, that is. She was the one thing that would keep me sane.

What remained of the City streets made them all nondescript, especially in the gloomy half-light. Totally disorientated, we blundered along, never stopping, just moving through the empty passages and lanes. I had slowed to her pace by this time, but she was doing well and her limp had all but disappeared. When we finally came to the mangled road that led up to the public arena I could hardly dare believe that I actually recognised it.

I shouldn't have done, in all honesty. It had taken several direct hits. The walls were down, broken into bite-sized chunks, the pavilion at the far end destroyed, nothing more than a gutted, burned-out shell. And yet...

And yet.

Somewhere amongst all this destruction somebody was playing a trumpet!

Instinctively, I pulled her back against the remains of a building. Squinting ahead, to the right a light flared from a window. A gutted, rotten tooth of a structure, the top storeys blown away, but from the first floor, a room. With a lamp burning within.

We gaped at one another. Despite the surreal moment, I was happy to find Yolanda looking good, breathing controlled, her physical fitness always something which made her stand apart. By the weak light of the lamp, I could clearly make out the healthy sheen to her skin, an inner glow from which I found it difficult to pull away. I longed to kiss her, but then that nagging doubt from before resurfaced. I had never stopped to ask myself the simple question, which once again rose into my head, causing me to scold myself for being so stupid. So intent on escaping, I had completely overlooked one very simple thing - Yolanda was supposed to have had surgery on her back and legs. It wasn't just a simple case of her limping, the way she sometimes had during our tramping through the debris. The Protector's wife had told me, quite emphatically, *there's a chance she may never walk again. We nearly lost her.*

How, then, could she run so far, without complaint?

Pulling in a breath, I prepared to tackle her about the reality of what had happened back in the hospital, when the melancholy sound of the trumpet drifted through the night air, sending a plaintive message to any who could hear.

"That's Clarke's Trumpet Voluntary," Yolanda said, her voice numbed with awe, or shock, or both.

I dragged my eyes from her and peered out into the darkness. It was one of the few pieces I could play reasonably well. Now, it seemed to be calling me, and not simply metaphorically. Seized by some invisible urgency, I crept forward, shedding myself from Yolanda's feeble grasp.

"Simeon, what are you doing?"

There was no time for explanations. Instead, I left her behind and crossed the road to the remains of the building. Moving through the open doorway, the lamplight flickered, casting wild, macabre shadows against the cracked walls. This close, the sound of the trumpet filled the void of what remained of the room. Mindless of my safety, I went towards the person who was playing, with his back to me. It wasn't until I tapped him on the shoulder and he turned to show his great toothy grin splitting his big, beery face that I recognised him.

It was my Dad.

Twenty-Nine

"*Simeon!*"

I snapped my head from side to side, blinking, intense white light invading my senses. Unable to focus properly, all I was aware of was the heavy pounding of my heart at the terrible shock I had just experienced.

"Simeon, are you all right? You were screaming."

I sat up, staring into nothingness, grappling with the myriad emotions swirling around inside my head. "Where the hell am I?"

Her voice came to me from out of the distance, beyond the glare. "You were having a nightmare, Simeon. You're safe now."

It had been a dream? All of it? A dreadful, realistic, horrible dream. My Dad. Why had I thought of him playing the trumpet? He had never played the trumpet, or any sort of musical instrument. They'd poisoned me again. Pumped me full of hallucinogenic drugs. Desperate to control me, destroy me, bring me back to the fold.

Groaning, I pressed the heels of my palms into my eyes, trying to blank out the glaring lights around me, trying to understand what was happening to me, find some focus. They say you only remember nightmares, and I remembered every detail of that one. Those images of Dad, so clear, and Yolanda – the wounds to her back and legs heeled. Where was she now, still in that hospital bed, her face swollen, unrecognisable? Blowing out a loud breath, I dragged my hands away from my face and turned to her.

The Protector's wife.

She sat next to me on the bed and slowly mopped my brow with a tissue. As if in a trance, I allowed her to care for me. It felt nice, it felt *normal*. No one looked after me now, not in these soulless, unloving days. There was no one who gave me a moment's affection, except Yolanda.

"Where's Yolanda?" I asked.

She stopped and gave me a measured look, then pressed her lips together. "Not good," she said quietly. I tensed and she placed her cool hand on my hot, sticky arm. "She *will* get better, Simeon. We just have to be patient."

"I want to see her."

"I don't think that's such a good idea."

"Please."

She thought for a moment, then brought out her interactive hand-device and spoke into it. Within thirty seconds, before she had put it back into her pocket, the door opened and two white coats came in. She nodded towards them and they helped me out of the bed to my feet. I was glad they were there. I was still weak, my legs barely able to support my own weight, and I had to lean on them for support. The Protector's wife sat on the bed, looking down at her feet. I glanced at her but she didn't lift her head. She seemed sad.

Very slowly and very carefully, they took me out of the room and down one of the long corridors, the sound of the orderlies' boots ringing shrill in the cold, sterilised air.

At last, they brought me to another featureless room and stepped aside to let me go in.

What confronted me caused my knees to buckle. Letting out a low groan, I had to use the doorjamb as a support. Before me lay Yolanda, stretched out beneath the starched covers of the single bed. My eyes filled up, the tugging at my heart becoming stronger. Yolanda, my beautiful, gorgeous, pure Yolanda.

She was nothing like she had been in my dream. Her face was a swollen mess, battered and bruised, bloated like a pumpkin to twice its normal size. Her lower body, encased in heavy plaster bandaging and supported by some sort of mechanical winch, was unrecognisable for the lithe, supple work of art that it used to be. Her breathing sounded ragged, the mucous bubbling in her chest. Every now and then she would change position slightly and utter a little moan, pain her constant companion.

Managing to shrug off my initial shock, I moved over to her and peered down at her purple-veined face. She looked dreadful and for a moment the world around me swirled as if stirred by some great, invisible mixing device and I almost collapsed as I flayed around for support, vaguely aware of a chair close by. One of the white coated orderlies loomed beside me all of a sudden, held onto my arm, and eased me down onto the seat. I smiled my thanks and took a moment to recover my senses. Glancing towards Yolanda again, my tears came unchecked, the awfulness of what had happened truly hitting home. I held onto the edge of her bed to stop myself from sliding to the floor. I closed my eyes, waiting for the nausea to subside, and hoped, in some crazy way, that when I opened them again everything would be all right. But it wasn't. She was still a mess and there was nothing I could do to help her. Wiping away the trails of tears from my cheeks with the back of my hand, I pressed my forehead against her naked arm and mumbled, "Oh Yollie … Forgive me." Then, in silence, the two men helped me to my feet and gently, but assertively, returned me to my own room.

It was cold outside. Summer had rapidly retreated and already the air was changing, meaning that autumn would soon be here. The Protector's wife slipped in beside me in the hover-car and soon we were whispering through the broken, deserted streets towards my waiting apartment. She'd promised me a fresh start, in a new place. I was past caring.

We were there before I had time to think through any of the many things she had told me. My apartment was kitted out with all the very latest technology; I would want for nothing. As we stepped out from the hover-car, I strained to look up at the sterile, featureless, bland building that towered above me. We were just outside City Centre, an area unscathed from the recent attacks. Touching my arm lightly, the Protector's wife took me through the main entrance. A guard inclined his massive, armour encased head, scanned us both before we moved into the fully functioning lift – a rarity in itself. She stepped aside when we made my floor and motioned for me to move on. The door to my apartment – the only one of that floor as far as I could tell – opened automatically and I stepped inside. The hover maid appeared and helped me with my coat. Already it had produced freshly chilled orange juice. It tasted delicious and I carried on sipping at it as I moved through the interior. A nice place. Clean, bright, airy. I couldn't argue with that. Everything was new; clothes, computers, furniture, everything. The smell was sharp, clinical, untainted by human kind. It was small, but wonderful. If I hadn't been in such a terrible mood I would have thanked her. Instead, I just crossed to the window and looked out.

What I saw was the one part of the dreams I'd been experiencing which remained unaltered. Just over the way, perhaps a couple of hundred metres or so, the streets had taken a terrible pounding with the evidence of fearsome fire-fights everywhere. No one moved in those streets. Not even a Sweeper. It was disturbing to see bodies lying about, to rot like so much rubbish. I looked over to her. She stood leaning in the doorway, arms folded, waiting.

"What happened?" I asked.

"We were attacked."

"I know that," I snapped, clicking my tongue. I sat down on a chair. It was soft and seemed to sigh as I fell into it. Suddenly, I felt very tired. "Can't you be a little more…specific?"

It was her turn to sigh, obviously not wanting to go into details. She pushed herself off the wall and came closer, that same steely look in her eyes that never seemed to leave her. She sat down opposite me and made a face. "It's not really important, you know. What happened, happened. It is in the past now, securely locked away. You have no need to trouble yourself with all the whys and wherefores."

"Well, I think I do – especially after what happened with Yollie…"

She nodded, seeming to cave in, accepting my need for truth. She exhaled slowly. "Very well. When the news of the Protector's death—" She stopped, looked away for a brief moment, biting her lip. After a short inner battle to regain her composure, she took another breath and resumed. "When the news of his death was announced, other states took it upon themselves to attempt to…overthrow us. They didn't succeed, needless to say. Their technology is not as advanced as ours. My husband, you see, was only the figurehead. The *real* power lies with our programmers. Our enemies don't understand this, Simeon. They believed that without the Protector we would simply collapse, our society pitch into some sort of Dark Age. They were wrong. We defeated them. Sweepers are formidable, Simeon. The pinnacle of modern inventiveness. The fusing together of advanced micro-technology and human capability. And if they fail, the Sandmen will come."

"*The Sandman cometh…*" I pressed my face into my hands. "It was a song, you know."

"Yes. Very old. Very silly."

"You think?" I looked at her through my fingers, then sat back. "I was taught, when I was little, that the Sandman would come and throw sand in my eyes when it was time for bed. That all I had to do was sleep and everything would be fine. It was a story designed to scare me into doing as I was told. And every night I'd put my head on my pillow and I'd hear them, pounding down the streets, looking for those who had not quite made it to the safety of their beds."

"And then what? What would happen to them?"

"Where you at the first gathering? When the Protector introduced the Sandmen? Did you witness what they could do, what they *did*?"

"Yes, Simeon, I was there."

I shook my head. "And you...you still stayed with him, even after that? You still stood at his side and watched innocent people – men, women, children, being carved up by those hideous things?"

"The few needed to be sacrificed in order for the majority to survive. It was an acceptable cull, Simeon. We had to show everyone what would happen if anyone chose not to conform."

"And our parents? Why did you take them away?"

"They were a bad influence, Simeon. Everyone knows that. Everyone has *always* known that. In the past, if a couple could not have a child, they applied for adoption. They had to go through a very rigorous process of investigation to see if they were *suitable*. What process did a natural mother and father have to go through?"

I looked at her blankly and shrugged my shoulders. "I don't know."

"None. Anyone could have a baby, bring a new life into the world. Drug addicts, serial offenders, anyone. Some would argue that *love* brought couples together, that love produced the offspring, but that was only for the very tiny few. Mostly it was about *lust*. And the outcome was an unloved, unwanted child, who would grow up knowing it was unloved and unwanted." She breathed hard. Obviously this was a subject close to her heart and affected her adversely, her cheeks reddening, her eyes pooling with tears. Blowing out a long, hard breath, she continued, her voice not quite so assured now. "So...decisions were made. Harsh, but necessary. Parents were not deemed to be essential. They made too many mistakes. The State would provide for our children."

"But...grandparents too? You got rid of those?"

She nodded. "Eventually our children will have no family ties at all. Their only loyalty will be to the State."

"And the next generation? What about them?"

"Well...the same."

"So, let me get this straight – what you're saying is that the idea of us no longer requiring parents was dreamed up by the State, to ensure our conformity. Our *loyalty.*" She stared at me blankly, no need for an answer. "But what I don't understand, what I just *don't get,* is how do we have more children? How will the world continue?"

A slow smile crept across her face and she told me, in great detail, the answer to my question.

Thirty

I spent the next few hours exploring my new apartment, a huge place, with more rooms than I could ever use. My wardrobe was full of new, neatly pressed clothes, the gadgetry was all up-to-date, everything working smoothly and seamlessly. On accessing my computer files, I learned the Academy had accepted me. My programming would begin in one week's time. One week! Was that how much time I had left at being plain old Simeon Allis? Because I knew, beyond any doubt now, that once I stepped into the virtual classrooms of the Academy my life would change forever, perhaps even my ability to think rationally, for myself. I'd be reconfigured. Instinctively I felt the scar behind my head and frowned. There was something not quite right about it, even now, after all their tampering and refitting. Ever since Warren had taken it out and played around with its configuration, all sorts of strange, inexplicable events had followed. Re-inserting it proved problematic, and the Protector's wife told me infection had set in, causing me to hallucinate, become confused, irrational. So they replaced it. But running my finger lightly across the scar line I couldn't feel anything at all, no evidence remaining of where they'd inserted the chip. Perhaps they were experts at what they did, those nameless, faceless technicians at Central Control. Perhaps.

The hover-maid provided me with my daily dose of barbiturates. Some weeks had passed since I'd taken any – or least, I assumed so. During my stay in the hospital they may have infused them intravenously. I couldn't be sure, but I felt good. Fit, healthy. Ready to start afresh. So, I swept them up and swallowed them down. An array of blue and green lights rippled across the surface of the hover-maid, so at least it seemed pleased. Already it would have reported back to Central my conformity, but I no longer harboured any desires to resist, escape, or disobey. The State, the provider of everything that was good and clean and pure, knew what it was doing.

I ran a search on the computer, looking up some of the words the Protector's wife mentioned during our many talks. I still didn't know her name and I chided myself for not asking her. Thinking of her now, a pleasant, warm glow spread through my stomach and I realised how much I missed her. I wondered about what she did all day, to whom did she speak. No matter how hard I tried, I couldn't get her out of my mind. Her slim, lithe body, legs that seemed to go on forever, the tussled hair, finely chiselled features, sun-kissed skin. Sitting close to her as we went through the archives of world history were just about the happiest moments of my life. I breathed her in, taking little notice of the images and facts swirling around me. What Warren told me was nonsense. Why he told me those things, I have no idea. To confuse me, turn me against authority, who knows? Who cares? All I cared for now was the close proximity of her body, and when she pressed her thigh accidentally against mine, I recalled the thrill, the desire exploding in my loins

I rubbed my face vigorously with both hands, trying to rid myself of the picture of her face. But I couldn't. She kept looming up in front of me, smiling that smile. Making me feel weak.

I slammed my fist down on the desk in frustration and stood up.

"Do you require refreshment, Simeon?" The somewhat concerned voice of the computer filled the room.

"No. I just want answers."

"I have answers, Simeon."

"I want to know about Stem Cell Technology. I want to know how it is possible that scientists have been able to do away with males, making them redundant. I want to know how long it will be until the world has no more men in it." There was silence. Defeated, I sighed and ran a hand through my hair. "Yes, I'll have some refreshment."

These were the other things she'd told me. The Protector's wife. Society no longer required men to carry out their 'natural function', as she'd so clinically put it. Everything was now going to be done in the laboratory. Only very few men would be required. Exceptional men. Leaders. A way had not yet been found to do away with the natural function of women, their ability to develop children, give birth. Perhaps one day. But not yet.

The hover-maid brought me a drink and I took it. It tasted slightly salty. There was very little fresh water now, most of it coming from the desalination plants all around the coast, wherever that was. "Computer," I said, suddenly having a thought, "map of the world."

Instantly the wall blinked to show a detailed map of our world. Or, should I say, the parts we were allowed to see. I stepped up close and ran a hand over our own country. Very small, compact, the cities highlighted in red. Only four remained after the ravages of the Wars. Central, Northern, Far Northern and Island One. Island One. I wondered where that was. My geography was pretty awful, having learned nothing at school. Just the names of places, not their actual location. I wondered what they feared we might discover. Corrigan had given me a map, a map showing the location of a secret area, but I had few clues of how to find it. Nothing but a red line, a thin scratch across the surface. Where to begin? And was it really so important anymore?

The door hummed. I gave a start, causing my drink to spill to the floor. The hover-maid appeared and did its job, sucking up the mess in a fraction of a second. "Would you like another?" it asked.

I ignored it and looked up to the screen to see who it was at the door. It was a Sweeper.

I felt sick.

Why would a Sweeper come calling at my door? At anyone's door? Why didn't he just step through, they had passkeys to every building in the city.

It hummed again. I told the computer to open it.

"Hello, Simeon," the Sweeper said brightly as he stepped inside. Without thinking, I moved past him and checked down the corridor. He was alone. This in itself was unusual. Sweepers almost always patrolled in pairs, often in threes.

Closing the door I watched him as he scanned the room. He was colossal. They always were, of course, but this one was truly huge, the bunched muscles across his shoulder straining beneath the dirt-brown material of his coat. He turned to me and smiled. "Yes," he said in a kind voice, aware of what I was doing, what thoughts were racing through my mind. "I'm a unit commander, Simeon. You've never met a unit commander before."

He said it as a statement, because he knew everything about me. Every single detail of my life, embedded in the chip. Slowly he lowered his bulk into a chair. Then he did the most remarkable thing, he reached up with both hands and pulled off his helmet, pressing a little plate in his chest to disconnect the neuron cables that ran from his brain into the back of the casing. He sighed deeply.

His face looked like anyone else's, except paler than most. A broad nose, thin lips, eyes which appeared bloodshot and tired. His short, matted hair, flattened onto his head, sparkled wet with perspiration. Taking a white tissue from one of his coat pockets, he dabbed at his forehead and blew out a long breath. "Questions and explanations," he said softly.

I sat down opposite him, waiting. Before long, he launched into a speech, and I listened without interruption.

"Simeon, you've learned some things that you shouldn't really have been told about. Things that, if the general populace discovered, could well lead to disturbances. We've had a few days of intense violence, Simeon. You yourself have been affected by it. Surely you don't want it repeated? Those terrible wounds? The danger, the fear of death…" He shook his head. "Simeon, we all know what happened. The good Protector's wife has made everything very clear to you, and now you have a responsibility, Simeon. A responsibility of silence. Do not speak of these things, do not pursue them. Simply accept them, Simeon. You have your place in the Academy, a place you have earned through your own, exceptional endeavours. You are, to put it mildly, an outstanding student, gifted, supremely intelligent. Life will be different once you enter the Academy. *You* will be different, Simeon. Very, very soon everything will become clear and you can stop worrying so much about why things are the way they are. Indeed, you will become such a part of them that you accept them without question. You will embrace our new society without fear and you will feel all the better for it. Until then, stay at home, study, take your medication and play some virtual games. You used to like them, so rediscover them. Stop beating yourself up with what has happened, or thoughts of what might happen. Become a vessel to be filled with new knowledge, Simeon. Acceptance is the key. Anything is possible now, Simeon, from the comfort of your own armchair. No one goes outside now. No one needs to."

"They did the other night, when they were summoned."

"The other night?"

"Yes. I mean, I *think* it was the other night. Perhaps it was weeks ago." I leaned forward. "What happened to that red-headed girl?"

He bristled, shifting his weight uneasily in the chair that was obviously too small for him, and dabbed at his forehead again. "You see, that is *exactly* the sort of thing I'm talking about. What has the other night got to do with anything? A few people became alarmed at the news of the Protector's death and they panicked. That's all."

"The girl? Why was she singled out?"

"A malcontent. That was all she was. Her partner attacked you, did he not?"

"But *why* did he? What have I got to do with any malcontents? What possible threat could I be to them...?" I stopped, turning my face away to gaze into the distance. Was that the reason? He'd attacked me because I actually *am* a threat to anyone seeking to undermine our society? I turned to him again. "All right, let's just assume that what you say is correct. The girl was a malcontent, so she had to be...removed. What about what happened afterwards? Those paratrooper-droids? Why did they attack, where did they come from? And what happened?"

After a final mop of his brow, he began to refit his helmet, the cables bleeping as they connected. "You have to report to Programming in two days."

"Why won't you answer those questions? She never did, the Protector's wife. What are you afraid I'll do with the information?"

He paused, the helmet in his great hands, his eyes mere slits, alive with anger. "Your tone is disrespectful, Simeon. Remember who you are – and who I am."

The room grew ice-cold. He'd come here to press home the idea I needed to accept. I thought I could, but seeing him, being so close, made me realise that no matter what anybody said or did, I would always question. She knew that. The Protector's wife.

He stood up and I joined him, moving to the door, which opened with a swish.

He paused, readjusting his helmet then turned and scanned me. "Programming Central. Don't forget. Be early." He went to step outside, then slowly turned and placed a hand on my shoulder. "And no more questions, Simeon. Just acceptance."

I stood in the steely, sterilised whiteness of my room, going over all he said. They were afraid. Despite all they had done, to thwart me, I was still the rebel. My new chip had not succeeded in removing my knowledge of who I am. Who I was.

Checking my pockets, I found it was still there, taken from under my pillow in the hospital, so tiny I almost missed it. The nurses and orderlies' may have purposely over-looked it, or had its minute size caused it to remain undetected by the authorities. A broken chip, but with the information cell still intact. If they'd found it and scanned it, they'd know as much as I did. If they hadn't, and I truly believed they hadn't. I retained the advantage.

I patted my jacket where Corrigan's map was. Undoubtedly, they'd studied it. If I followed the route, I'd be followed. If I didn't, what would Corrigan do? He said he'd kill me if I didn't show. Well, I hadn't and I was still breathing. I'd been laid up in hospital for goodness knows how long. A chance to gather my thoughts, work things out. It would be best to simply do as the Sweeper had advised. Stay indoors. Play some games. Corrigan couldn't find me here. I was safe.

Being safe, however, no longer applied. I had to get the answers. That, at least, had remained unchanged.

Thirty-One

I retraced my steps of that first night, skipping from one wrecked building to the next, groping my way in the darkness until I stood in the freezing cold room where they'd beaten me and coerced me into going to the Protector. Just as then, right now my options were limited. I'd made the decision to come here, to the place where it had all begun, but I doubted there was anything in that abandoned place for me. It was just an old, derelict house.

I heard the tramping of marching feet and I instinctively crouched down in the darkness, a futile action, of course, as a Sandman's scanner could penetrate any material and would be able to find me within seconds. I held my breath. This was all so utterly stupid. They'd pick me up, interrogate me, then the Unit Commander would scold me and I'd be confined to my apartment, under guard, a prisoner in my own home. It was all going to end as abruptly as it had begun.

Crouching there, I remembered that first terrible night when I'd stumbled, lost, through the streets and made it to this place. The Sandmen had come...but then, as now, they hadn't followed me. In the darkness, I struggled to surmise why. Something had prevented the Sandmen from scanning me that night. It couldn't have been my chip, any fault would have been noticed long, long before. No, there had to be another reason.

Coming closer, the tramping feet continued on into the night. They didn't stop.

I squatted there for a few more moments, staring into space, thinking things through. I couldn't work it out. Something had blocked the Sandmen's scanning devices. The obvious place must be the door, so I shuffled across and ran my fingers down the metal panel separating me from the street beyond. Metal, but not hard, soft and giving.

Lead.

Lined with lead, Stoker must have fitted it to prevent the Sandmen scanning the interior. Simple, but was it true? Could lead prevent the Sandmen finding me? I wasn't sure, but it seemed reasonable.

I reached for my scar again, this time exploring it more carefully, searching for the outline of the chip.

There wasn't one.

Taking in several breaths, feeling as if a great heavy clamp was crushing my chest, I tried again. Again, despite the scar, I could feel no outline, no evidence of there being a chip beneath my skin.

Slowly, it dawned on me. That niggling doubt which had haunted me for so long. All this time I'd been walking around without the one thing that would ensure my capture. The Sandmen were good, but they couldn't scan you if there wasn't anything to scan. Despite myself, despite the dark and the cold, I couldn't help but grin as broadly as I could.

I was free.

Finding the crumbled house completely empty, with no trace of Stoker or any of his technology, I abandoned my search, eased open the door, took a swift glance down both ends of the street, and slid outside.

I jogged through the streets without fear. Old habits die hard, and whenever I heard a Sandman patrol – which was easy as they made so much noise – I'd hide in a doorway or down a coal-black alleyway and waited for them to pass. It was difficult to suppress the urge to run up behind them, tap them on the shoulders, then disappear again before they spotted me. In those cold, clammy streets, such thoughts were great fun.

Soon, buildings grew less, city streets giving way to wide, open stretches of blank ground. Occasionally, I would come across a dead body, and I studied the first few. They lay in twisted piles, blank faces staring upwards sightlessly to the night sky. Paratrooper drones, every one. Not being living creatures, I felt nothing for them, no revulsion, no glimmer of regret. Their failed task was to kill, destroy our society. One of their missiles almost killed Yolanda. Now, they were discarded junk, destined for the rubbish pit. I felt good knowing what awaited them.

A single question nibbled away in my brain as I moved through the broken wrecks of our attackers. Who had sent them? It was clear we had enemies – every country has enemies – but who were ours? The only thing we were ever told about foreign lands was that most of them lay in ruins, or was that just another lie? What if, and this was the burgeoning thought taking over now, none of it were true? What if *we* were the only country to have been affected by war and destruction? Perhaps other states, other nations, remained intact, untarnished by ideas of order and acceptance? Could there be other places where freedom and individuality were still values to be promoted, defended? Is that why we had been attacked – that we were the threat, the enemy?

I was growing tired. I'd been on the move for hours and by the time I reached the main supply road that ran into the city, I was in desperate need of rest. About half a kilometre from where I was, the great entrance gate to the city stood. Sweepers checked anything and anyone passing in or out. When I'd gone to the Protector's home a lifetime ago, the public transport system simply went through unhindered, everyone on board already scanned, as was the hoverbike which took me to his door. Anyone else, essential suppliers, officials on important business, all had to pass through a strict process of scans, checks, double-checks whilst Sweepers stood, gyro-lasers at the ready. I'd seen it but briefly on my journey to the Protectors but now, up close, I realised just how massive those gruesome gates were. Huge green blast doors, taller than a house, were locked together in the centre, supported on either side by tall pillars of solid metal, the tops bristling with multiple batteries of lasers. Spreading outwards from either side of these towers was the ring wall, a ten feet thick barrier of solid steel which encircled the entire city. Punctuated with more weaponry and festooned with scanning devices, it was a virtual impossibility to try to break out.

Keeping low. Although there appeared to be nobody about, I weaved my way towards some grim, featureless blockhouses. Dilapidated and forgotten, I forced the door of one and went inside. It offered some meagre shelter, and I tried to make myself comfortable. In the morning, with welcome daylight to lift my mood, I would have to try to think of a way to get through. Pulling my coat tightly around me, I curled up in a corner as an icy wind built up, cutting into the exposed flesh of my hands and face. With my knees clamped up against my chest, I let myself drift away as images of Sandmen and Yolanda danced through my mind.

I woke as the first streak of grey dawn filtered through the open roof of the bunker. The night had passed, with me in extreme discomfort, stretched out amongst broken bricks. I winced at the pain in my back and shoulders and when I tried to stretch I only felt worse. I had no food, no water and I felt dirty and cold. If I wasn't careful, the futility of my situation would overwhelm me and I'd start making my way back to the city and my home comforts, so I gritted my teeth, and made a conscious effort to push any negativity to the back of my mind. Scrambling over the debris, I wandered outside, dipped down behind a wall for a few seconds before I rolled over the coarse, brown grass and dropped down into a little dip.

I spent a long time lying on my stomach down there, well hidden thanks to the tall, tough grass which spread out across the plain. I watched. It was difficult to tell what was happening over at the gate from this distance, but the more I looked the more I realized that there appeared to be no signs of life at all. No traffic, no guards, nothing. After a long time, mostly spent chewing the inside of my cheek wondering what I was supposed to do, I took the decision to crawl forward, keeping myself as low as possible. It wasn't easy. The ground was flat, but hard, the grass as sharp as knives as it stabbed into me through my thin jacket. Rain rarely broke through nowadays, the weather patterns unpredictable, climate change accelerated after the nuclear winter of a dozen or so years ago, so everything was arid, hard, impenetrable. It hurt like hell but I was determined to push myself forward.

As I got closer I noticed two major things.

One, there was an enormous blast hole in the gate doors, big enough for a hover tank to get through. I'd missed it in the blackness of the night before. Secondly, not a living soul moved across that barren landscape. I looked, taking in every detail until I was certain before I took a deep, measured breath and stood up. If anyone was out there, they'd see me clearly – in that empty wasteland I would be as noticeable as a land battle cruiser, emblazoned with flashing lights. I had a plan of course, an explanation if someone, a Sweeper, challenged me, but it was feeble. But it would only be needed if I were spotted. Somehow, the longer I stood there, exposed, the more it became clear that nothing was going to happen.

I crunched on, constantly looking around, but growing more confidant the closer I got to the gate. It dominated my vision, rising high up into the sky, and was completely undefended. This unsettled me. The attack was real – what happened to Yolanda proved it. But, were the stories of defeating the attackers true? I was at the point where I doubted everything – but not the evidence of my own eyes. Whatever had happened here had caused the Sweepers to abandon the only entrance into the northern part of the city, leaving it completely open.

With the wind whistling through the mangled twists of shredded metal, I gazed up at the buckled, twisted doors. The missile, or shell, which had hit the gate, must have been of enormous power to carve such a gaping hole through the thick metal. It wasn't so much smashed as melted. The sheer heat from the projectile had simply sliced through without any resistance. Its awesome power was frightening. Such technology would be virtually impossible to resist, yet the Protector's wife had assured me that we were far in advance of our enemies in this field. But when my eyes settled on fallen Sweepers, corpses cut in two by lasers, dried, black blood leaking from shattered helmets, I saw it all for what it was.

More lies.

I could have stood there for longer, trying to work things out, but I knew I had to move on. Stepping between the mangled mess with caution, I threaded my way through piles of jagged, twisted metal. If I slipped and accidently hurt myself, it would be disastrous, alone in that empty place, no one to help me, so I took it slow. And as I edged on, I developed the unsettling idea I was being watched. Every few steps, I'd stop, listen, steadying my breathing, senses alert. But nothing stirred, the only sound the wind moaning through the debris.

On reaching the hole, I noticed a change in the metal beneath my feet. The pieces had fused together, the edges smooth where the heat had melted the metal, causing it to flow in tiny rivulets, folding over one another like liquid chocolate. Great boulders of this coagulated ruin were piled on top of each other and I climbed, probing with feet and hands, assuring myself of a good grip before hauling myself upwards to the top.

From my new vantage point, some twelve feet above the ground, I could see further evidence of attack on the far side of the gate. There were many more bodies. Paratrooper drones, and numerous Sweepers, which again caused me to doubt the Protector's wife. Our defenders, with their advanced technology, dead. Rooted to the spot, it was as if I too had melded to the metal heap upon which I stood. In every direction, stretching out into the distance, were the remains of the ferocious battle, the silent ghosts of charred hover tanks and fallen fighter-aircraft. Hover-copters lay in mangled mounds, bodies spewed out from their burst bellies. Great shell holes littered the ground, discarded weaponry and reactive-armour thrown around like so much litter. A horror scene, like some awful bloody throwback from medieval times, when battles were fought face-to-face, up close and terrible. Here was no war from a distance, conducted in the safety of control centres a thousand miles behind the lines – this was personal, hand-to-hand, and it frightened me to death.

The battle for the Northern Gate.

How many had died here, and what was the result? Why hadn't we been told?

Rubbing my face, exposed as I was, I knew this was not the place to be. Although it was over, the horrors still resided here, the ghosts of those who had fallen, the eerie silence hanging over that dreadful place, oppressive, dominating. I felt a trickle of iced sweat drip down into the small of my back and, keeping my eyes averted from the death around me, I mustered up my meagre courage, and got down on my haunches. Gathering my strength, I allowed myself to slide down the other side of my metal vantage point and tramped on, my legs heavy, stomach like water. Everywhere I looked I could see corpses. More and more of them with every step as I moved further into the battlefield. Drones, other humans dressed in black reactive-armour suits, and Sweepers, lots of Sweepers, littering the scorched earth. Earth that was no longer brown, but dyed red. Red with blood. The Protector's wife truly *had* lied. This was no glorious victory, but a massive defeat.

Breaking into a jog, I wanted to put as much distance between those awful scenes and myself as I could. I didn't care now if anyone could see me, I just wanted to escape. My legs pumped faster and soon I was sprinting, making for the nearest rise. As I hit that first hill the sudden scream of a siren shattered the still air. It was an awesome sound, massive and terrifying. I slammed myself flat down into the earth, covering my ears as the mighty wail filled the battlefield. Wriggling forward, I managed to find a hole and I slid into it, drawing myself up into a ball, head down, pressed into my knees, hands clamped to the side of my head, my whole body trembling with fear. This was it, I had been spotted.

Someone, or something, had been there all the time, watching me.

Thirty-Two

From out of the distance, it came – the steady tramping thud of a Sandman. There had been no evidence of Sandmen amongst the debris. The ultimate killing machine, it had once more proved its worth and it had prevailed. And now it was coming for me. I knew it would find me, the only living thing in that hellish plain, but I also knew it would take longer than usual because I had no chip. Once it spotted me, however, it would run me down with those great, long legs. My only hope was to try and remain concealed in that little dip. But it was so close, so close I could hear the whir of its mechanical limbs, imagining its head swivelling, scanning the horizon, searching. Searching for me.

Hardly able to contain myself any longer, I had an overwhelming desire to steal a look. Just a peak. It wouldn't see me if I was careful, but I had to know for sure. Curiosity was eating away at me, gnawing at my common sense. I'd be quick, it couldn't do any harm.

So I slowly raised my head over the lip of the hole I was curled up in. At first, I couldn't see anything. There were the gates and the battlefield, but no Sandman. Very slowly I looked around, checking. Nothing. Not a single living thing moved across that desolated plain. So, taking a breath, I half stood up.

My stupidity was laughable. Of course I couldn't see it because it was below the rise! As I stood up further, there it was, still and silent, like a watchtower, waiting. Its sensors must have been working over time, trying to locate my position. I froze, not daring to move, or even breathe. It may not be able to scan my missing chip, but it could certainly *hear* me, and that would be enough for it to pinpoint my position. So I remained as if in a trance, forcing myself to keep as still and as quiet as I could. Perhaps I *was* in a trance, fascinated by its sheer size, and also by its invulnerability. The Sweepers were good, but this thing was indestructible. It had survived this terrifying battle, had no doubt slaughtered hundreds of the enemy. And now it was after me. When it found me, I would be dead. There could be no other possible outcome.

All I needed to do was stay absolutely still.

As I stood frozen, I grew aware of a steady rumble from way off in the distance, initially a faint growl but growing noticeably louder. The Sandman swung round in the direction of the noise, then stood rock-still, listening. I listened too. The rumble came from the north and it was a sound I knew very well. Unmistakeable, like nothing else. Drawing closer.

The sound of a Harley-Davidson Sportster.

It exploded over the rise, moving at a frightening speed, the great bike jumping the hummock, engine roaring as it left the ground, tyres annoyed to be in mid-air. The machine hit the ground with a crunching thud and the rider slewed it to a halt, rolled off and, before he was fully upright, raced down the hill without a pause. I watched, spellbound, as he fumbled for something inside his coat and produced a small black box. The Sandman was spinning, its helmet up, laser ready to fire, all of its complicated technology working overtime. It moved in a blur, an elegant and precise action, surprising for something so big, and prepared to destroy its attacker. I held my breath, not wanting to look, but feeling compelled to do so, my morbid curiosity getting the better of me. Nothing happened. There was no blinding flash of light, no singe of burning flesh. The Sandman froze in its act of attack, teetered forward and then crumpled, falling flat on its face, lifeless.

Slumping to the ground, mouth gaping, I let my breath out in a long, slow stream, unable to comprehend what had just happened due to its suddenness. And as I sat, in stunned silence, a shadow fell over me. I looked up to stare into that face I knew so well. Grinning like a lunatic, inflating his cheeks, he ran the back of his hand across his brow and peered at the sweat glistening there.

"Intense." He looked down at me. "Hello there, Simeon." Stretching out his hand, he pulled me to my feet. "Still works," he declared, brandishing the immobiliser. "Are you okay? Not hurt or anything?"

My brain was numb, disengaged, and, unable to find any words, I shook my head.

Warren grinned again. "Well, in that case," he nodded towards the fallen Sandman, "we'd better get out of here before his mates come along."

He led me like a child over to his Harley and, once again, I found myself on the back of his bike as he kicked it into life, revved up the engine, and roared off into the countryside.

As I clung on, I slowly began to piece together what had happened and, more importantly, how. More questions for me to log away. More mysteries. With my head spinning with it all, the only good thing, I reassured myself, was that I was still alive.

Thirty-Three

Arriving some hours later at Warren's hideaway, I ate real food, not the synthesised muck served up for me back in the City. Bread. Unleavened, he called it, but delicious. We'd ridden to his place, hardly ever slowing down, even when we crossed bare, broken country, and I was feeling shaken and confused. He had sat me down and given me water and bread and, as the shock subsided, I gradually felt more normal. The Sandman was long gone. So was the battlefield, and the City. I'd made good my escape. Now all I had to do was find out how in the name of sanity Warren the Biker had known how to find me.

Munching through his own food, he sat there, staring as if he were scanning me. I wriggled about in my seat, his gaze boring into me, disconcerting in its intensity. The creaking, part-broken wicker chair beneath me felt as if it would collapse at any minute. Not unlike my courage. Laughing, Warren stood, knocking away the crumbs from his trousers, and went into his little house. After a few moments he returned, a small stubby bottle in his hands. "Beer?" he asked.

I stared blankly and he merely shrugged, raised the bottle to his mouth and drained it in one. Smacking his lips loudly, he came over and flopped down beside me. I could smell the beer on his breath and I pulled a face.

"Simeon," he said, laughing, "you've got a lot to learn." He reached over and felt the back of my head. "As I thought. They've taken it out. Who did it?"

"I don't know."

"You don't know? Just as dense as you ever were."

"I'm not dense, damn you. I'm just confused. After we were attacked, I woke up in a hospital bed, and ..." Catching his slightly amused expression, I took in a deep breath. "You know everything, don't you?"

"Most of it."

"I thought as much. But today, at the gate – how did you know where I was?"

"Scanned you."

"*Scanned* me? But that's impossible, I haven't got a chip – you said so yourself."

He shook his head and pointed to my jeans. "You've got a chip in there, Simeon."

I blinked and instinctively touched my pocket to feel the piece of micro-chip there. "But…but how could you scan it? The Sandman couldn't."

"No. That's because I made it and it's beyond his range. It's a homing-device."

"A homing…?" I stared like an idiot towards the ground, confused, lost in my attempts to comprehend his words. "You *made* it? But…but I found this…it was just lying there…"

"Convenient, eh? Didn't you ever suspect anything, Simeon? Did you really believe it was just an accident that you found it?"

"But a *homing-device*? Not a chip at all?"

"No. Just made to look like one. Simeon, I had to know how to find you. Look, I had an idea that you might go back to the place where you met Stoker, I even had an inkling that you might go and meet Corrigan back at the monorail station, but I couldn't be certain. The hospital too…I left it for you to find, and you did. You didn't question it, you just picked it up. You're too predictable, Simeon. That's a dangerous trait."

"This is all…so unbelievable…" I delved inside the small jeans' pocket and lifted out the tiny microprocessor. "So, with this device you could track me, you knew where I was?" He grinned. "But how come no one else could do that?"

"Because I'm clever," he lay down, stretching himself out on the hard earth, hands behind his head. "This is so much better than being in that awful city, don't you think? The City almost killed you, Simeon. When it was attacked."

"You know about everything, don't you – and you know who did it?"

"Of course I do – like I said, I'm clever."

"You're pompous, I know that much – a big-headed a user, a manipulator." I threw back the chair and strode across to the Sportster, lost in confusion and uncertainty as to what to do next. As I listened to its engine clicking as it cooled down, I had a sudden urge to kick it, to unleash my anger upon its hard, unforgiving metal body. I took in some deep breaths, giving myself some time to calm down. Yes he was pompous, arrogant too, but at he had helped me. I should have felt gratitude, not anger. "You saved my life, and I'm grateful for that. But I know you only did it for your own, selfish reasons, to further your plans to destroy the Sandmen. I wish you'd just left me alone."

"Do you? So you could become a pawn of the Protector's wife, is that what you mean?"

I turned to look at him, trying to read something in his words. He seemed to have such a knowledge, such an understanding of everything that had gone on. How was that possible, living out here, in the middle of nowhere? "What do you know about her?" He shrugged, non-committal. "She told me many things, showed me old newsreels and films. All of those things you told me, about our history and who were are, where we came from. All of it was lies."

"Really?"

"Yes, *really.* You told me we had *created* people from Asia, for our own reasons and when we had finished with them, we destroyed them. And black people from Africa. It was all nonsense, made up. How could you say those things? *Why* did you say those things?"

"You didn't check them, did you? You didn't go back home and research it. None of it. You just swallowed the whole lot, without question." He sat forward, clasping his hands together, "That's always been the problem, Simeon. Small-minded people, told lies that pamper to their own narrow-minded, bigoted beliefs. Leaders reinforced such prejudices, such phobias, and manipulate the masses, causing them effortlessly conform because they believe, wrongly, that these leaders are acting in *their* interests. But leaders only ever serve their own ends. I would have hoped that you, of all people, would see through such a charade."

"Well, perhaps I was confused, frightened, especially after the incident with the Wild Men."

"You've worked that out, surely? Holographic images, Simeon, created by myself, to confuse you, trap you, perhaps even make you feel grateful for my saving your life." He sat up, shaking his head. His lips formed the words, but I could see that he had no interest in their impact. What exactly was I to him? He'd said I was a pawn for the Protector's wife, wasn't the simple truth that I was just as much his pawn? "She showed you a lot of things, revealed a great many truths... but can you trust *her* Simeon, any more than you can trust me?"

"It was thanks to her that I began to do exactly what you said – question."

"Well, hooray for her."

I ignored his sarcasm. "Now, I don't know who or what to believe anymore. You – or her." I went back to the table and sat down, picking up a last scrap of bread, playing with it in my fingers. "Who *is* she?"

He gave a groan as he stood up, rubbing his knees vigorously, then ran a hand through his tangled beard. Finding the point of his chin, he scratched himself, making a face. "I hate this thing." He shrugged his shoulders a few times, as if he were trying to ease some tension. At last he deemed he should answer my question. "I know a lot about her, Simeon. Not much of it very…palatable." Sitting down opposite me, he leaned forward, clasping his hands together and fixed me with his icy glare. "Did she tell you about the stem-cell technology developments?"

"How…No, not in detail, not really. Only some vague words about society having no use for men…What has that to do with anything? More to the point, what's it got to do with *me*?"

"You've made the Academy, Simeon. You're in. Do you know what the Academy is, Simeon? Do you know what happens there?"

I chewed my lip for a moment, ruminating over the question. He was tying me up in knots, not answering my questions, going from one topic to the next. Where they linked? The Protector's wife, stem-cells, the Academy? The Academy…In truth, I didn't really have a single clue what it was or where it was. All I knew was what others had told me, that it was a real place, not virtual, that only the very top-rated students went there, to learn how to become the very best scientists and programmers. Nothing mysterious, or at least I didn't think so. From what Warren was hinting at, it was something much more. "Perhaps you should tell me."

He nodded, closed his eyes for a second before tilting his head back and looking at the sky. He sighed. "It's getting cold. Let's go inside, and I'll make us a hot drink. Then, I think you need to know the truth, Simeon. All of it."

* * *

Warren handed me a steaming hot cup of something dark brown in colour. I arched an eyebrow, not absolutely sure what it was. Giggling, he fell into a chair and crossed his legs at the ankles. "It's hot chocolate. Give it a try – you won't regret it."

I eyed the drink suspiciously for a second before taking a small sip. It tasted delicious. I nodded my appreciation, "My God, this is …" I licked my lips and took a second sip. "This is wonderful. I don't think I've ever tasted anything so—" I stopped when I saw the expression on his face. "What's the matter?"

"The Protector's wife – took a fancy to her, did you?"

"Are you mad? Why do you think that?"

"Because everyone does." He shifted position, reaching out for a poker to stir through the spluttering logs piles up in the hearth. "She is quite delicious herself," he nodded towards the mug in my hand. "You'd swap her for that, I'm sure."

"You're insane."

"Am I?" He threw another log on the fire and sat back, wallowing in the luxurious glow. "Let me tell you how it is, Simeon. The Protector was out of control. He, together with his wife, had allowed huge advances to be made in genetic technology, unchecked, unregulated. The Sweepers and the Sandmen were only the *visible* parts of this. The real danger was the development of stem-cell technology, first begun over fifty years ago and now advanced to a geometric rate. In the first decade of the twenty-first century, scientists discovered the beginnings of how to develop life. *Life,* Simeon. Not quite artificially, but in a way that would mean that the male of the species would eventually become redundant. I'll not bore you with the details, but twenty years later the advances they had made caused the government – *all* governments, actually – to outlaw the research. That didn't stop it, of course. It simply went underground. Then, in the early twenty-forties, sea-levels gradually began to rise and the world had to finally wake up to what it had been doing to the environment. Low-lying areas became deluged, causing massive destruction. With millions dead, everyone took their eyes off the ball. Research into stem-cell technology was forgotten, and so it continued at an even greater rate than before."

I watched as his eyes suddenly darkened, as if the knowledge he was sharing was too great, too painful. I saw then a man who cared, not one who lied.

He jerked his head up, as if snapping himself out of some self-imposed hypnotism. "As China and India reeled from the effects of the sea rising, war was inevitable. The outcome was horrendous. Both countries had awesome stockpiles of nuclear weapons…" He jammed his fist into his mouth, a single tear spilling down his face. When he spoke again, his voice sounded frail, like that of someone far older. "The Far East became a wilderness. Billions died, Simeon.

Billions. We tend to ignore all of that now, having successfully buried it for so long. What we were left with, however, was a vacuum. A vacuum that was filled by Europe. It was almost as if the clock had gone back to ancient times, with Rome at the centre of the world. You know about Ancient Rome? Empire? World domination? Well, it was like that again. Except this time, there wasn't much of the world left to dominate. The air was poisoned, millions were starving, it was chaos. Our own government became more despotic, more tyrannical. The Protector was seen as just that, a protector of what was left. As we managed to survive, to find some sense of order, other nations were jealous, envious of our technology, the advances we had made. War broke out again. The Fourth War as some call it. Someone once said the Fourth World War would be fought with sticks and stones. Well, it wasn't. It was fought with the most advanced technology known to mankind, and we won, Simeon. The Sweepers won. Our society survived, with all its flaws, all of its weaknesses, all of its dangers. We found ourselves at the top of a very precarious perch, and we had to think about what exactly we were on top of – a ruined, bleak and desolate world. The Protector took measures to preserve what was left. Parents, grandparents, relatives, were all removed. Systematically and ruthlessly. Only the children remained. It was the beginning of the end, Simeon. An end brought about by revived research into how to produce life without the need of males. And the champion of this, was the Protector's wife. It was she who has pushed the research forward, it is she who wants it to succeed. Not because she hates men, but because she can see the logic. A world without men, *thinking* men, could well be a better world. A more caring, cleaner world. But at what cost. The cost of love and togetherness. A cold world. A world without emotions. Safe, but empty."

He put his head in his hands for a moment. I sat rigid, playing with the mug between my fingers. I didn't know what to say, how to respond. I had no words, I just felt overwhelmed by what he had told me, numb.

Pulling down his hands, he blew out a long sigh. "So, I made a decision. Not an easy one, not a quick one. I took months thinking of what to do. Then I learned about you."

"Me?" I'd found my voice, but perhaps it would have been best if I'd remained silent. His answer was not something I wanted to hear.

"You were the rising star of your year, Simeon. *Any* year to be precise. Every now and again, someone comes along who is exceptional. Plato, the Buddha,

Jesus, Jung, Einstein…Right now, that someone is you. You passed every test, you completed every assignment, you had a *thinking* mind, Simeon. The ability to question, despite the chip. In a world without men, you would be king! Think of that. It's what she told you, surely? That there would be some men needed, exceptional men? Men to lead."

"Yes, but I never thought she meant *me*."

"Well, she did. You have been groomed from an early age. Did you never stop to think why your chip was malfunctioning all the time? Why you, unlike anyone else, had memories?"

"Yolanda had some."

"Yes. *Some.* You had masses of them. There is no one in that city, or any other city in the world, who remembers the things you remember, Simeon. No one. And despite everything they did, all the times you had to have things reconfigured, reprogrammed, new downloads, et cetera, nothing changed. You still had memories. Your school was contacted. There was no sense to it. You were lazy, haphazard, sometimes you'd work, sometimes you wouldn't. Assignments were late, often just scribbled down notes. But everything, *everything* was perfect. Whether you were late or not, it didn't matter – you got everything right. You were a total mystery, a glitch in their software. So, they had a choice. Eradicate you, or develop you. They chose to develop you."

"But why? I just don't get this – why do that if I posed such a threat? I must have posed them a threat, surely. Is that true?"

"Oh yes, very true. There were some in government who were convinced you had to be killed. Fortunately, there were powerful voices in your corner, Simeon. The Protector was one. His voice was the most powerful of all, of course. Then there was his wife. His wife saw in you the hope of a new future. She saw you as the natural successor to her husband."

I shook my head, a head swelling with the bombardment of facts. "That role would pass to the Deputy-Protector, surely?"

Warren gave a scoffing laugh. "The Protector's wife hated him. She would do anything in her power to prevent him ever gaining control."

"But why? I don't understand. Why would she hate him so much?"

There was a long pause during which time Warren seemed to look back into the recesses of his memory. His eyes misted over slightly, affected by something, or someone. Then he looked at me, and smiled warmly. "Because he was in love with her."

He spooned some strange looking worm-like things onto a plate and placed it before me. Laughing, he sat down opposite and spooned pieces of the revolting slime straight into his eager mouth. I had to look away. "It's pasta," he said between mouthfuls. "Cheese, grated on top. It's delicious. Try some."

I stared down at the white mound and felt my stomach lurch again. Closing my eyes I pushed the bowl away. "No thanks." I drank the water he'd given me as hunger gnawed away at me, twisting around in my gut, making rational thinking difficult. The bread I'd munched only served to make my stomach yearn for more. I glanced down towards the bowl, poked at it with my fork. How could I eat *that*?

Warren sat back, his plate empty. Licking his lips, he closed his eyes for a moment; I couldn't help but focus on the little shreds of pasta that populated his beard, an even more disgusting sight than the food. He caught me looking, noticing my reaction and took a napkin to wipe his face, which resulted in only a slight improvement. "Sorry," he muttered. "You know Senior Administrator Taylor Andrews?"

"Who?"

"Taylor Andrews? He's the head of all education within our society. He's your Principle's boss."

"I don't think so. How should I know him?"

"Because you've met him. At Stoker's."

I gawped at him. "What the hell do you mean by that?"

Thoroughly pleased with himself, he sat back, and folded his arms across his chest as if he were waiting for something.

It wasn't a long wait.

The door opened and I turned to see two men striding in. Two men I knew well.

Pushing my chair backwards, I jumped up, instinctively pressing myself against the far wall, my mouth suddenly very dry, a squeezing tightness clamping my heart against my chest.

Corrigan was grinning. It wasn't a friendly grin, not at all. More like triumph. Looming up behind him, the second man, the man I'd seen so long ago in that little room of Stoker's. The man who I sensed was evil, twisted. He was there, and his eyes glinted in that same maniacal way. As before, he didn't speak, he just stood, measuring me with his unblinking stare.

It was Warren who broke the silence. He sat unmoving, smiling. "Have you got the piece of paper Corrigan gave you, Simeon? The map."

I gave him a quick glance, feeling trapped, helpless. I nodded, dumbly, like a fool. Because that's what I was. Trussed up, like a prime turkey. I wasn't brave or single-minded anymore. I was lost, alone and confused. The evil one shifted position slightly, the movement snapping me in to action and I brought the paper out. At once, Corrigan stepped forward and snatched it from my grasp, slapped it onto the tabletop and smoothed it out. He was smiling. The evil one looked at me. He seemed pensive. What was he concerned about? The hairs on the back of my neck were rising.

Catching my mood, Warren leaned over the table. "Don't worry about him, Simeon. He used to be a Sweeper."

I gaped at him. "A Sweeper? How can anyone 'used to be a Sweeper'?"

"You never completely forget."

He'd spoken. Turning my face to him, I saw the glint in his eye, as if he were scanning me. The Sweeper's helmet is fused into the cortex of the brain. I'd seen the Unit Commander detaching his, but there were still some wires connected, onto his spine. But how could the entire contraption be removed without causing irreparable brain damage? But here he was, standing there, speaking to me in a flat, almost robotic tone. Was this the payment he had made for his freedom?

"This," Warren was stabbing at the paper, "this is a plan. A map. No doubt *she* took a copy and is right at this very moment sending an army of Sweepers to this very spot. By 'she', I mean, of course, the Protector's wife." His finger jabbed the large 'x' that glared out from the surface of the paper. "They'll know that you've left the city by now, Simeon. Even without your chip to guide them, they'll deduce where you've gone. The trouble is, there's nothing there."

"Not quite," said Corrigan, smiling again. "Thing is, Simeon. We knew you'd be careless. We knew you wouldn't commit this to memory. We knew that sooner or later, the Protector's wife would get to you and you'd let your guard drop."

"My guard...look, no one 'got to me', all right. I was wounded, caught in the blast from a missile..."

"So you say," said the ex-Sweeper.

"What?" The trap was closing, the very air around me squeezed of all its goodness, leaving it poisonous, cold. I grew desperate, the heat rising to my jaw line. "Fuck you – of course I was wounded! Yolanda and I were both injured as the missile came through the window. I was knocked cold and woke up in a hospital bed."

"With the Protector's wife holding your hand."

I looked from Corrigan to the others, blank stares betraying nothing. They simply watched me. A bead of sweat ran down the side of my face but I didn't dare wipe it away, feeling that even such an insignificant movement would be judged as an admission of my lying. "It's true she showed me kindness, but she was also angry – angry that I'd helped you to kill her husband."

"Tosh!"

The ex-Sweeper's voice spat venom, and he took a menacing step towards me. I tried to back away from him, but already pressed up against the wall, I couldn't. I turned my face towards Warren, praying he would step in and help me. Surely he knew what I had said was the truth. "What do you think I am," I yelled, "some sort of informer? That I've led them here?"

Warren smiled, putting his chin in one hand and giving me an amused look. "But you couldn't, because I rescued you."

"Exactly! So why don't you stop with the accusations."

"No one's accusing you of anything, Simeon."

"Insinuations then."

"You're clever," said the ex-Sweeper, standing so close to me I could smell his sweat. "Perhaps too clever. Why didn't you get rid of the map?"

"I didn't know I had to. Look, if they did take a copy, well they'll go to wherever this place is," I nodded towards the map. "Then they'll find nothing and they'll have missed their chance."

"More than that," said Warren, his voice steely, cold.

I frowned at Warren, hearing something in his tone. Something like triumph.

He continued, still smiling, "You see, the thing is, we *knew* you'd 'forget' to get rid of it. So, they've gone there," he tapped the 'x', "and when they get there…just around now…" He reached inside his waistcoat and brought out a small digital device. He quietly spoke into it and suddenly the far wall metamorphosed into a large viewing screen. I stared at the view blankly. It was nondescript, just a flat plain. There was nothing there that I recognised and I shot a puzzled glance his way. "Just watch, Simeon. Watch and learn."

So I did. The scene on the wall came into sharper detail; two ramshackle buildings, surrounded by a collapsed fence. The view was obviously taken from a high-powered telescope and showed everything from a wide-angle lens. There was no sign of life at first and I shifted uneasily from one foot to the other. Everyone else watched in silence, all of them waiting for something to happen. And then, it did. Unexpectedly, three or four hover bikes loomed into view, appearing over the far distant rise of hills, quickly followed by two hover-copters. As they ground to a halt, two dozen or more Sweepers spilled out, spreading out, taking combat positions, gyro-lasers ready, surrounding the entire area. They trained their weapons on the building as voices crackled from loud speakers, 'You are surrounded. Give yourselves up!' I watched in disbelief as another figure stepped out from one of the 'copters. It was her, the Protector's wife. There was no mistaking her elegance, her striking beauty. She stood, hands on hips, casually observing her servants going about their job. She snapped an order which I could not hear, but which I nevertheless knew and I winced as the Sweepers charged forward, their lasers ready. Ready to kill.

I turned to Warren, willing him to tell me what was going to happen. He shrugged his shoulders. "She thought you were in there, Simeon. With us. She wouldn't have baulked over killing you. How does that make you feel?"

I said nothing and turned my eyes back to the screen just as the first Sweeper went through the main building's door.

Almost at once, there followed an enormous explosion. I jumped, instinctively shielding my face. The others laughed and I looked up. The screen had blurred, or was it smoke? Yes, it was a pall of thick, black smoke and as it slowly cleared everything came back into focus. And what I saw chilled me to my very bones.

It was all gone.

Everything.

I stood rigid, my brain not registering what my eyes had seen. From somewhere a distant rumble seemed to swell and grow, becoming louder and I felt it reverberating throughout the little house, shaking it to its very foundations. The explosion had been massive. And nothing had survived. Sweepers, 'copters, bikes, buildings, all obliterated in the wake of the terrific blast.

And her. The Protector's wife.

Dead.

Thirty-Four

We all stood for a long time, looking at the wall-screen in silence. There was little to see, the only remaining evidence of anything a blackened smudge in the centre. None of us could tear our eyes away from the smouldering remnants of that tiny homestead, nor come to terms with the horrific fact that nobody remained alive, all of them blown to pieces.

The first to find their feet, I went to the table and sat down. From somewhere within in me I hauled up the courage to sample the pasta still waiting in a bowl. Too hungry to resist, I pushed away any lingering revulsion and munched through the food in record time.

"It's over," said Warren quietly. I sat back and studied his blank expression. His words, not addressed to anyone in particular, brought nods of agreement from the others. A curious atmosphere clung to that room now, one of depressed resignation. There was no sense of triumph, or joy, or excitement. A sense of shame lay heavy upon us all.

"Why aren't you shocked, Simeon?"

I glanced towards the ex-Sweeper and frowned. He was giving me that look again. I shrugged. "Why should I be shocked?"

"Surprised then? You don't seem in the least bit bothered, almost as if you'd been expecting it."

"Really? Well, perhaps it's simply because I don't care."

"You don't even care about her?"

I avoided his eyes, staring down at the empty bowl. Of course I cared about her – she'd captivated me, and I longed to be with her, wishing the fleeting moments we shared would last forever. She showed me a new world – the past, and awoken so many buried emotions, so many memories. Much more than any of this, she had cared for me and I cared about her. I couldn't tell these men that, however. Once the mocking laughs had faded, they'd use my admissions to their own advantage, to ensnare me ever more deeply into their web of deceit. So I kept my face stoic, masking my feelings. "I care for her least of all," I lied.

That seemed to silence him, at least for the moment. He muttered something under his breath, turned away and strode outside. It was now Corrigan's turn to take a swipe at me. "I think you *do* care, you're just damned good at hiding it."

I knew my best tactic was to stay quiet, but I still had questions to ask. One question in particular had been gnawing away at me since the explosion. "What happens now?"

Exchanging glances, Warren and Corrigan took a moment, a silent agreement passing between them. Warren blew out a breath. "In around ten minutes or so, the first cohort will arrive and will move to the city to begin our takeover."

Stunned, I looked from one to the other. "Cohorts? Takeover? What does any of that mean?"

Corrigan laughed. "Perhaps you should show him."

"It'll certainly be a relief," said Warren.

"Well, there's no point anymore, is there?"

"No, I suppose not."

I had no idea what this exchange meant but as I turned to Warren, it all gradually grew so much clearer. With his eyes squeezed tight shut he slowly, and painfully by the look of it, gripped both sides of his beard and began to pull it away from his jaw. Mesmerised, I watched the beard part from the skin in a single sheet of tangled hair. He dropped it onto the table before moving first to his eyebrows, then the bulbous nose, made from some sort of rubber material, and finally, with a great theatrical flourish, the hair extensions. He tossed the whole mess into a far corner. Rubbing his face furiously, he stretched out his arms and beamed. "God, that feels better!" Now transformed, Warren the Biker bobbed his head, chuckling at my bemused expression. "Did you ever guess, Simeon?"

I wanted to say something, but my senses were reeling, my throat constricted. All I could do was force a feeble whimper from my quivering lips. He wasn't the Biker anymore.

He was Stoker.

* * *

Sometime later I sat motionless in front seat of a hover-copter. Never having seen one so close before, its sheer size staggered me. Stretching back into the interior, serried ranks of identical, black-clad paratrooper drones waited in silence, huge laser blasters at the ready. Pacing up and down between them was a large commander, who was human. He spoke in a language I didn't recognise, but he sounded tense and anxious. I knew now the battle for the Northern Gate was a curtain raiser for the conflict to come – the conquest of the City.

The strike-force arrived not long after Warren had completed his transformation into Stoker, effectively cutting off the multitude of questions were circulating in my head. Stepping outside, I turned my face skywards, the sun blocked out by swarms of aircraft, whilst all around rumbled heavy land battle-cruisers, tanks, assault vehicles, bristling with every conceivable type of armament, disgorging an endless stream of massively armed individuals. Officers barked orders, as the armoured machines assembled into battle formation. Soon the entire plain filled with an army of unprecedented size and I gazed upon it as one might do at rows of ancient toy soldiers upon a table-top. A fug rose from the bodies, a haze of grey clinging slightly above their heads and I turned to Stoker, who stood, arms crossed, grinning like an ape. I swept my hand over the incredible scenes before me. "Where the hell did this lot come from?"

For an answer, he rammed a battle helmet into my midriff. "You may need this," he said, the grin gone, his features now grim, hard resolve replacing his former carefree attitude.

"You can't be serious?"

"Deadly serious, Simeon. You're going to lead us to victory."

Corrigan appeared, suitably attired in reactive armour, and without a word he frog-marched me over to a waiting hover-copter. Clambering into the bench seat beside the pilot, I baulked at the sharp smell of sweat. The taste of fear caught at the back of my throat and when Corrigan slammed down next to me, I noticed his lips trembling. I realised then, if I didn't know before, that there really was no way back from this. We were going into battle.

Beyond the blast windows I saw the whole countryside bristling with a mass of armoured fighting vehicles, crammed with soldiers and droids, all waiting for the command to advance. "We're fighting for freedom, Simeon," said Corrigan, voice faltering slightly, "justice and righteousness. We've been making preparations for years – this is the moment we've all dreamt of."

His words, no doubt designed to instil pride and courage, did nothing of the sort for me. All I felt was a burning sensation in the pit of my stomach, every fibre of my being enmeshed with fear.

Over to my right, in another 'copter, sat Stoker, transformed from a tangle-bearded ruffian into a shimmering, white uniformed officer, golden chevrons on his shoulders, fully enclosed inter-active battle-helmet adorned with insignias of high rank. "How has this happened?" I snapped my head towards Corrigan. "Why would such a man skulk around in the dark of an abandoned house when he has the ability to lead so many, without question?"

Corrigan punched my knee and I glared at him. He was grinning, choosing to ignore my words like the fawning idiot that he was. "Don't you feel pride, Simeon?"

"Pride? Why should I feel pride?"

"Being part of all this," he swept his hand across the vista to the left and right of us. "This is one of the great historical moments of our age, Simeon. *Any* age! And you're part of it, my friend. You made it all possible."

I wasn't to be drawn by his flattery. I hoped my dull response reflected my depressed mood. "I did? How did I do that?"

"By helping us kill the Protector, of course. Hacking off the rotten head of the beast, Simeon. That's what you did."

"That's what she said, his wife. But you're both wrong. I didn't kill him."

"You may not have done the deed, Simeon, but your hand was on the knife. And, anyway, 'she' is dead."

I looked away, hardening my eyes, trying to prevent the sting of the first teardrop. "Yes. I know. So, now you and Stoker can step into her shoes. Is that it? What about the Deputy? Don't you think he'll have something to say, and the Sandmen? Whilst he's in control of them..." I stopped. Corrigan was laughing, and it was a mocking sound, contemptuous almost. "What's so funny?"

"You! You're such a fool, Simeon. For someone so bright, you really are very, very dense."

"Really? And you're so very, very wise, I suppose?"

"Well, let's just say I'm a damned sight better informed. You know how you've always been told about the war in the Middle East? How all of our resources were being put into that conflict? Well, it was all a lie. We'd lost that war over a year ago. All we were doing was surviving. Some of us took the decision to end the catastrophic system that had led us into virtually total oblivion. We made peace with our former enemies, made a pact. And that pact has almost come to fruition. We've got the chance to start again, to rebuild a world which is clean and bright. A world for our children. Children of nature, not of petri-dishes."

"But you'll still have to overcome the Deputy and his forces. Is that what this attack is? You've allied yourself with powers from the East? Is this your 'new age'? You've sold us out to a foreign regime?"

"Tripe. It's our only chance for survival. The Protector's dream was a future of clinical, sterile conformity. What we offer is humanity."

"Through death." I looked away, suddenly angry. If what he said was true, then my entire life had been built on dishonesty. All of the promises, empty. I chewed my bottom lip, struggling to understand. "You're no better than the Sandmen. And the Deputy will swat you like flies once he unleashes them."

"Simeon, haven't you worked it out yet? Are you really that stupid?"

I dragged the back of my hand across my nose, sniffed loudly. "Don't play games with me, Corrigan. I've had enough of those."

"Very well." He nudged me to turn around and then pointed towards Stoker's gleaming command vehicle. "There he is."

I followed his finger and frowned deeply. Then it all slowly dawned, the veil pulled back. I didn't need him to say anymore, I had all the answers right there in front of me and it was all so ridiculously simply – Stoker was the Deputy Protector.

Thirty-Five

The rumbling ranks of fighting vehicles went through the Northern Gate as if it wasn't there, whilst overhead a hundred and more flying vehicles, a black swarm filled to bursting with men and material, floated over the broken walls and headed towards the interior. No one stopped us, probably because no one was there. We swept over the outer suburbs and I heard the sirens begin to wail. I peered down. What few people there were on the streets ran like frightened rats, scurrying away to the limited safety of their homes. I watched in fascination as we banked away to the right, the great clouds of hover vehicles beginning to fan out across the sky, slipping between high-rise apartment blocks, swooping across city squares and central park, laser blasters shooting out streaks of death, hitting the occasional Sweeper as he tried to dodge out of the way. Nothing could impede our advance, we were simply too many, too powerful and I gripped my arm rest, grimacing, not knowing whether to feel elated or terrified. Is this how everything changed, through death and destruction? Could anything ever begin afresh without violence?

A group of Sweepers rolled over in various directions, gyro-lasers shooting out long streams of light. A nearby hover-copter took a direct hit, burst into flames and spiralled down to the ground out of control. It exploded on impact and I looked away. I met Corrigan's eyes. They told me nothing.

We came to the main city square, the great building of Programming Central looming up before us, black and foreboding, and the vehicles touched down, drone-troopers already running out of the vehicles before they had even come to rest. Apart from the occasional group of Sweepers, it had all been very easy. No doubt the battle for the Northern Gate had taken its toll on the City defenders, and no one seemed surprised at how little actual defence there had been.

Corrigan was pulling me out of the 'copter, grinning. I took a moment to scan the deserted streets and noted the piles of dead dotted here and there. My stomach lurched and I fought down the desire to throw up. Corrigan gripped me by the shoulder and we ran, bent double towards some over-turned, burned-out vehicles. I took in a sharp breath when I saw a dead Sweeper close up, his helmet pushed back to reveal his sightless eyes staring towards the sky. Before I could even begin to muster any kind of revulsion, Corrigan tugged me down, putting his face close up again me, so close I could smell his breath. "Something's not right," he muttered.

I didn't say anything, but I knew that what he said was right. There had been so few instances of resistance. The only thing that gave any clue that someone, somewhere was aware had been the sirens. The lack of any concerted opposition was curious and I felt the knot in my stomach tighten. Corrigan looked wide-eyed around him as the paratroopers poured out across the square, weapons angled towards the Programming building. I could see Stoker, standing up in his command vehicle, directing the troops forward. Beside him was the ex-Sweeper, the man whose eyes always held so much hatred and malevolence. They were some way off and, with us crouching down, I doubted he could see us. I was wrong. Perhaps his old skills had never left him, for his head seemed to revolve with all the deliberate slowness of a machine, and he spotted me, eyes like beacons picking me out, holding me in their virulent glare. I met his gaze and became lost in a sort of detached world, losing all sense of time and place. Corrigan shook me and I blinked, releasing myself from the ex-Sweeper's glare. As I continued to watch I saw it all unravel before my eyes.

The ex-Sweeper spoke into Stoker's ear, then he vaulted over the side and ran in the direction of the Programming building, head down. Stoker screamed furiously, but at that distance I couldn't make out the words. There was no need really.

I felt them rather than saw them. As Corrigan fell back, whimpering like some wounded puppy, I stared upwards. From over the top of the building they came, swarming over the roof like so many ants. They came down the front of the building, using their great long legs to eat up the distance, gravity as nothing to them. Like steamrollers of old, their progress was relentless, nothing able to stop them.

I looked back, to see Stoker as he fumbled for the immobiliser. A glint of triumph must have shone from his eyes, the certainty of victory overcoming him.

He swung it outwards, pointing it directly at the Sandmen as they steadily advanced. But the program had been nullified, the immobiliser's intricate circuits bypassed. Even from this distance, I could see Stoker's face crumple, disbelief etched into every line. How could this be possible? He tried again, pointing it at them, squeezing the black box as if more pressure might have an effect, but nothing worked. The thing was useless, its machine code assimilated by the Sandmen.

The Sandmen were immune.

Corrigan was screaming at me to move; half standing, trying to pull me up to my feet he had the look of an ensnared beast. Which was what he had become, what they had all become. I looked at him, feeling a strange sadness seep through me. I wanted to explain to him what was happening, but then the huge shape of a Sandman loomed over us, its great arm curling around Corrigan's midriff, slicing him in two as if he were a melon. Great gouts of blood spewed outwards and I turned away, shielding my face from the grizzly spray.

Not hanging around to see what the Sandman might do next, I sprang to my feet and ran from the utter chaos enacted all around me. Corrigan wasn't the only one to fall victim to the Sandmen. With the screams of the dying ringing in my ears, I sprinted over to Stoker, standing open-mouthed, watching Judgement Day playing out before him. I saw drones slaughtered, their weapons useless against the Sandmen, who swept their great cutting arms through the air, slicing off heads and limbs with ease. Human soldiers died in heaps, hover-copters and battle cruisers disintegrating as those who were too far away to feel the razor edge of the cutting arms were vaporised. Commanders screamed in terror, all control gone. Drones clattered to the ground, the sound of metallic limbs filling in the gaps between the cries of the human beings who died in their thousands. They ran, they routed. They all died. As the tanks and battle-cruisers approached, they met the same fate, Sandmen leaping on board, tearing away cupolas and turrets, slaughtering those inside, the blood flowing to the ground, turning it from insipid brown to vibrant red.

I tugged at Stoker's trouser leg and he stared down at me, his face ashen. I shouted to him, "Come on, we have to get out of here."

Our rolls were now reversed, he the helpless child, me the valiant rescuer, pulling him from his vehicle, rescuing him from the Sandmen. We made it across the square, just seconds before his vehicle was hit by a laser. It erupted into a great ball of flame, the blast throwing us to the ground. I lay there, stunned, spitting out bits of gravel from my mouth, a dreadful ringing thundering through my ears, enveloping my brain in a mass of white noise. From somewhere, I found the strength to get to my hands and knees. Stoker lay someway off, on his back, one knee arched, his other leg twitching. I crawled over to him, unable to hear anything except for that infernal ringing. I reached him and gazed into his face, saw those eyes wide with fear, moving from left to right. I breathed a sigh of relief – at least he was alive.

Shaking my head violently from side to side, the ringing gradually faded and I checked the distance between us and the steps leading up to Programming Central's entrance. Nothing barred our way, the Sandmen too intent on dealing out death far behind us. Mustering my strength, I dragged Stoker across the broken, blistered ground towards the main entrance. He was a dead weight, limbs as heavy and as unforgiving as lead. Blood leaked from his neck but I knew I had to continue. There was no time, simply no time at all. We had to keep moving.

We made the steps where I stopped, lungs bursting, every breath a monumental effort. My hearing had returned, and I registered a great roar filling the air overhead. From out of the blackened sky came more hover vehicles, flying low, their lasers trying to pick out the Sandmen. The huge mechanical beasts took the blasts without a flinch, invincible, and their returning fire knocked out machine after machine, some bursting apart instantly, others careering away out of control to smash into buildings, or the ground, where they erupted into great gouts of red and black flame. This must have been what it was like at the Gate. The air filled with the sound of defeat, all consuming and terrible.

I took a breath and pulled Stoker up the steps towards the huge doors.

Sandmen spilled out from the interior, their great legs making them move incredible fast. They strode past, ignoring us. I realized it was for the same reason – neither of us had chip. Perhaps, in the confusion of the fighting, their sensors didn't pick up our laboured breathing, perhaps they were too intent on killing others. I didn't care which it was, I only knew we had to keep moving.

Each step was like a movement up the north face of the Eiger. I'd climbed that mountain many times from the comfort of my room, knew its dangers, its hidden pitfalls. A virtual mountain in a virtual world. A lost world. The world of my past, to be filed away with the world my parents had inhabited, my Nan also. The only constant, the Sandmen. Then, and now. Would it ever be any different?

At last we reached the top step. I stood, gathering my strength, or what little of it was left, and chanced a look behind me. It was almost over; I could clearly see that. Burning hulks and mangled bodies filled my vision. Striding between them, the massive, resolute figures of the Sandmen. I turned away, went over to the doors and steadying myself, flattened my palms against the thick, solid oak panels, and pushed them open with all my strength. With painful slowness, as my shoulders screamed, they moved inwards.

I went back to Stoker, who by now was sitting up, and helped him to his feet. He looked at me, eyes unblinking, lost in his nightmare world. I led him inside.

Huge, wide and bright, the enormous entrance hall yawned back at us, completely empty. A cathedral to our sovereign state, its vaulted ceiling adorned with ancient paintings of gods, this magnificent edifice usually thronged with people waiting for chips to be re-configured, downloads completed, homes re-programmed. Sweepers were forever on guard, but not today. Today there was no one, the only sound the echo of our footsteps as we crossed the marble floor towards the central reception desk. The sounds of death and destruction from without were blocked by the great bomb blast doors through which we had just come, making the building a surreal centre of peace.

The reception desk matched the rest of the interior. An enormous, semi-circular affair, fashioned from brightly polished rose-wood, topped with dark brown leather, behind which receptionists once sat, locked into the massive mainframes. All that remained now was the bank of electronic equipment they had once used, with lights continuing to play across the panel. Stretching over, I spoke into one of the mouthpieces. Something flashed and I had the answer I wanted. I eased myself around and gave Stoker a reassuring smile. "Fifth floor. It would be safer if we take the stairs. If anyone knows we're here, the elevator will be the first thing they shut down." I didn't think Stoker needed that information. He seemed unable to register anything, his eyes like black pebbles, empty of emotion. He was in shock. Even the blood trickling down the nape of his neck didn't appear to cause him concern. It did me, however. I studied it more closely and hissed at the shard of bare metal protruding from his flesh. It looked nasty, the wound deep. I held his empty gaze. "Do you think you can make it?"

His face came up, but nothing registered in his expression. It was as if he were in a trance so, steering him by the elbow, I guided him towards the main stairway and slowly made our way upwards.

Successfully negotiating the first flight, it soon became apparent however that Stoker was suffering. A daunting climb at the best of times, a sedentary lifestyle, with everything provided at the wave of a hand, meant physical exertions were alien to most of us. Add to this the trauma of the battle and his wound, I did not think he would make it. Reaching the end of the third flight, he collapsed, breathing hard, face washed with sweat.

I sat next to him and peered upwards, groaning at what still lay ahead. Next to me, Stoker gazed at the little black immobiliser in his hands, no doubt wondering why it had failed. I placed my hand on his shoulder and he looked at me, a flicker of recognition returning to his eyes. "It'll be all right," I assured him, doing my best to form a smile.

He shook his head. "We've lost, Simeon." His voice sounded tiny, unsure. "I thought we could overcome them. I thought..." He looked again at the immobiliser in disgust and hurled it clattering down the steps. I watched it in silence until it finally came to a halt on the landing. It wasn't broken, but it was useless nevertheless.

"What went wrong, Simeon? I'd worked on the programming, used everything I knew about how the Sandmen worked, their computer systems. Here, here in Central Programming, I'd been able to move freely, doing what I needed to do before *she* became suspicious. I tried, tried so hard. I wanted her to see the awfulness of what she was attempting to do. But she wouldn't listen. She hated me and I...I loved her."

How do you help someone in the depths of despair? Someone blinded by love? I ballooned my cheeks. "Perhaps that was the reason, Stoker – you were too close, too blind to her. That's why you failed."

"No. No, I don't believe that. I was betrayed. Betrayed by Melling. You saw him run."

"Melling?"

"The ex-Sweeper."

I sighed. My recent experiences had taught me the lesson, the mantra repeated endlessly in my head, *Trust no one.* Now it was my turn to wonder how someone as intelligent as Stoker could be so easily taken in, be so gullible. "Didn't you ever question the notion of him being a Sweeper once, linked to Central Computing? His mind melded into the mainframe? How can anyone, ever, be an *ex*-Sweeper?"

Stoker's face crumpled, shoulders sagging, chin falling onto his chest. His voice was small and fragile as he continued, "I thought he could be trusted. I was wrong." His hand came up and I saw it was shaking. He ran it through the tangled mess of his hair. "I've known him for years. We met here, in this very building. He was a unit commander back then. We grew friendly, talking endlessly about our society, where it was heading, our shared dreams for the future. We had so much in common and he seemed to be in tune with everything I believed in. The first moment he removed his helmet and disconnected the leads to his cerebral cortex it was as if he were surrendering his role as a Sweeper to me." He put his face in his hands, the tears sprouting unchecked. "It was all a trap. He betrayed me. It must have been him that reprogrammed the immobiliser, given the codes to the Sandmen." His body became convulsed by great sobs. I sat there and waited, not speaking, just allowing him the time to drain himself of the terrible sense of betrayal that he so obviously felt.

After a few moments, I helped him to his feet. I had no intention of telling him about my suspicions of Melling, the terrible fear I felt the very first moment I laid eyes on him back in that derelict house. I knew then there was something very wrong about him. Nor did I wish to reveal the real identify of who reprogrammed the immobiliser. Not yet.

Taking him by the arm, we continued trudging up the stairs, I for one trying to keep my mind clear of how much farther we must tread, until at last we stood outside the entrance to the room where I knew the answers lay.

"This is it," I said but Stoker no longer cared, all of his former confidence, faith, call it what you will, replaced by the countenance of a defeated man. I touched his arm. "Let's go in," and I gently led him through the door.

It was a large square room, the desks arranged around the edges, buckling under the mass of blinking technology arranged on top. A huge panoramic window standing opposite the door dominated everything. It looked out like an all-seeing eye across the city and I noted how black the sky was, plumes of inky smoke drifting across the horizon. Leaving Stoker's side, I crossed over and gazed down to the square, where the battle was rapidly ending, the last few pockets of resistance wiped out even as I watched. And everywhere, the dead. Stoker's dreams erased. Sad. Sad and pathetic.

I stepped away and turned towards the computer array to my left, the many machines humming into life. Above them a liquid pool of undulating silver slowly materialised into a screen, and the voice, soft yet determined. "All ready?"

I nodded without speaking and motioned to Stoker for him to sit, turning my back on the screen, knowing there was no need for any further communication.

Stoker, like a man lost in a dream, stumbled over to the nearest chair, fell into it and gazed out of the window whilst I leaned back on the desk and waited.

It wasn't a long wait. The far door slid open and they came in. Three of them. They stood there, looking at me.

"You've done well, Simeon."

I looked down at Stoker, whose face registered the bafflement he must have been feeling at that point. For an age he was like a stone, perhaps not able to fully grasp what was happening. He leaned forward, eyes round with terror, imploring me to give him some sort of answer. "Simeon?" I shrugged my shoulders and he blinked rapidly, lips starting to quiver. Everything was coming back, little by little, his senses struggling to make some sense of what must have been dawning in his mind. He hadn't turned around yet, so it wasn't the entrance of the three people which had brought him back into reality, it was the voice of the person who had spoken. The voice of someone he knew only too well.

The Protector's wife.

Thirty-Six

He appeared as if he were a frightened child, lost, unable to find his parents. Abandoned. All of his dreams and ambitions were now as dust and he sat, mouth open, saliva drooling from the corner, incomprehensive written in every line of his haggard, drawn face as he turned to face the woman standing in the doorway. "But ... I saw you. I saw you blown to pieces."

For one fleeting moment, the urge to reach over and grip his arm, assure him he wasn't going mad, that actually things had all turned out for the best. The moment came, and it went. I remembered how they treated me, back in that old house, how they punched me, abused and used me. And Yolanda. How she was almost killed. How she was most probably never going to be able to walk properly again. It was all down to Stoker and his miserable, pathetic attempts to overthrow our ordered society. Some vestige of mercy may have ruminated deep inside my gut, but for the most part I wanted justice to be served – despite him loving her and seeing her now, standing before him, triumphant.

She glided across the room, her long fingers flickering over my arm as she passed by. Smiling, she gazed through the window, not giving Stoker the courtesy of a glance as she spoke to him. "It's all finished. You've lost. If you'd have been sensible, not so arrogant, and joined us none of this would have happened. But you were impatient and you were blind. So blind that you thought you could use Simeon to further your pathetic plans. And look where all of it has got you – to this room. Nowhere else. This is the limit of your ambition."

Clenching his fists until the knucklebones showed white beneath the flesh, Stoker groaned with barely contained fury. He made to stand up, but one of the others stepped smartly up to him, pressing him down into his seat. Stoker looked up into the face of the man and withered when he saw Melling measuring me with his hard eyes; the man whom Stoker had trusted, believed, now the one in control. If Stoker had wanted to resist, he showed no signs, his body sagging, his defeat complete. I doubted he had the strength, or indeed the will to do anything. To confirm my thoughts, his tired voice sounded like a death rattle as he turned to her, her back still towards him, "How could I join you in your loathsome deceits? I wanted a future for our people, not a living laboratory where you could indulge all your wild, insane ideas. Taking away parents was one thing, perhaps there was even some *reason* for that, some method in the Protector's madness. To create a world for the young – ordered, without fear, a world where everything was provided, and opportunity and success given to all." He shook his head. "But he want more – and so did you. Ultimate power, ultimate control. *You* would decide the type of people who would populate this planet. You yearned to be gods and I could not allow that."

"You pompous bastard," she spat and turned, motioning for Melling to step away. "It must be wonderful to be so perfect, so righteous. What gives you the claim to have all the answers?"

"I don't claim to have anything, all I know is that you had to be stopped. I tried to co-operate, I tried to talk some sense into you, but you wouldn't listen. And now – now it's all going to come tumbling down."

"Really?" She said mockingly, folding her arms, a sneer transforming her lovely face into something hard, maniacal almost. "And how is that going to happen – now, with all your dreams shattered? You've tried and you've failed, so who is going to bring about your Utopia now? Simeon?"

I started at the mention of my name but she merely smiled at my obvious alarm.

Stoker shook his head. "The people will rise up. You can't stop that."

"The *people*?" She laughed, a single biting barb and I saw him flinch. "The people will do as they're told. Why should they resist anyway, they'll have everything they ever wanted. Just as it was before you started your meddling. Your problem is that all of your ideals were set in the past. You never could look forward. You never could find the courage to change."

"I could have done, with your help."

"Oh yes, your well declared love for me. I suppose I could have relented, taken you in, let you think that you were a welcome part of my world...The funny thing is, I couldn't bring myself to be that cruel. Besides, I have other ambitions and they have nothing to do with love, or commitment, or any of those old-fashioned, dead ideas."

"Could I really have been so blind? You … The moments we shared. I thought…hoped…" He ran a hand through his hair, pausing in this position, as if overwhelmed.

"The moments we shared were nothing but biological functions. I had an itch, you scratched it. And not all that well, I might add."

His eyes flared. "You bitch." He directed his next question to me, teeth clenched, close to losing control. "What of you? How do you feel about all of this? Your betrayal?"

I spread out my hands, palm up. "You talk to me of betrayal after all you did to me? The things you said – your threats, your lies? I had little choice in any of this. From the very start I've been a pawn in this *game.*"

"Don't blame Simeon," she said, her voice crackling with a spark of anger. "The poor boy had no choice, like he said. You see, we have Yolanda in a state of perpetual suspended animation. She won't age, she won't become ill, but if he doesn't conform…we switch off the life support."

I looked at Stoker's despairing eyes and I nodded. It was true, all of it made clear to me during my time at the hospital, in one of our more private 'meetings'. She'd told me, in simple terms, what I had to do, how I had to use my superior knowledge of technology, how I had to worm my way into Stoker's confidence. Of course, I didn't know how any of it would pan out. My plan was to use Corrigan. But Warren the Biker, as I had called him then, had been my real ace in the pack. When he revealed himself as Stoker, I felt I wanted to shout out with glee. Everything had fallen so neatly into place. Of course, I hadn't revealed my thinking, my part in the plan. I kept up the charade. I kept it up very well. I even managed to hide my feelings for her, the Protector's wife. Or should I say, the Protector. Because that was what she had become. She had it all. Absolute power, in her grasp, to do with as she pleased.

"So, Simeon," Stoker's eyes were without expression now, but I knew that inside he was breaking apart, "all the while, you just played me – even whilst I tried to play you." He sniggered. "You were very good. You should be proud."

"I didn't play you all the while, Stoker. Only for most of it."

"That should give you some compensation then, shouldn't it?" His hand flopped down from his hair and landed on his lap. "I thought you were going to be the key to a new world-order, Simeon. A new beginning."

"How dare you be so sanctimonious," spat the new Protector, crossing to him in a single stride, her voice threatening, her features hard. "You were fully prepared to destroy anything that got in *your* way. And don't try and deny any of it. You're no better than the system you wanted to replace."

"At least in my system there would have been some element of choice."

"It was choice that destroyed the world in the first place. There had to be order. Order and control. Your system was the system of the past. Mine was of the future."

"Yours? You're taking all the credit are you?"

She laughed at that. "You're so naive. You don't understand anything of human nature. How it can be corrupted, as well it having the ability to corrupt. That was another of your many mistakes. I simply wanted to *cleanse* the world. You wanted it to carry on, in the same way. A lost cause. Dead. Medieval."

Stoker lowered his head. From where I stood, I could see the others watching him, waiting for something. But there was nothing. He was finished, along with his dreams. I wanted to tell him, as far as choices went, that I didn't have any either. It was as the new Protector had said, they had Yolanda. If I didn't do as they commanded, they would turn off the life-support. I believed them. Without question.

The room changed in atmosphere, a palpable air of relaxation wafting over us all. The new Protector had triumphed, her victory complete. Stoker was squashed, all of the fight gone from him, the realization of how he'd been strung along complete. The one person whom he had never suspected, bringing him to this place, this final chapter in his hopeless dreams. Me. If I had been a more uncaring person, I would have smiled at my part in his downfall. However, any feelings of elation had no place in my soul, not at that moment.

As I turned away, I could saw her exchanging grins with Melling and then, without any warning or discernible change in his demeanour, Stoker leaped from his chair and charged, full pelt, towards the window, launching himself against the glass with all the strength he could muster. He hit the surface with his shoulder with a tremendous crash, and rebounded, like a rubber ball, onto the ground, the glass wobbling dramatically but otherwise completely unscathed.

Everyone stood stunned, frozen into immobility for a moment. Stoker writhed on the floor whimpering and clutching at his shoulder, a broken man, hopes destroyed.

I took this as my cue to action.

As the others closed around him, I casually waved my arm over the computer array, and gave the command for the window to slowly dissolve, revealing before us the wide, open sky with nothing to prevent him now from carrying through his desire. The wind howled through the opening and, from far below, the occasional, weak scream as someone else died.

We stood there, like gunfighters of old, waiting for one of us to flinch. I saw their indecision, their bafflement. "It's time to reap the changes," I said.

They exchanged glances, turning questioning looks towards their new leader. But she had none. "What have you done, Simeon?"

"Something I should have done a long time ago."

They all turned as the entrance door opened and the Sandman strode into the room, stooping awkwardly he was so huge. They screamed, frantic now, knowing there was no escape.

Save for the open window.

Stoker broke into a run but even as he dived through the open window in his second attempt at suicide, before he'd fallen a metre, the Sandman's vaporiser hit him and Stoker simply disappeared into a slight wisp of grey, swirling smoke.

A stunned silence followed. The Protector tore her wild, disbelieving eyes away from the monstrosity before her and gazed out of the window, as if she didn't believe the evidence of her own eyes. Breathing hard, her face a hardened mask, she snapped her head around and gave an unspoken command to the two men. Perhaps they continued to be hot-wired into the central control system, for they acted as one, laser blasters appearing in their hands.

And in Melling's – an immobiliser.

I barked my own command and the Sandman moved, far more quickly than any human being, Sweeper or not, could ever move. He struck with his great scything arms, hitting Melling across the torso, parting him as if he were ripe fruit. The other man screamed, fumbling for the laser under his coat, but even as he brought it up, the Sandman struck him, parting him neatly down the middle, from the top of his head to his groin. He fell, in two perfect portions, blood spurting outwards in a fine spray. As he died the silence in the room was tangible.

I waved my hand over the sensors and the great window reappeared, shutting us in, cocooning us from the outside world. All that we were left with now was the horror within. I stepped away from the array and allowed my eyes to wander over the scene of carnage in front of me. My stomach heaved, forcing me to turn away. I may have instigated such violence, but I didn't like it.

"What have you done?"

Her voice was barely more than a whisper. I turned to her, grateful that I could divert my eyes to something a lot more pleasant. I smiled and shrugged my shoulders. "What had to *be* done." I patted the standing, silent Sandman on his 'arm' and took a glance through the window to the slaughter below. All appeared quiet now, the only movement coming from a few Sweepers probing through the fallen enemy. In the far distance, those who had survived – either on foot or inside machines – were making their hasty retreat. There few left. The battle now over, who won or lost, depending on one's point of view, was a simple question for me to answer. Gloriously simple. I glanced towards the Protector. Her face drawn, ashen, eyes wide, mouth trembling slightly, waiting for what she assumed would be my order to have her sliced apart by the Sandman's cruel scythe. I revelled in that moment, tasting her fear, lapping up the pathetic look on her face. Vulnerable, afraid. I curled my mouth into a sneer.

"If we're going to carry on," I said, "we're going to have to learn to trust one another."

She blinked. "Trust – what? Who, *you*?" Taking a few faltering steps backwards, she fell into a nearby chair. "I once thought I could trust you, Simeon, but now ... Now, I'm not so sure. How have you managed to do this – to bring the Sandmen under your control?"

"A simple act of programming, nothing more. You shouldn't have left me alone for so long in that blood hospital. That was *your* mistake."

"Left alone ... you mean, all the time you were there, recuperating, you were actually ..." She shook her head, chuckling, "You really are a class act, Simeon. You're cleverer than any of us ever imagined."

"Too many lies and too many deceptions, Protector. You and I are going to have to learn to..." I didn't want to say anymore. I believed I'd said enough.

"What is it you want?"

I titled my head and relished the way she squirmed in that chair, all of her bravado nothing more than a memory. "I want Yolanda safe, Protector. That's my demand. I want to go back to my apartment, live my life, do my studies and wake up every morning with her lying next to me. And I want every person in this shit-hole of a world that you've created to be able to the same. But most of all…" I leaned forward, my eyes boring into her. I watched her eyes dance with uncertainty and total, abject terror. "I want my family back."

She gasped, a perfectly manicured hand clamping over her beautiful mouth. "That would mean a return to how it once was…" She shook her head, those deep, limpet eyes that had so captivated me, attached themselves to my heart, slowly filled up with tears. I watched as her nightmare vision of the future disappeared in that single instant.

"You have the power now, you're in charge, and I will do nothing to thwart you, so long as you carry out my instructions. But trust me," I nodded my head towards the Sandman, standing silent and huge in that room, "you cross me and I'll unleash Hell. I'll unleash the Sandmen. After all, they are mine now. I control them."

She had nothing to say. What could she say?

I'd won.

I've kept this account of my life since the coming of the Sandmen in a number of secret locations, both as hard copies, in the cloud and as programme files. If you're reading this, it means I'm most probably dead or, less likely, somebody has managed to break into the machine-code which keeps my words safe. Let us all hope, that if I have died, it was through natural causes, that my life was long and happy and ran its course well into old age. If I'm dead through any other means, then the Sandman will come. And you all know what that means, don't you…

The End!

About the Author

Stuart G Yates is the author of a eclectic mix of books, ranging from historical fiction through to contemporary thrillers. Hailing from Merseyside, he now lives in southern Spain, where he teaches history, but dreams of living on a narrowboat in Shropshire.

Lightning Source UK Ltd.
Milton Keynes UK
UKHW011157091120
373077UK00001B/249

9 781034 021896